PYGMY WARS

Ronald K. Myers

PYGMY WARS

DOUBLE DRAGON

A DOUBLE DRAGON PAPERBACK

ISBN 978-1-78695-624-8

Double Dragon
is an imprint of
Fiction4All

Published 2021
Fiction4All
www.fiction4all.com

CHAPTER 1

In one of the last pockets of civilization struggling to survive, Eippy, the little pie pygmy, hid in a sheltering thicket. With his silky-black tail partially blocking his vision, he crouched in the shadows and peered through his small eyes. Beyond the shore and across the water, the setting sun inflamed the horizon, causing an orange dusk to linger, but all was clear. It would be safe to come out.

Eippy took one step.

Angry sounds of his dog barking at a pygmy hunter cut through the last of the filthy rain sluicing down through the dead trees. Eippy froze in place, swished his silky tail to the side, and looked to where his dog was barking.

The pygmy hunter ignored Eippy's little cream-colored dog, reached down, and grabbed an orange pygmy's wrist. As the rat tail of the pygmy formed a threatening S, the hackles on the dog's back flared up and accented the green, spinach-shaped blotches on its back.

With his small eyes open wide, Eippy's excited voice rang out, "Sic him, Spinach!"

Growling, Spinach barreled toward the pygmy hunter's ankle.

With guttural grunts resonating from his hollow pig-like nose, the pygmy hunter reared back and kicked Spinach. Spinach yelped once and went flying across the rugged ground. He tumbled to a stop, rolled to his feet, and ran into the forest.

With mouthwatering expectation, the pygmy hunter grinned and straightened the orange pygmy's arm straight out. Holding it with one hand and using his other hand, he reached toward the sky and brought his fist down.

Snap!

The hammer blow broke the pygmy's arm.

Screaming in pain and with his tail lashing violently, the pygmy staggered back and tried to free his broken arm from the pygmy hunter's powerful grip.

He couldn't.

The pygmy hunter pulled out his ax, chopped the pygmy's arm off, raised it to his mouth, and took a huge bite out of it.

As if a switch had been pulled, the sun dropped below the horizon. Everything became early night gray.

Like a quickly moving ghostly shape, Spinach came barreling back. He grabbed the pygmy hunter's ankle, hung on, and twisted. The pygmy hunter dropped the arm and swung his ax. It sliced the tip of Spinach's ear off. Spinach let loose of the hunter's ankle and ran into the bush.

The orange pygmy's half a meter high son, Eippy, whose small eyes had been staring from the shadows, gasped in shock, his panic temporally immobilizing him. With his long, fluffy, black tail curved into a threatening S, he sprang out of a pocket of rolling fog, hopped up and down, and excitely waved his little arm. "Come on, Papa, I have the gold. Follow me."

Eippy looked toward a flickering orange glow on his right. The light from torches in their hands revealed a new band of wild-eyed pygmy hunters with sweating, contorted faces yelling and running down the hill. But the pygmy-hunters, pig-people with IQ's equivalent to a bag of stones, were going the wrong way.

While the other pygmy hunters' attentions were focused on where Spinach had gone, Eippy's father held his blood-spurting stump, where his arm used to be, and took off running. With his rat tail standing straight up behind him, he zipped along the dark shoreline of the red algae bloom. But the blood loss caused his rat tail to droop. He slowed to a limping walk.

Searching for the escaping pygmies, the revealing beam of a carbide-gas searchlight streaked down from the side of the mountain. As the beam bounced along the rolling red water, it only revealed a few isolated waves that creased into the filthy shoreline.

The pygmy hunter adjusted the beam to a spot of land between a set of towering boulders. Here, old tree roots had raised the soil. Like black, bony fingers waiting to reach out, grab a toe or a foot, and send someone flying, the roots twisted along the ground. This would be a good execution place, and the pygmy hunter wasn't disappointed. Even though Eippy wore a black and white stripped polo shirt, the blur of his running legs and his swishing tail cut the beam and was gone so fast the hunter must have wondered if he were seeing things. He rubbed his eyes and focused the beam again. The moment it touched Eippy's father's limping, orange form, Eippy's father took off running. Wildly screaming, with his long, black hair flying back, he rushed toward the safety of the concealing dark.

The gas in the carbide lantern hissed. The revealing white of the light turned blue, sputtered, and flicked out.

Eippy's father fell.

Eippy ran to him. "Come on, Papa. The light went out. We can get away."

His father struggled to his feet, bent over, and placed his hand on his knee. With weary eyes and blood spurting from his severed arm, he looked toward Eippy. "You came from a village with pie pygmies just like you." He tried to breathe in but coughed up blood. "I always tried to take you back to your village, but I never could find it. If I don't make it, take your mother and sisters and find the village. It is an archaic dream of two old men that came true. The magic there will make your world normal again."

Eippy held back his tears. "Get up, Papa. We'll go there together."

"I believe we can." His father peered into the darkness created by the carbide light that had flicked out. "It's dark enough to get away. We're out of danger."

For a moment silent dark enveloped them. Then the boisterous grunting of pygmy hunters cut the dark. Eippy looked back over his shoulder. He and his father weren't out of danger. The dreaded, flickering, orange torch light from guttural-grunting pygmy hunters, fifty meters behind him, gave substance to both of their silhouettes.

Eippy's father lifted his hand from his knee, took two steps, and tripped over the tree roots. His legs crumpled. He thudded to the ground.

The grunting of the pygmy hunters grew louder.

The gap closed.

Eippy tugged at his father's arm. "Get up, Papa. Get up!" He looked toward the grunting. The pygmy hunters all wore dirty-black jackets made from irregular pieces of pygmy skin they had dried and sewn-together. Consisting of a diet of pygmy and dog meat, most were tall and lanky. Shaggy goatees, the color of dirty straw, hung down and over their double chins. On their heads, tight fitting baseball caps, with long bills, covered most of their short bristles of hair that looked as if it had been gnawed off by a sewer rat. On the fronts of their baseball caps, crudely cut tin letters, reading "PH", caught torch light and flashed like bright badges of unearned authority.

Even though ordinary pygmy hunters had the characteristics of pigs and looked alike, Eippy knew from their grunting that these weren't ordinary pygmy hunters. These were the feared "top-of-the-line" pygmy hunters. They never failed to kill their quarry.

Eippy pulled at his father's arm and tried to help him to his feet. He didn't respond.

Spears rained down, swished past Eippy's tiny body, and sank into Eippy's father's back. Blood exploded around the spearheads. More spears came. They sliced into the sand and zipped past the thorn canes. Grabbing his back and moaning in agony, Eippy's father rose. Spinning in the sand and oblivious to the pain, his one hand pulled at the jagged thorny canes. More spheres sliced his body.

As the spears flew all around Eippy, none hit him. In a state of shock and fear, he stood helpless.

Whimpering, with blood flowing from where the tip of his ear had been sliced off, Spinach hid under a small bush.

Still trying to escape, Eippy's father's small orange hand clawed at the sand. After he had crawled the length of his body, he quit breathing.

With the renewed bright beam of the carbide lights stabbing at his eyes, Eippy looked into his father's face. His glassy eyes looked up. Eippy knew his father was dead. With pain welling up in his chest, Eippy took one last sorrowful look at his dead father and wondered how pygmy hunters could be so cruel. He felt it wasn't any mortal person's right to decide who should survive or parish. That great right was reserved for Orange Man.

Eippy turned, and plunged toward the trees. With weeds and tall grass lashing his face, he sprinted toward the thick cover of the forest. Breathing in ragged gasps, he held his hands in front of his face and warded off tall grass that blocked his vision.

As thick bushes flanked him and overhanging branches of densely leaved trees cast shadows behind his tiny body, the gruff voice of a pygmy hunter rang out. "Where's that little one?"

Huffing for breath, another pygmy hunter walked up to the pygmy hunter standing next to the thorn canes and peered into the tall grass. "I don't know where he is," he said with his eyes darting back and forth. "Did you see the long fur on its tail? It's a pie pygmy. Even if it doesn't have gold, it's really good to eat."

"Get back to the one we got," the other pygmy hunter commanded. "Kick his teeth out before he bites someone. I shouldn't have to remind you, those teeth are poisons."

Although the pygmies' teeth were not poisons, to instill fear in the pygmy hunters, the pygmies had spread the rumor that their teeth were poisons. If the pygmy hunters would have known Eippy's father had hid a weird magnet, they wouldn't have worried about kicking his teeth out. They would have been searching for the magnet.

With Eippy at his side, his father had been using the weird magnet to search the shoreline. They had been finding gold. But gold wasn't the only valuable thing the pygmy hunters were after. Because of Eippy's half a meter high size and his distinctive blaze of silky-black fur that ran from high on his forehead down the center of his head, down his back, and to the tip of his tail, he was considered a pie pygmy. Pie pygmies were considered top shelf. Made into pies, they were a much sought after delicacy, and their black fluffy tails were prized as the most tasty and tender of all pygmy meats.

Eippy's small size and his black fur gave him an advantage: It made it difficult for pygmy hunters

11

to find him, and his great lightning speed allowed him to go where no other pygmy dared to go. But if he made one misstep, or one mistake, or if one pygmy hunter, hungry for pygmy meat, caught him, he would be somebody's evening meal.

With a knot of pygmy hunters bunched before him, Eippy hid under a bush, crouched into a ball, and labored to quiet his gasping breath.

One of the pygmy hunters with fat hanging like slabs of bacon under his arms raised his blood-covered hand and rattled the bush. Praying to Orange Man that the pygmy hunter hadn't seen him, Eippy froze with fear.

Cocking an ear, the pygmy hunter leaned forward and took one step.

Snap!

The pygmy hunter's thick boot clumped down on Eippy's tail. Pain raced up his spine. He wanted to scream out, but he held it in. Although the bush blocked the pygmy hunter's vision, he had broken Eippy's tail.

The pygmy hunter excitedly yelled, "There's something here!"

To protect himself, Eippy placed his hands on his head. Before he could be seen and struck, Spinach came barreling out of hiding and stopped at the feet of the hunter. With the hackles on his back rising, Spinach growled.

"It's a dog!" the pygmy hunter yelled.

Holding his spear in a ready position, the other pygmy hunter rubbed his stomach in anticipation. "We can eat that."

"I'll kick him your way. Spear him." The pygmy hunter drew his foot back to kick. Before he could swing, his foot into Spinach's side, Spinach turned and scampered off into the brush.

Afraid to come out, Eippy crouched amongst a thick tangle of vines, held his broken tail, and wondered if the hunters would quit searching for him.

But he didn't have to wonder long. The sparkling show in the sky was just beginning. It was the aurora borealis. Soon the sky would be filled with magnificent flowing colors of blue, green, yellow, orange, and red. Eippy knew it was harmless, but the pygmy hunters were afraid of it.

They immediately stopped searching.

With fear-filled eyes, the pygmy hunters hoisted Eippy's father's body onto a wooden wagon. As they were pulling the wagon away, a trailing pygmy hunter leaned askew.

Splat!

His lifeless body fell flat onto a stretch of cement-like ground. Afraid of the growing lights from the aurora borealis, the other pygmy hunters didn't stop. Holding his foot, the fallen pygmy hunter stayed on the ground. One pygmy hunter turned and looked back. As if the fallen pygmy hunter had now become worthless, the staring pygmy-hunter's mouth locked in a sickening leer. And the fallen pygmy-hunter's band of former friends walked away.

After Eippy had watched the pygmy hunters wheel his father's torch-lit body into the darkness, he hoped Spinach would come out of hiding. But

Spinach never came out. Making sure the fallen pygmy hunter was still on the ground and hoping Spinach would be behind a tree, waiting, Eippy pushed away the concealing vine and fled into the forest. And his broken tail trailed behind him.

Before he could look for Spinach, Eippy had to do something about his broken tail. He reached up, snapped a smooth stick from a tree, and broke it in half. Then he placed the sticks on the break in his tail and wrapped them with a thin vine. His tail still hurt, but it wouldn't be dragging on the ground colleting dirt and getting infected.

After hours of searching, Eippy could not find Spinach. Eippy's years of weaving through the forest and experiencing its changing temperatures told him that the black rain was coming to Blue Town and the surrounding area. He wanted to go home and be safe, but he would never cover enough ground to get far enough away to avoid the black rain, and he didn't want to go home without Spinach. It would be better to find a place where the black water wouldn't cover his body and fill his clothes with soot, especially his horizontally-striped black and white polo shirt that his mother had made from a leathery cloth that had taken four weeks to grow using live kombucha cultures, water, vinegar, sugar, and tea.

He decided to go to a place where the pygmy hunters would never think of looking for him. He would go where Spinach had gone the last time he had been kicked. He would go into the storm culverts under Blue Town.

CHAPTER 2

Even though none of the Dinkies were taller than a pig-person's waist and did nothing to harm the earth, not long after pig-people had begun going off the blue grass, the Dinkies were blamed for all the pollution problems of the earth. As a result, thousands of Dinkies had been killed. At that time, a few pig-people had called them midgets, and believed their short stature had evolved from a race of miners who hadn't had a decent meal in hundreds of years, and the lack of food had caused them to be dim-witted and inferior but perfect to be slaves.

Unknown to the pig-people, the Dinkies were strong survivors of radiation exposure. The exposure had not only resulted in small, strong bodies, it had also blessed them with superior minds.

The pig-people were the opposite. Their inferior minds, constant fighting, and burning of buildings, had left most of Blue Town in ruins. The necessity to rebuild had been so urgent that unreasonable physical demands had been placed on the shoulders of the few surviving Dinky slaves. The demands were met with sabotage and resulted in chaos that had caused Blue Town to be reconstructed in a disorderly fashion.

Labyrinths of streets, many dead-ending into the sides of dilapidated buildings that were fronted with crooked sidewalks and sewage running alongside, were just a few of the botched rebuilding legacies.

On the outskirts of Blue Town, Ivan Law, the half-breed pig-person, wanted to relax. It had been a tiring day. He sat down, pushed his reclining chair back, propped up his feet, and opened one of the many ancient books he had rescued from a demolished museum. Many of the books he had tried to read were so ancient that the pages crumbled or turn to dust. But the book he held in his hands was in pretty good shape.

He began reading a page about the diseases marasmus and kwashiorker. These diseases attacked people who did not eat enough protein. He was glad he had learned enough from the ancient books to grow plants that were protein rich and that he didn't suffer from fatigue, diarrhea, or have a belly that stuck out.

He looked through the window of his half-brick, half-wooden house and admired his long rows of corn and beans. He was thankful that he had learned corn had protein but needed the enzymes in beans to be absorbed by the body. But what he was most thankful for was the solar panels that electrified the fence that protected his corps. His feet ached from walking the long rows of corn and beans, and after a day of constant bending over to pick beans, his back hurt even more. But the pain was a small price to pay. Tomorrow, while others wondered where their next morsel of food would be coming from, he would be eating corn on the cob with a side of fresh green beans.

After he harvested more beans and sold them at an outrageous price, he would dry the corn and give "some dumb ass pig-person" a few kernels to turn the crank and grind the corn into cornmeal. Then he would have enough corn to last a year or more, and better yet, he could sell it at an even more outrageous price.

Just as he was about to close his eyes and reminisce about the golden age of Blue Town, a staccato of footsteps echoed through the wall. A band of strange stringy-haired, purple pygmies rounded the corner of his house. Although he had never seen purple pygmies before, he thought they were only walking across the blue grass of his yard to keep their bare feet from being burned on the steaming hot sidewalks.

The crowd of perspiring, purple pygmies began pushing ahead of each other. Tugging one another away and pressing their faces against the window, their foreheads and fingers smudged the glass.

Law had worked long and hard to construct a house like no other pig-people in Blue Town could build. He had hand-cut the heavy, rough-hewn beams that supported the ceiling above his head. When it got cold, he had a fireplace in the living room, and the dark, rich wainscoting in the dining room always made him feel as if he were someone special.

But he hadn't always lived like this. For years, he had been homeless. He had survived in one of the one hundred meter long culverts that the sunlight never found. At first, when he had ventured out into the seedier and less populated section of Blue Town, tall, lean pig-people with shaved heads had taken everything he had.

On the verge of starvation, he had fallen to the ground. His hand had slipped through the ground and broken through a rotted board. When he pulled his hand out, he discovered a tunnel that led to an underground storage chamber. The chamber had more preserved food than he could ever consume.

After a few months of eating enough food and getting good exercise, he became stronger than any of the homeless pig-people, but when he realized food was a big equalizer and could be traded for gold, he didn't have to use his physical strength. But more important, he found out that the ability to control the lives of others with impunity required a lot of gold.

Exchanging food for gold, the homeless pig-people in the culverts had stolen, enabled him to control them and the strong pig-people, too. But every time he had taken control of the culverts, pig police had swooped down, rousted the denizens from their fetid beds, and burned their makeshift homes.

After months of exchanging food for gold, Law's food supply began to dwindle. He sold just about all the food that remained and bought and improved the house he was sitting in. He had thought he would have an easy life. But even though it was a new place, he found out that it was just the same old crap: You lived and died by your wits, and the stupid did not survive for very long. He didn't need purple pygmies or anybody else smudging his windows. And he didn't want them close to his life-enhancing crops.

He jumped from his chair. Flapping his arms at the purple pygmies, he shouted through the glass, "Go away! Go away!"

The purple pygmies at the window drew their faces away, intentionally flashed rows of sharp pointed teeth, and smiled in Law's direction.

The sharp teeth were threatening, but Law didn't back away.

Snapping their pointed-toothed mouths, the purple pygmies raised their grubby fists and pounded on the window.

Law had heard of cannibalistic pygmies filing their teeth into points to make it easier for them to tear flesh from a pig-person's body. Although the pygmies outside his window were half the height of him, if they decided to attack, their pointed teeth would be like voraciously carnivorous piranha. Within seconds, their snapping teeth could easily clip the flesh from his body.

He jerked back.

If he could get to his shed, he could mix up his secret mixture of brown soap and gasoline. He would create a Molotov cocktail that would burn right through their bodies. There would be no more bothersome purple pygmies. But for safety reasons, the glass containers, wicks, wires, and incendiary ingredients were in his garden shed. And the shed was outside, inside the fence.

Again, he excitedly flapped his arms at the pygmies and yelled through the glass. "Go away!"

The pygmies turned and walked away from his window. Relieved, he sat back down. Before he could tilt the recliner back, ten pygmies hurled stones over the cornfield fence. The stones smashed down on the top of his solar panels. A myriad of cracks, spider-webbed across the panels. One pygmy cautiously touched the electrified fence around the cornfield. The pygmy jerked back. Law wasn't sure, but it looked like the pygmy had monetarily turned red. But it didn't matter. The solar panels were still working.

More rocks rained down on the solar panels. They sparked and broke along the spider-webbed cracks. The pygmy reached out and fearlessly held his hand on the fence. He didn't jerk his hand back. He didn't get shocked. The solar panels were no longer operational. The fence protecting Law's crops was no longer electrified.

A hoard of pygmies, with their rat tails undulating like slithering snakes, charged the fence. Their combined weight caused the fence to sag and fall to the ground. More pygmies than Law could count rushed into his cornfield.

He jumped up. A good dose of napalm from the shed would get rid of them all. He rushed to his back door and yanked it open. Like an army of ants, purple pygmies bowled him over. As he lay on the floor, more pygmies streamed into his house, pushing, grabbing, and snapping their pointed-toothed mouths.

With the hard, bare feet of the pygmies tramping on his body and their rat tails snaking over his legs, Law grabbed the doorknob and managed to pull himself to a sitting position. He screamed at the purple pygmies, "Get out of my house!"

Three pygmies stood right next to his face, opened their smiling, pointed-toothed mouths, and turned red. A high-pitched staccato of, "Yay! — Yay! Yay! — Yay! — Yay! — Yay!" streamed from their throats. They were about to bite the flesh right off is body. They were going to eat him alive.

He rolled out the door and took off running.

When he arrived at the pig police station, he stepped inside, and the door automatically slammed behind him. He looked around. No one was there. He tried to go outside. Not only was the door that had slammed shut locked, all the doors that led outside the room were locked. If he broke the locks, he would be arrested. The only thing he could do, was wait.

After Law had waited and slept on a cold metal bench all night long, the lock on the main door clicked.

The door opened.

Law jumped up off the bench.

As if looking for a place to take a nap after lunch, a pig policeman, wiping cherry pie off his face, walked into the station yawning.

"Officer," Law said with great relief. "I've been waiting for hours. I need your help."

As if he didn't want to be bothered, the pig policeman waved his hand down. "Good. Hire yourself a partner."

"You don't understand," Law pleaded. "A band of purple pygmies are eating my crops. They are destroying my home."

The pig policeman's forehead wrinkled with suspicion. "Have you been drinking?"

"No, I haven't been drinking. Come on. Get help. They're tearing my house down."

A door with rusty hinges that led to a side room squealed open. The chief of the pig police walked in. "What's going on here?"

The pig policeman laughed. "Noting to be alarmed about, chief. It's just another one of those drunks who thinks he's seeing purple pygmies."

"We had three last week," the chief said. "When we went to check out the claims, we found they were all unfounded. The complainers were homeless people who wanted to be arrested for giving a false complaint. They figured if we threw them in jail they would get a free meal." He cast a suspicious glare in Law's direction. "I think I've seen you in the culverts. Are you a homeless person looking for a free meal?"

"I'm not homeless. I have all the food I'll ever need."

"Oh," the chief said with realization. "You're one of those greedy people who grow food and won't share."

Trying to give the impression he was ashamed, Law lowered his head. "I can barely take care of myself. I would share if I could."

"Don't lie to us," the chief said with finality. "You're not getting a free meal. Get out!"

Law pleaded, "But purple pygmies are destroying my home."

A spasm of irritation crossed the chief's face. "Get off it, buddy. There's no such thing as purple pygmies."

The chief and the pig policeman grabbed Law by the arms and threw him out of the station.

Law tumbled onto the sidewalk and lay still.

Shaking his fist, the chief shouted after Law, "If you come back here, we'll have you certified insane and committed to a lunatic asylum." He slammed the door and locked it.

Law struggled to all fours and yelled back. "I'll turn you into the Friends of the Earth Corporation."

His threat was met with silence.

He stood up, brushed himself off, and ran back to his house. A mound of hot brick dust and smoldering ashes was all that remained. The purple pygmies had broken into his shed. They had used the secret mixture of brown soap and gasoline, created napalm, and used it to heat the bricks of his house so that they crumbled to the touch.

When he looked toward his cornfield, not only were the beans and ears of his corn gone, every stalk had been gnawed off clean to the ground. The broken solar panels were gone. The shed was nothing but a pile of splintered wood, and the fence was gone, too.

On his way to file a complaint, with the Friends of the Earth Corporation, the stink and squalor of Blue Town was appalling. The heavy metal gates that protected the windows and doors of the storefront buildings broadcasted that thievery was a regular occurrence. When he passed pig-people on the street, they were dressed in ragged clothes and frayed homespun. Although Law didn't thrive on parties and the pomp of officialdom and he didn't adore all the outward signs of success, these pig-people were way below his wealthy, privileged and elite status. He hurried away from them.

He stopped at a faded storefront and peered into a window where the heavy metal gate had been pushed aside. His reclining chair and many of the things that had been in his home were there. He breathed a sigh of relief. Some kind people had saved his things.

Inside the store, a pig-person behind the window smiled and motioned for Law to come in.

Law stepped past the retracted metal gate and opened the door.

The pig-person wearing a three-piece suit stepped up to him. "Our window display seems to have caught your interest. Is there something you wish to buy?"

"Very funny," Law said. "But thank you for saving my things."

"You seemed to be mistaken," the pig-person said with a furrowed brow. "We've had those items in the window for three days."

"Quit joking. Those items were in my house before the purple pygmies burned it down. And that was yesterday."

The pig-person's eyes turned cold. He looked back over his shoulder. "Hey, George, looks like we have another one of those purple pygmy freaks."

With the veins of his bull neck sticking out and his face red with rage, George stomped across the floor and yelled into Law's face. "If you're not out of here in one second we're taking you to the police station."

Law held up his hands in a defensive posture. "Gentleman, there is no need for that. I'll go there myself."

Law turned and walked away, but he didn't go back to the police station. He was no longer a culvert person whose complaints would be met with apologizes and promises of investigations and be left to die in mystery. They didn't know who they were dealing with. He was Ivan Law, an important homeowner. He had class. He was going to get his belongings back. He was going to file a complaint. He walked out of the store and trotted toward the Friends of the Earth Corporation building.

On the way, he weaved his way between heaps of trash and jumped over sewage running into channels along the streets where young pig-people sat under plastic cardboard shelters doing nothing.

The young pig-people's looks of hopelessness did not bother him. Their pig-people parents had descended from a long line of lazy humans who had been pampered and cuddled to the point of dependency and helplessness.

If the young pig-people would do as he had done, they wouldn't be sitting around projecting a "Hey-look-at-me!" demeanor and sitting next to garbage. They would be doing something to help themselves.

At the Friends of the Earth Corporation building that housed a jail, Law stood in front of the high desk, looking up.

The judge looked down at him. "Can I help you?"

"Yes, your honor. I want to file a complaint against the police."

A stern look filled the judge's face. "Just what do you want to complain about?"

"Purple pygmies burnt down my house, destroyed my crops, and now my stolen belongings are in a store front window."

The judge rolled his hand in encouragement. "And?"

"And the police won't do anything about it."

The judge banged his gavel three times. A side door to the room opened and was slammed shut. In front of the door, a jail guard with a scar on his right arm stood with his arms folded across his chest.

The judge looked in the guard's direction. "We may need your help."

Law felt his body slump with relief. He was going to get some help.

As if in thought, the judge tented his fingers. "Are you sure purple pygmies did all this?"

"Yes I'm sure. Go to the store. You'll see my belongings. The owner says they have been there for three days, but they have not."

The judge cast him a suspicious eye. "So, you're saying the items are yours?"

"That's what I've been trying to tell you since I came in here,"

The judge looked to the jail guard. "Write him up for receiving stolen property, and escort him to the jail."

In complete bewilderment, Law jerked back. "What?"

"You have to be dimwitted," the judge said, shaking an accusing finger at Law. "You are trying to get the things in the window that are not yours."

"But I can prove those items are mine."

The judge leaned back with self-righteous. "Our records show those items were stolen months ago."

Law persisted. "That's impossible. Only yesterday, purple pygmies took them from my house and burned it down."

"Nice try." The judge smiled. "But a messenger told us a maverick might come here with a cock and bull story about purple pygmies."

Over the years, planned obsolesce, 3-D printing, and robotic manufacturing, had eliminated all manufacturing jobs, and videos had replaced reading. When one of the many magnetic pulses had destroyed all computer and video data, many skills and ancient knowledge on how to physically manufacture items had been lost. Law was one of very few people who could read and had the skills to create things others could not. Because he could do this and refused to abide by the dictates of the pig-people's government and live off of a society that encouraged people to feel as if they were owed something, he was branded a dissenter. He was a maverick.

Knowing the judge's sense of right or wrong wasn't based on law, but on how much he could get out of a victim brought before him, Law wanted to offer him a bribe. But first, he would have to make the judge feel they were the same class of people.

"Your honor," he said. "We're not common people. Would you agree that it's not our fault that common pig-people are too lazy to grow their own food and are too ignorant to learn how to make the things they need?" Waiting for an answer, he squirmed uncomfortably.

The Judge's head bobbed with sadistic laughter. "We cannot allow common people like, *you,* who are a menace to our ordered society, to come in here and tell us there are purple pygmies."

Law didn't like being called common, He flared up. "Not only is this malfeasance in the extreme, it is not an arcane subject." He paused and studied the judge's face. He seemed to be coming around.

With finality, Law defiantly stated, "There *are* purple pygmies."

Instead of extending his hand for a bribe, the judge let a rasping snort erupt from his pig-like nose and banged his gavel once. "Use all the fancy words you want. There is no such thing as purple pygmies." He gestured to the guard. "We've had his kind before. They think because they have an easy life, everyone else is worthless. Lock him up."

The guard grabbed Law by the lapels of his suit coat and slammed him against the wall. "You're going to be on the inside looking out!"

As Law was being escorted to the jail, he couldn't believe he was going to jail. It was going to be a big change.

Although other houses in Blue Town were surrounded by clusters of trash and dirty plastic shacks clung to the hillsides, creating slums that spilled into the once pristine streets, Law had grown accustomed to his spacious house with the board green lawn and his cornfield. He had considered himself aloof from those who lived around him. After all, he could sleep anytime he wanted, and wear beautiful clothes others never dreamed of having, and he never went hungry. His efforts had allowed him to exist in a world of his own creation. His world had been a place where he had importance, a world in which he was somebody. Now, a tyrannical judge had taken it all away. Jail would be a far cry from his luxurious life style he had worked so hard to obtain.

For three months, shackled at the wrists and ankles and chained to the floor, Law had stayed behind bars. He had to put up with the dirty clothes, the continuous odor of feces, the horrible feeling of starvation, the total lack of privacy, and the unending boredom of a totally pointless existence. If that weren't enough, the anger, the scorn, the mocking jibes, and the pink-faced rage of the guards tore at his sanity. Waiting to be set free, he felt defeated and helpless.

When the guards had tried to starve him to death by feeding him left over bones from roasted pygmies, he had broken the bones, sucked the marrow from them, and managed to survive. But the ordeal had caused him to hate the odor of pygmy meat.

For a reason unknown to him, a mysterious person had arranged an early release. Suddenly free, he vowed to take back everything that he had been denied and more. He would never eat pygmy meat again, and he was going to right the wrong that had unjustly ruined his life. As a final crowning achievement, he would return Blue Town to a time of human exploitation. He would get the Dinky slaves back into Blue Town.

CHAPTER 3

In the dank cellar of an abandoned house on Main Street, Ivan Law hunched over and peered through the slat in the blanket-covered window. Outside, Peep, a dim-witted pig-person, hurried across the street. With one arm jerking grotesquely, he glanced back over his shoulder. Even though a band of pig-people were following him, a tsunami of adrenaline began to rush through Law's veins. The notebook Peep had clamped under his short arm caused Law to go on instant alert. The notebook contained valuable information he needed to place his plan into action. Over the centuries, other books had been heavily edited by copyist who had exercised their own judgment and cut out what offended them. What remained was devoid of common sense. If that information were put into use, it would result in the complete disintegration of Blue Town and any other town that chose to use it. But the book Peep was bringing was an original copy.

If the band of angry pig-people following Peep caught him, like most pig-people who didn't understand something, they would destroy the thing they didn't understand. Years ago, hand-held computer-controlled screens that sent and received video and audio messages had caused reading and writing to become obsolete. Few pig-people knew how to read or write. The notebook was something the illiterate pig-people would not understand. They would rip it to shreds.

Swinging his arms that were half as long as other pig-people's arms, Peep hastened his steps.

Not being fast or coordinated enough to keep up, the pig-people waved their weak carbide flashlights in many directions and grunted with frustration.

Years after the pygmies had eaten most of the Dinky slaves, who had grown and harvested crops for the pig-people, food had become a valuable asset. If the pig-people got it into their heads that someone could lead them to food, they would follow that person until they were led to food or the person managed to slip away. That was what was happening now.

Above Law's head, footsteps rumbled on the plastic boards of the floor. He felt his tsunami of adrenaline begin to ebb. Peep was inside the ramshackle building. Outside, the angry pig-people pounded on the door and screamed for him to come outside, their trailing voices begging him to give them something to eat.

Ignoring their calls, Peep bent over. Using his sausage-sized fingers, he opened the trap door, tramped down six steps, giggled, and closed the trap door over his head. "Those beggars won't catch me now."

At the bottom of the steps, Peep tried to adjust his night vision by squinting his one eye, and Law studied his appearance. His arms functioned just like any other pig-person's arms, but they were so short that his hands were where other pig-people's elbows were. One skinny, black suspender draped across the scant muscle that clung to his sunken chest. The suspender held up his felt pants that had a loose waistline and resembled the edge of a little tub that circled around his ample waist. Little ears on each side of his close-together eye sockets stuck out. His only eye was the reason he was called, Peep.

Law stepped out of the darkness. Peep's eye twinkled with friendship. He was usually a ceremonious shaker of hands, a likable man who knew jokes, but, tonight, he tensed with fear, and Law was glad that he had.

Although, Law's mentor, Derrick, was controlling him like a puppet master pulling the strings on a marionette, Derrick had taught him that fear was control, and it was working. If Law wanted to control someone, at any moment and without warning, he would let his temper flare. With his superior intelligence and what Derrick had taught him, Law could keep just about any one awkward with fear. His use of convincing arguments and promises of a better life had swayed many a nonbeliever over to his side. When someone disappointed him, his actions were like the dirty black rain of Blue Town: He would let the disappointment freely rain down on them and choke out any expected forgiveness. A single glance from him could cause many people to cower and limp away as if they were physically disabled.

Law extended his hand. "Nice to see you, Peep."

Peep relaxed and extended his short arm. With his stubby, three-fingered hand, he grasped Law's hand. A full-toothed smile spread across most of

Peep's face and caused the top of his head to look smaller than was. Being entitled to grin showed he was used to getting what he wanted without working for it. Peep was a typical pig-person.

When Law had gone to a secret meeting to select someone to be the new Chief Earth Officer, to his surprise, he had been selected. Although he felt he wasn't qualified, the few pig-people at the meeting had assured him that many educated people would show him what to do, but only a deformed person called, Derrick had accepted the task.

It was nothing new. Most pig-people didn't care much about anything except themselves. And the environment showed it.

With the Dinkies no longer caring for the land, most of the growing fields had been polluted, poisoned, or flooded. In many areas, poisonous gas hovered above the land, and most of the pygmies who had taken over the Dinkies' task of growing food had escaped or moved away. Although rumored to have hydroponic gardens under the ground, the escaped pygmies only provided enough food for themselves. When pig-people with little knowledge of gardening tried to grow edible crops, only nameless weeds struggled to exist. The few who created compost and weeded and watered their gardens didn't fare much better. Their gardens were usually raided or destroyed by marauding pygmies.

Food for pig-people was no longer easy to get. They didn't go outside much, and the lack of sun had caused a good portion of them to take on a pale ashen look. If the pig-people had enough ambition to find a solar panel or construct a windmill to provide electricity, sun lamps may have helped, but they were not as beneficial as the real sun, and most of the time it was blocked with filth-filled clouds. To counter the cold weather caused from the sun being blocked, pig-people burned more coal, used the outlawed process of cracking, and drilled for more gas which resulted in the dumping of radioactive brine into the streams and rivers. Uncontrolled fires added to the filth-filled air. Sometimes black smoke covered the sky and caused night to last for three days. Meetings were set up to try and stop the practice, but just as no one had showed up at Law's meeting, no one had showed up at those meetings either. It was difficult to find anyone who cared.

Dressed in a suit and tie of a politician, compared to Peep's appearance, Law thought Peep's was comical. He wanted to laugh, but he suppressed a smile. "Did you bring it?"

Peep took the wrinkled notebook out from under his short arm and presented it to Law. "It's very old," he said. "But I managed to get a newer copy."

Law took the book. "Thank you."

Overcome with emotion, because he had done something Law approved of, Peep's nostrils ran, and the corner of his one eye formed a tear. He reached up and wiped his pig nose on the back of his wrist. "Do you think it will work?"

Law glanced at Peep's wet wrist but didn't comment. "It has worked many times." He opened the notebook and thumbed through pages yellow with age. "It's a simplified version of the original scheme for world conquest under pig-person rule."

"But will the people fall for it?"

"People are nothing but useful idiots. They can object all they want. But in the end, we'll convince them that everything will be just fine. They have always been useful idiots, and they will always be useful idiots."

"What do we do first?"

Law really didn't need the entire book, but he pretended he did. He held up his hand. "Let me look."

Making a pretense of studying the notebook, he turned to its center. Cannibals were supposed to have killed and eaten all the Dinkies. But a map that revealed the location of the new land of the Dinkies was before him. His dream of getting them back into Blue Town and making things as they had been was now possible. He turned to another page and looked to Peep.

"Most of what's on this list has already been done."

Peep leaned over and looked at the list. "What's there left to do?"

Law ran his finger down the list. "Increase the poverty level. It makes it easier to control people. We can't get that much higher. And if you are giving them food to live, they will not fight back. We've been feeding them pygmy meat. So that's covered." He paused and read on. "Deny education. That's already being done."

Although he didn't tell Peep, most of the pig-people were born ignorant and because slaves had done mostly everything for them, they stayed that way. The ones who did learn usually forgot what they had learned and had to be constantly retrained. The adage was, "Don't give them a lunch break. You'll have to retrain them."

Law ran his finger down the page, felt a surge of excitement, and held his finger on the page. "Here's one we can start with: Control what people read and listen to."

"How do we do that?"

"Most people are not very interested in hearing what another person has to say, unless there is something in it for them." Law paused. "A rally may do the job."

Peep lifted one stubby finger. "Ahh yes, first thing in the morning. Get an early start."

Law's rock like jaw bunched into quivering knots. "No way!"

"What?"

"After sitting around all day, doing nothing, pig-people's minds are more susceptible to suggestion, especially after dark. And they are fascinated by torch light. To make them even more susceptible, we'll have the meeting in a glorified beer joint and give them free beer."

CHAPTER 4

Under Blue Town, for over a week, amid the broken beer bottle shards, garbage, and fetid odors, Eippy skulked in the shadows of the storm drains. Sometimes, his soaking wet clothes dripped like rags, and his face and his black fluffy tail were glazed with dirt and grease, but he didn't quit. He continued to search for his dog, Spinach.

During his search, he occasionally slipped out of storm drains and ate whatever he could steal or whatever he could scratch from the pig-people's weed-choked gardens. All the while, the nightmare of his father's murder stayed with him, and his heart yearned for the companionship and warmth of Spinach.

In the dark night, to get some fresh air, Eippy slipped out of the storm drain. As he wove his way through a maze of streets and alleyways, he was always amazed at how much Blue Town had changed. It had once been a shining example of what a decent town should look like. Immaculate blue buildings had stood tall and had offered shops, restaurants, and places to reside in luxury. Outcasts of society, emaciated dogs, bone-thin cats, and toothless winos were confined to back alleys and the seedy side of town.

Now, only a trace of faded-blue color remained on the dilapidated, once-blue buildings. Haphazard placements of corrugated plastic shacks, encrusted with dirt, were the homes of the outcasts. The bone-thin cats and emaciated dogs had been eaten, and the winos had shriveled up and died, their mummified bodies left to turn to mold-covered leather. Although defecating in the shadows of thatched huts next to a river gray with pollution was obscene, it was accepted as a money-saving necessity for the pig-people of the new and unimproved Blue Town.

Out of breath and hiding in the shadow of a trashcan, Eippy breathed in deep drafts of air, but suddenly stopped. An acrid trail of smoke brought back an obnoxious odor that could never be forgotten: The unmistakable smell of burning flesh.

Breathing in shallow breaths, Eippy walked toward the odor. When it became almost too strong for him to breathe, he stood against the wall of a dirty-red brick building and looked to the center of the foot-hammered dirt street. A fire pit had been dug. Two dead orange pygmies had been skewered onto two long rods that ran over the pits. On both ends of the rods, long handles, used to turn the spit, sat motionless. One side of the pygmies was being brunt.

Although boiled pygmy meat was regularly consumed by the lower class of pig-people, roasted pygmies were sold as exotic meat to high class, gullible pig-people who were too ignorant and too lazy to grow their own food. But this night, only one pig-person was tending the spit. That meant something more important was going on someplace else.

The pig-person tending the spit looked around. Satisfied no one was watching, he took a deep breath and leaned over the body on the spit. The body's bulging eyes were permanently fixed in death, staring back at him. But those eyes would never see again, and the body's mouth was open in a scream that would never cry out again.

The pig-person wiped the blood from the pygmy's face and looked around. Satisfied no one was watching, he leaned over, bit off the pygmy's nose, and swallowed it in one satisfying gulp. After he saw the pygmies were burning on one side, he grabbed the handle of the spit and rolled them over.

Although Eippy tried to suppress it, the sight of the pig-person biting off the nose and swallowing it was too much for him. Memories of the pygmy hunter biting into his father's arm came flooding back. He closed his eyes and backed away. Leaning against the wall, he felt as he were going to vomit.

When he opened his eyes, he didn't know if it was because he was woozy, or it had actually happened, but something that resembled a little purple blur ran up to the pig-person and stabbed something into his butt. In pain, the pig-person squealed, jerked his hand from the handle, and whipped around to face his attacker. But the purple blur had vanished as mysteriously as it had appeared.

After his sickness had subsided, to get away from the grotesque sight and the odor of burning flesh, Eippy ran down the sidewalk.

The usually noisy café at the end of the narrow thoroughfare was silent. Dirty-yellow light from oil-fed, naked wicks of streetlights shone weakly in the eerie mist. Doorways and centuries-old blue asphalt amplified the sound of footsteps at the end of the alley. Eippy strained his tiny eyes to see who or what it was. But the figure never materialized. The sound of the footsteps vanished into a gauntlet of shadows.

Eippy continued down the street. Alert to the black spaces of threatening silence, he walked cautiously. But he sensed something was wrong. In this part of town, carbide-powered floodlights usually washed the streets all night long and illuminated activity that never stopped. Pig-people would be standing in groups. Pygmy hunters would be mingling with and crisscrossing the groups of pig-people. Some would be pointing to areas where electric lights used to brighten but were now dark and deserted. Here, idle OvalCars, once powered with electricity, lined the streets. Before the food shortage, brown and beige pygmies had brought mounds of glutinous food into Blue Town. Instead of preserving the food or storing it away for another day, pig-people had jammed it into their slobbering mouths and swallowed it until their stomachs became bloated, and they had difficulty breathing.

But it didn't matter how huge their stomach became, they still entered broken-down bars that lined the mist-laden alleys and drank bad whisky and cloudy beer.

Eippy slipped into a dark alley and peeked between the broken boards of an ancient bar. Inside, pig-people who seemed to be half devil wallowed in the raucous squalor of the place. Cigar smoke, thick with the stench of stale whisky filled the bar like a thick greasy fog.

Already wasted, a rough-looking pig-person with crossed eyes and a shirt collar ringed with dirt, stumbled up to the bar. Seeking out additional means to do further damage to his limited brain, he banged on the bar and demanded a double shot of rotgut whisky. When it came, he looked around for approval and lifted the glass to his slobbering lips. In one smooth motion, he dumped it down his throat. As if he were expecting applause, he looked around and smiled a satisfied grin.

No one applauded, but pig-people shouted across the tables. Pygmy hunters lurched at each other and broke into loud drunken laughs. A few had passed out, collapsed where they sat, heads limp on folded arms. Spilt pools of beer surrounded their dirty hands and filthy faces. These pig-people wouldn't be much of a threat to Eippy, but Spinach wasn't there. Eippy walked out of the alley and continued on down the street.

Next to a tipped over garbage can, Eippy stopped. A pygmy hunter with a sour face walked out of a side street and looked in Eippy's direction.

Eippy was one of many pygmies that had survived when most of the bigger pygmies had been killed because of their size and bright orange color. Eippy's father had told him that breeding with orange aliens may have been the cause of the bright orange color, but was probably caused from eating too many carrots. The pygmy hunters claimed that only black pie pygmies and bright orange pygmies were good to eat, so they passed over brown or beige pygmies, saying that they were not ripe yet. Being a black pie pygmy, Eippy was always hunted.

He was certain he would spend most of his life in a state of fear.

Afraid the pygmy hunter had seen him, Eippy jumped up onto the steps of a dilapidated building and crouched behind a garbage can. The pygmy hunter surged up out of the darkness and stopped right beside him. The pygmy hunter's rear end was right in front of Eippy's face. It was close enough for him to touch. But the pygmy hunter did not see him. He lifted his leg to pass one of the most obnoxious horrors of the world: Pygmy hunter gas. Eippy held his breath. But the pygmy hunter only grunted and walked away.

As Eippy breathed again, around the street corner, pig-people created chaos that became compounded when volatile pygmy hunters' tempers erupted. Using his tiny size to his advantage, Eippy crouched to an even smaller size and made his way in the shadows until he stopped between a fallen metal sign and the wooden wall of a dilapidated bottled water building. He peered from his vantage point. A ways from the quarreling pig-people, empty wine bottles had been strewn in the gutters around a broken fountain. Uncollected garbage had been piled against a purple-mold-covered brick wall. It was once a place where raucous revelry, laughter, gambling, fights, and whores parading their wares, would go on all night and all day. It was where it had all begun. The fountain was the first place that the announcement had been made.

"It is okay to go off the blue grass," the Chief Earth Officer had announced. "Go back to the green lands. The virus is a cruel hoax played on you to keep you away from the good life that only the pygmies enjoy."

For years, the Chief Earth Officers of Blue Town had controlled the pig-people by keeping their expectations low. After they were permitted to go off the blue grass their expectations soared. Out of control, they cut down most of the forests, polluted the streams and lakes which resulted in gigantic fish kills, and much of the vegetation of the earth began to die, but the pig-people did not care or believe they could harm the earth. Immediate self-gratification was paramount in their misguided minds. After ruining most of the earth, they had retreated to the confines of Blue Town, where they had lived off the labors of Dinky slaves until the Dinkies had escaped or were replaced by cannibalistic pygmies who ate Dinkies.

After a few minutes, the chaos and violent tempers around the street corner subsided. The rowdy pig-people flowed under a broken, filth-covered plastic sign and into a large bar.

Sometimes after a flare up, uncertain of their own value and having no reasons for being where they were, the amateurishly, conspiratorial pig-people wandered around in circles or met on street corners to exchange nonsense. But this was one of the times they didn't. The sudden movement of all the pig-people going toward a specific place made it obvious that something important was about to happen.

Silvered in the moonlight, Eippy slunk to the alley next the bar and shimmied up the drainpipe that ran up to the roof. Once on the flat roof, he took up his secret viewing place at the edge of the skylight.

As patches of escaping light from the blotchy skylight slid across Eippy's face, he peered down. The room was big, and the ceilings were high. But to tiny Eippy, all rooms were big, and all had high ceilings.

The center of the crowded room was profuse with plastic tropical plants in huge fake wood-grained plastic boxes. On the tables around the boxes, candles, within lanterns, provided yellow light that caused shadows to flicker against the dull-green, plastic foliage. As quiet crescendos of laughter filtered through the room, it seemed as if the patrons were waiting for the usual nocturnal games to begin. They were waiting for people to get drunk, make fools of themselves, and provide entertainment.

Below Eippy, and off to the right, pig-people and pygmy hunters gathered around a pig-person with short arms standing on top of the bar. With their eyes locked on his face they were listening to every word he spoke.

"We need a new leader," the pig-person said, and because he had only one eye, he moved his head from right to left. "We need a man for all seasons, a man for all the people, a man with the propensity for going right to the core of the matter. We need a man to eliminate the pygmy race."

A pig-person stood up. His voice rose in anger. "I don't recall the Chief Earth Officer quitting. Who gave a short-armed person like you the job?"

As if it were an invisible ice pick, Peep's one eye pierced into the complaining pig-person's eyes. "My short arms do not affect my brain. And for your information, I don't claim to be the new Chief Earth Officer."

A laughing pig-person yelled from the back of the bar. "You couldn't make a pimple of the Chief Earth Officer's hind end."

Peep shot back, "I wouldn't want to be a pimple of a Chief Earth Officer who rapes defenseless women and molest little children?"

Eippy knew the Chief Earth Officer would never do that. Apparently, false information about the Chief Earth Officer had traveled through the gossip grapevine. It was believable, and for some reason, Peep was taking advantage of it.

The pig-person at the back of the room cringed and sat down.

Then a pig-person with a floppy hat and a happy face jerked his finger toward Peep. "You tell em' Peep."

Eippy wondered why Peep wanted to eliminate the pygmies. Not only was it possible that they had been cross-bread from an incredible race of orange aliens, for years, the pygmies had lived with the earth and cherished its life-giving gifts. Their small bodies did not disturb the delicate plant life. Their actions and way of life had greatly helped the earth to regain some of its former wetlands and pollution-free forests.

Peep continued talking. "Tonight, a new leader is with us." Although Peep's short arms made it almost impossible to applaud, he clapped his hands in front of his chest and began walking backwards. "Give a rousing welcome to the man who is going to turn Blue Town around." He quit walking and held out his short arms in a welcoming gesture. "Our next Chief Earth Officer, Ivan Law!" In a show of excited support, Peep applauded and tried to jump up and down. But only the blubber of his ample stomach bounced inside his loose-fitting pants.

Law hopped up onto the bar and turned to the pig-people. Being a half-breed pig-person, Law didn't have all the characteristics of a pig-person. He was more like the ancient human people. His eyes set further apart than a pig-person's, but his nose had a piggish look to it. His head didn't narrow at the top, and he had a full head of red hair that hung down to his shoulders. Compared to the three-fingered pig-peoples' hands, Law's four fingers and a thumb looked odd. Although he had a slight paunch, his stomach was nowhere near the size of a pig-person's. He could almost pass for a normal human being.

As if amazed, he looked around the bar. "What a wonderful turnout." He beamed his smile toward the pig-people, but Eippy saw one side of his upper lip curl up. It was a sure sign Law was lying, and it was a phony smile.

Law held his phony smile and said, "Thank you for being here tonight."

A drunken pig-person, wearing a red striped beanie, lifted his round head from the table and stood up. With a piggish sneer and a nasal sound to his voice, he shouted, "Who died and left you in charge?"

Law didn't falter. "It doesn't matter," he said with the utmost confidence. "When a pig-person knows he can do a job that needs to be done, he cannot be modest."

Baffled, the drunken pig-person's red face flushed with puzzlement. Avoiding eye contact, he looked down.

Law grunted through his pig nose and continued. "The misery of our people is horrible. Many are starving. The whole of the middle class has been impoverished. When this collapse reaches the homeless in the culverts, we will be faced with a disaster never experienced before. Not only will Blue Town collapse, the devastation it causes will cause the civilization of pig-people to grind to a most painful end."

A round-faced, jovial pig-person called out, "Don't be a worrywart." He held up his empty mug. "They lowered the price of beer. Everything's going to be just fine."

Law turned toward the pig-person with the empty beer mug, smiled, and gestured toward the bartender. "Give that man another beer."

As the crowd laughed and cheered in approval, Law turned toward the crowd and held his big pleasing smile. "I'm glad you are with me." He turned toward the bartender. "I'll only be a few more moments. When I'm finished, give everyone another beer."

As the pig-person scrambled to the bar to fetch his beer, Law turned to the other pig-people. With

48

one side of his upper lip curled up, he continued to lie. "We deserve something better than a reduction in the price of beer. The pygmy's regulation of the price of bottled water and confiscation of salt and sugar and other impossible economic proposals make you wonder who the geniuses are advising the pygmies."

A pig-person with dark, inquisitive eyes and a forehead lined with wrinkles that made him look attentive and studious, stood up. "But aren't economic measures being taken to solve all of our problems?"

Law vigorously shook his head. "Nothing is going to be accomplished by petty economic measures. The pygmies have all the gold. Their conspiratorial actions are an ever-present nuisance. Their use of gold has caused our Chief Executive Officer to order more reform programs than he can possibly control. Bribing by the wealthy, aristocratic pygmies has become an all-too prevalent way of life."

The pig-person with the beer blurted out, "So what?"

It was apparent that he didn't understand what Law was talking about.

"Good point," Law said to make the pig-person feel important. "The fight is against the pygmies. To solve this pygmy problem, administrators are not needed. Strong pig-people" — he waved his arm in an arc — "like the ones before me, right now, are needed."

The crowd nodded in approval.

Law smiled and continued. "Many times, I have pointed out to the Friends of the Earth Corporation that they are not behind us common pig-people and that they should help us ameliorate our situation." He paused to see if there were effects from using the word ameliorate that meant "to make better", but there were none. Apparently, not one pig-person in the bar was highly intelligent. They would be easy to sway. He raised his voice. "I am for the common pig-people. The Friends of the Earth Corporation wanted me to join them in their quest to find the gold the pygmies have stored away. I informed them that I would join them only on the condition that this ongoing political struggle be placed into my hands alone."

A pig-person with dark inquisitive eyes raised his hand. "Every time we get close to a hoard of gold, the pygmies move it. If you are given power, just what is your great plan to find the gold?"

"Simple. When there are fewer pygmies running free they will not be able to move their hordes of gold as easily as they do now. I say we hunt and capture this excellent food source until their numbers have diminished to the point that they can no longer move their hordes of gold without us seeing where they are taking them. Once we have their gold, we can buy all the food we'll ever need."

Toweling sweat from his swollen, lead-colored face, a pig-person spoke up. "Our former Chief Earth officer claimed that wasting disease called Kura is caused by cannibalism. Do you want us to eat pygmy meat and go mad?"

"Yeah," a pig-person with a large jaw shouted. "What about that?"

Nodding and smiling pleasantly, Law answered. "We all know Kura causes its victims to stand and walk as if they are intoxicated, have a loss of muscle control, slurred speech, tremors, and have uncontrollable laughter."

The pig-person with the large jaw turned to a drunken pig-person slumped in his chair. "Hey, Tony, you've had Kura disease all your life."

Tony jerked his head up and blinked his eyes. "Hey!.. I wanna tell ya! And back that way again."

As his eyes closed and his head eased back down, the crowd erupted in friendly laughter.

Laughing, Law held up his hand. "Gentleman, we shouldn't make fun of a horrible disease, but all our former Chief Earth Officer has done is babble and create confusion. He has fed us a most incredible lie." One side of his upper lip curled up and almost touched his pig nose. "No transmission of Kura disease to pig-people has ever been reported."

A white-suited pig-person with black, greasy hair plastered down on a round skull stood up. "Just because the Friends of the Earth Corporation haven't reported it, it doesn't mean Kura hasn't been transmitted to the people who have eaten pygmy meat."

Law raised one finger. "Good point," he said and continued to lie. "Although cannibalism *is* the eating of human flesh, pygmies cannot transmit Kura disease. Pygmies are not human."

The hard blue eyes on a brick-red pig-person's face flew wide open with alarm. "But if we eat all the pygmies, we will have no one to grow our crops."

Law gestured to the pig-person. "I'm sure my learned friend, here, has seen pig-people suffering from fatigue, diarrhea, bellies that stick out, enlarged livers, and swelling of the body."

A bewildered look filled the pig-person's face. "I don't understand."

The medical terms for those diseases are marasmus and kwashiorker. Those diseases attack people who do not eat enough protein."

With a dumbfounded look on his face, the pig-person's mouth dropped open. "I didn't know that."

"Now that you do, you may be surprised to know that the junk the pygmies grow is not like the crops the Dinkies used to grow. The pygmy crops do not have enough of the life-giving protein that we need to live. We need more than pygmies' crops. If we want to be healthy, we need to eat pygmy meat."

Still amazed, the pig-person goggled at Law. "So what do we do when we have eaten all the pygmies?"

"May I remind you" — Law shook his finger at the pig-person — "we have a proclamation that came directly from the chief earth officer's lips: 'Inferior pygmies in the brown and beige stage are to serve the fine people of Blue Town.'"

"But we are not served by any pygmies."

Law held up his hand in protest. "Where have you been? We *are* served by pygmies. When they are in the brown and beige stage and not fit to eat, they grow our crops. But when they turn orange they become tricky little buggers and are most difficult to catch."

As if demanding an answer, the pig-person stared at Law. "You didn't answer the question. What do we do when we have eaten all the pygmies?" His eyes seemed to make Law uneasy.

Law quickly looked away, but knew it was time to break the news. He continued. "After we kill all the pygmies, it won't matter."

Whispers and a state of confusion spread across the crowd.

A huge smile spread across Law's face. "Tonight, I have good news for all of you. The pygmies have not eaten all the Dinkies."

A murmur of excitement rippled across the crowd.

"That right. I have information that the Dinkies have built a new city. They have grown more protein-giving food than they'll ever need."

The mention of food caused the gathered pig-people's eyes to jerk wide open.

The pig-person with the dark inquisitive eyes stood up. "Are you saying that the Dinkies who used to grow our food are still alive?"

Law nodded. "That's right. And I have a map that shows us how to get there."

A pig-person with calm intelligent eyes jumped up. "So what? If you bring the Dinkies back, the pygmies will only eat them, again."

"Not after we eliminate the pygmies. When that's done, we'll bring back the Dinkies."

Squinting one eye, the intelligent-looking half breed pig-person reasoned, "Dinky are an insular tribal society. There may be a few humans with them, but they have no say in the government of Blue Town. What if they don't want to come back?"

Peep raised his hand. "May I cut in?"

The half breed pig-person blinked his inquisitive eyes and gestured to Peep. "Knock yourself out."

Peep smiled. "After we eliminate the pygmies, Blue Town will be a safe place for the Dinkies to live and work. They will gladly come back. Blue Town will return to its golden age."

"That's right," Law added. "But just in case the Dinkies don't want to come back, we'll offer them so much gold, they'll be standing in line to come back."

The pig-person with the inquisitive eyes asked, "Will we still need a few pygmies?"

"When the Dinkies come back, Blue Town, we will not need a single pygmy." As if in thought, he paused. "Do you all remember when Blue town was a respectable place to live?"

Heads of pig-people silently nodded.

"Everything will be just the way it was before the pygmies ate most of the Dinkies and forced them into hiding."

The man with the free beer raised his mug. "I'll drink to that."

Cheers of approval along with a thunder of cheering and ovation filled the bar.

After the ovation died down, Law continued. "But until we make that happen—" He held up a cage. Inside, a dog whined. Law jerked the cage toward the crowd. "Until that time, we'll have a fine source of protein to surge through our veins. Tonight we are going to roast a dog."

As bits of pygmy meat dribbled from the greasy lips of an enormously fat pig-person slumped in the corner, his bloodshot piggy eyes brightened. "A dog? I love dog meat."

A pig-person using a paper cone for a hearing aid held up his hand in protest. "But haven't the pygmies made pets of dogs?"

Defending his chance to eat dog meat, the piggy-eyed pig-person jumped to his feet and jerked his finger at the pig-person. "If you don't shut your trouble-making mouth, I'll shove that cone down your trouble-making throat."

Cowering, the man dropped the paper cone from his ear and lowered his head. "I just wanted to know."

"I'll be glad to answer your question," Law assured the pig-person. "Sure, the pygmies have made pets of dogs. In the old days the pygmies knew a belly full of food was enough. Now they make pets of the health-giving dogs we need to survive. They have mixed up survival with wanting no one else to have food at all."

"That's right," Peep yelled.

A cheer of support roared from the crowd.

Eippy peered over the skylight and struggled to see what kind of dog was in the cage. A splash of cream-colored fur, accented by a splotch of spinach, flashed from inside the cage. The dog turned. The tip of its ear was missing. It was Eippy's dog. It was Spinach. They were going to roast him.

The drunken pig-person's head fell back. With his eyes looking up, he suddenly came to life. As if clearing his vision, he shook his head. With stark realization, his eyes opened wide. Jerking his stubby finger at the skylight, he shouted, "Hey! And back that way again. There's one of those little pie pygmies right above our heads. He's spying on us."

As if he hadn't touched a drop of alcohol, the drunken pig-person stood up and threw his empty beer mug at the plastic skylight. The mug bounced off the filthy plastic, came down, and crashed onto the hard floor.

"Get that little bugger," the pig-person with the red-striped beanie yelled. "Tonight, we'll eat dog, topped off with a pie pygmy."

Stumbling over each other and shouting with determination, a hoard of pig-people rushed toward the door.

Eippy jumped back from the skylight, scurried to the side of the roof, reached out, and grabbed the drainpipe. As he descended, like a fleeing spider, his hands and legs became a blur. Toward the end of the pipe, his little body rushed into a sheer slide. He hit the ground with a force so great that his knees came up, hit him in the chin, and knocked him backwards. He landed on his back, but only remained there for an instant.

He jumped up and turned to run out of the alley, but a band of pig-people blocked that escape.

He turned and hurried the other way. When he came to the end of the alley, three round-bellied pig-people, eating greasy pygmy meat, were waiting for him. Using his quickness, he zigzagged around their dirty, grasping hands, but one greasy hand with sausage-sized fingers managed to grab his wrist and jerk him to a stop.

The horrible sight of Eippy's father's arm being chopped off, flashed in Eippy's mind. Trying to free his wrist, he planted his feet on the ground. Even before he could begin to pull away, the pygmy hunter raised an ax. With an adrenaline rush surging through his tiny body, Eippy wiggled and jerked. The greasy, sausage-sized fingers on the hand could not sustain the grip. Eippy's wrist slipped free. He leaped away and sprinted down the sidewalk.

A few meters down the street, Eippy stopped next to the curb. Breathing heavily, he lay flat and slipped into the horizontal opening of a storm drain.

Although it was no longer safe to stay in Blue Town, Eippy had to try to save Spinach. He would have to use the gold he and his father had found.

If he could rescue Spinach, together, they would go back into the forest. There, the pygmy hunters would be in Eippy's element. It had befriended him and his father when they had no one to depend on. They would be safe there.

Eippy hoped he could save Spinach. He had saved him before. But Spinach had been a puppy then. Eippy had simply snuck to the cage behind the bar, opened the door, picked him up, cradled him in his arms, and carried him away. Now,

Spinach was too big and too heavy for Eippy to pick up. But he didn't care. No matter what had to do, he was going to save his best friend. He was going to save Spinach, go through the secret tunnel, and go home.

CHAPTER 5

After the bulk of the pig-people had run out of the bar to chase Eippy, most of the lights had winked off. As if signaling that he wanted to close early, the bartender noisily stacked chairs on the unused tables.

In the subdued amber light, the odor of stale beer, pig-people's dirty clothes, and urine, intensified. The air being blown from a ceiling fan was not fresh, and at times, it became noxious. While an old pig-person with a hunched back tramped around the bar searching for dropped or forgotten change, Law, Peep, and a few other pig-people sat at a table sipping cloudy beer and ignoring the bartender. Everyone but Law picked at a platter of pygmy meat that sat in front of them, and a pig-person with a lead-colored face constantly erupted into fits of sporadic laughter.

The sporadic laughter seemed uncontrolled and was a sign of Kura disease, but Law pretended the man was only drunk.

With his foot resting on the cage, the dog was in, Peep took a huge drink of beer and set the mug on the table. "Well there goes the rally."

Although the adrenaline rush from the speech, he had just made, still churned in Law's mind, he was glad he had lied. At first, when he had begun to lie, he had felt that it was wrong and against the supreme laws of Orange Man. Everyone knew that lying was wrong and that good could not possibly come from doing anything wrong. After Law had

59

lied, about cannibalism being the eating of human flesh, and that pygmies cannot transmit Kura disease because they are not human, using Derrick's guidance, he had felt good. Not only had he felt good, he had felt elated. Using the technique of protective rationalization, he had convinced himself that because telling lies made him feel good, he could not be wrong. Now, with a clear conscience, he could easily deceive the pig-people. He was surprised he had not thought of doing it sooner.

The exertion from his energetic, impassioned speech was causing him to sweat, and he was at the peak of exhaustion, but looking around the empty bar gave him new energy to speak. He raised his hand and gestured to the people sitting around the table. "You see what happens when people don't have leadership?"

In unison, Peep and the others nodded.

Law took a swallow of beer and continued, "Without leadership the pig-people of Blue Town will continue to be sociopaths."

Holding a piece of pygmy meat on the end of a pointed stick, a pig-person with a red-striped beanie jerked the meat at Law. "What can we do about it?"

"Simple," Law said. "We break the prisoners out of jail."

The pig-person lowered the stick and stared, stunned. "Oh my, Orange Man! Why would we do that?"

Law spoke with certainty. "The number of people in a group is directly proportional to the number of people who will support a cause."

The pig-person shook his head in numb bewilderment. "I don't understand."

"I'll explain it to you." Law settled back into his chair and lifted one hand. "If a group of people were walking down the street claiming they knew where to find free food and one person was walking in the opposite direction claiming he knew where to find free food, which person would you follow?"

"I'd follow the crowd. That many people couldn't be wrong."

Even though Law knew a crowd of people could be wrong, and many times they were wrong, he didn't bring up the point.

"That's right," he agreed with enthusiasm. "With prisoners joining our ranks, we'll have the persuasion of numbers." His voice rose with emotion. "And besides, we don't need pig police interfering with our efforts. When we break out the prisoners, we'll throw the pig police where they belong: in jail."

With his eyes glaring with trepidation, the pig-person asked, "But won't it be difficult to overpower the pig police?"

"Years of sedentary lives have caused the pig police to become flabby and weak. We can easily outnumber them." Thinking about how he would get even with the judge who had sentenced him behind bars, Law let out a revengeful laugh. "Then they'll be the ones on the inside looking out."

The pig-person with the lead-colored face picked up a roasted pygmy forearm, ripped off a healthy chunk, and held it to his mouth. "That's all well and good, but after the pig police are eliminated we'll have to find someone who can lead the pig-people."

Law leaned toward the pig-person's lead-colored face. "Do you want to be a leader?"

The pig-person held up his hand and defensively backed away. "I'm too dumb for that. But years ago, someone had a notebook with things a person—" For no reason the pig-person stopped talking and broke into uncontrollable laughter. When it subsided, as if he had never laughed, he asked, "Does anybody know what those things are?"

Confusion and uncertainty seemed to freeze on the faces of the pig-people sitting around the table.

If someone with a little intelligence studied the guidelines the pig-person had referred to, Law was afraid they might figure out what he was trying to do. Then his and Derrick's plan would fail. Law couldn't let anyone know he had the notebook with the guidelines.

"I've never heard of such a notebook," he lied. "But the most important thing is to communicate with one another. Don't try to be a hero and go off on your own. "We need a common bond to unite all of us. People who don't unite are of no value to us or themselves."

As if bored, the pig-person with the red-striped beanie leaned back in his chair. "Unite all you want. Nobody's going to do as they're told."

For a moment Law twisted in his chair and struggled for a reply.

The red-striped beanie pig-person pressed on. "Come on, Law, just how can you make anyone do what they're told if they don't want to do it?"

Faking anger to control the pig-person, Law leaped to his feet. "What are you doing? Trying to kill the movement before it starts?"

The red-striped beanie pig-person lifted his hand in a defensive mode. "Of course not. I just wanted to know."

Law slowly sat back down. "For their own good, we'll make them do as they're told." His tone was low and deadly.

The red-striped beanie pig-person opened his mouth to reply but didn't.

The chair the pig-person with the lead-colored face was sitting on creaked under his weight. "Good luck on that," he said and laughed. "Free beer couldn't keep them in here."

"We won't need luck," Law said and grinned. "People don't know it, but we have the power to take over our useless government." He stood up and rubbed his belly. "However, before we do that, we have a dog to roast."

Peep tore a chunk of pygmy meat off the pygmy forearm. Holding it, he looked to Law. "Do you really believe Kura disease is caused from eating pygmy meat?"

Law knew eating pygmy meat caused Kura disease and people were going insane from eating it. But if he let it be known, it would ruin his plans. He wasn't going to eat pygmy meat, and he wasn't overly concerned about the people who had, especially the pig-person slumped in a chair next the wall who looked like a breathing skeleton and probably had the disease. But the deaths of a few pig-people didn't matter. It was more important that he had a cause to unite the pig-people so he could lead them and bring back the golden times of Blue Town.

With his shoulders shuddering with fake laughter, he lied again. "Nobody in their right mind would believe Kura disease is caused from eating pygmy meat."

Peep took a bite of pygmy meat. With his mouth full, he mumbled, "Do you eat it?"

Law considered pygmy meat poverty food, but it was okay for low-class pig-people to eat it. Sure, a few of them would go mad, but that was better than letting them starve to death. Law figured that because he was more human than the other pig-people, he was probably immune to the Kura disease. But he wasn't going to take a chance and eat pygmy meat, again.

Avoiding an answer, he said, "I'm not going to eat pygmy meat when I have a dog to eat." He gestured to the cage setting under Peep's foot. "Get it, Peep."

Before Peep could lift the cage, the pig-person with a lead-colored face picked up the pygmy forearm. Before he could guide it to his waiting mouth, he dropped it. It fell to the floor and landed with a greasy splat.

"I d-don't feel so good," he stammered, and his eyes were blinking.

Peep looked concerned. "Are you going to be okay?"

"M-maybe if I-I walk around," he managed to mumble. But when he tried to push himself to a standing position, his right arm didn't move as much as his left. It wasn't moving at all.

Law knew the symptoms. The occurrences of pig-people having a Kura disease attack that resembled a stroke seemed to be becoming an everyday thing. The man's speech became thicker and more forced. His arm was hanging limp. His head lolled to one side, and he gave off an odor of meat starting to rot.

The rotting meat odor confirmed it. The man was about to die from Kura disease.

Law shook his head. "He is not going to make it."

Saliva ran down the side of the man's chin. His breathing became deep and sonorous. After one final labored breath, he fell to the floor.

"There goes another one," Peep said as if it were an everyday occurrence. He turned from the man and picked up the caged dog."

His actions seemed callous, but there was nothing anyone could do. There were no doctors or medical care in Blue Town and very little of any other luxuries.

With amused contempt, Law stared at the dying man until the life faded completely from his eyes.

Law had a suspicion that the dead pig-people were being secretly roasted and sold as pygmy meat. If they were that would surely be cannibalism. It would cause Kura disease quicker than eating pygmies. He stood up and signaled to the humorless bartender. "You have a clean-up over here."

Keeping his stone-faced expression, the bartender nodded and mumbled, "Ground meat special tomorrow."

Law and the pig-person, with the red-striped beanie went outside. Peep picked up the caged dog and followed. They were going to roast a dog.

CHAPTER 6

Eippy stopped at the end of the storm drain culvert and gasped. The sea before him was littered with what looked to be hurricane wreckage. Uprooted trees, huge clumps of seaweed, splintered plastic boards, and ancient boat hulls bobbed and lifted on the swelling water. In silence, he stared toward the horizon. The heaving carpet of flotsam seemed to stretch to the sun. A few days ago, the earth had shaken as if there had been an earthquake, but there had been no aftershocks. Eippy figured an inverted red lightening sprite had struck a gas well. But he never believed such an explosion could cause so much damage.

With twilight deepening, Eippy stepped out of the storm drain culvert and ran to the spot where his father had been killed. He looked at the stretch of hard ground where the pygmy hunter had fallen. Clean white bones of the pygmy hunter formed a haphazard heap. Eippy wondered what had killed the pygmy hunter and had carefully licked the bones clean.

After making sure no one was watching, Eippy took three steps past a brown rock, dug into the black sand, and extracted a leather bag that contained a rare magnet and what he hoped would save Spinach: Gold.

With the leather bag of gold securely tucked into his pocket, Eippy traveled back up the storm drain culvert, stopped at the skinny, rectangular opening under the sidewalk, and looked out. Barely visible in the spill of an orange light, a filthy street sign slanted to one side. Streaked with runny letters that had not been repainted in years, it read "Pit Street". He crawled out of the storm drain opening and looked down Pit Street. With drooling mouths and huge expatiations, pig-people stood around a roasting pit. Waiting, they held knives and forks. As saliva ran down their chins, a few noisily ground their teeth and burst into uncontrolled, sporadic laughter.

Eippy knew the people who seemed half-witted were in one of the stages of Kura disease and would soon go mad, but Law was acting like they weren't there. He held the cage door closed with one hand and held a knife in his other hand.

He was going to kill Spinach.

At first Eippy figured there were too many pig-people surrounding Spinach for him to do much of anything. But when he realized that their backs were turned toward him and all their attention was being focused on Law and Spinach, he knew he had a small opportunity.

Law opened the cage. The pig-people lifted their fork-and-knife-filled hands above their heads, stabbed the air, and grunted with anticipation.

Making sure no one was watching, Eippy jumped up, grabbed onto the side of the rectangular storm drain opening, and slid out onto the street. With his hand in the leather bag, he weaved his way between the legs of the pig-people. As he hurried toward Spinach and Law, no one looked down. They seemed to be mesmerized not only by what

Law was about to do but by what a huge human was doing.

Licking his lips and running his hand through the stringy hair of his misshapen head, the human swayed his undulating hips. Law handed him the huge knife. With the clumsy posture of an intoxicated halfwit and with the front of his dirty-white apron swelling with his ample paunch, he rotated his huge belly in a slow, obscene grind and swung the knife to and fro.

The gathered pig-people hooted, cursed, and began a dog roasting party. High-fiving and exchanging guttural grunts, they celebrated with animalistic glee.

Law reached into the cage, grabbed Spinach by the back of the neck, and violently yanked him out. Whimpering in pain, Spinach curled his tail between his legs.

Eippy stopped right in front of Law and Spinach. Clunk! The stick Eippy had been using for a splint on his broken tail hit the cage.

Surprised, Law jerked his head down and stared at knee-high Eippy. "Pie pygmy!" he shouted. In his excitement, he let go of Spinach.

Spinach landed on the ground and got set to run, but at the sight of Eippy, he immediately jumped around and impatiently whined.

Law bent over and reached for Eippy, but the huge belly of the stringy-haired human blocked his view. As Law tried to reposition himself to catch Eippy, Eippy pulled a handful of gold out of the leather sack and flung it onto the ground next to the pit.

As if enlivened with electricity, the gold brightly flashed and twinkled in the firelight.

All eyes snapped toward the sparkly gold.

For a long moment, the pig-people seemed to be in shock. They stood still and stared. Then as if they had just come out of a trance, they stampeded over each other, grasping, grappling, pushing, and mauling one another for the gold. In the process, they caused Law to step aside. The stringy haired human tripped over Law's foot, tumbled to the ground, and landed onto his back. As if he were a gigantic cockroach, struck upside down, he helplessly waved his chubby hands and kicked his thin legs.

Back where the pig-people had just been, Eippy threw more gold. Those pig-people turned and scrambled after that gold, too.

While Law stood with his mouth agape, Eippy jumped on Spinach's back, wrapped his arms around his neck, and held tight. Together they made an end run around the moving, mauling people, raced down an alley, and slipped into another storm drain opening. It has cost Eippy all the gold he had in the leather pouch, but Spinach wouldn't be on the menu tonight.

Now, they were going to a place where there were no pig-people. With Spinach's compact, strongly built body keeping up a sedate pace that didn't tire them, they would easily make it home.

CHAPTER 7

After Eippy and Spinach had rushed through the storm drain system, exhausted and gasping for breath, Eippy stood just inside the end of the culvert. With his ears erect and his keen eyes watching, Spinach stood beside him.

The barrier of the sea before him and the sounds of the pig-people off in the distance, celebrating, caused Eippy to feel he and Spinach could leisurely walk along the beach until they came to the cover of the forest.

Eippy took one step out of the culvert. Spinach backed up and let out a low growl. Something wasn't right. Eippy looked to his left. Lit by the torches in their hands, a band of pygmy hunters, with spears, were marauding down the beach. But they hadn't seen Eippy or Spinach, yet.

Eippy turned to go back into the safety of the culvert, but the strong odor of smoke entered his nostrils. Someone must have seen him slip down the storm drain opening. The pig-people were trying to smoke him out. All the culvert openings that led to the sea would be watched.

Eippy hoped it was still there. If it were, he might escape. Holding his breath, he ran back into the smoke-filled culvert and stopped at a place that had been dug out and covered with a sheet of black plastic. He moved the plastic to one side. The smoke prevented him from breathing a sigh of relief, but what he was looking for was still there: An old plastic bell he and his father had converted into a diving dome. Ropes with weights on the bottom of the bell made it possible for him and Spinach to travel under water. When Eippy had used the dome to find gold, his father had constantly reminded him that while walking on the bottom of the sea, he would have to be careful to go more than nine meters deep or he would get sick from an embolism.

Eippy tried to pick up the dome, but it was too heavy to carry to the sea. He tipped the dome over and grabbed one of the ropes. Spinach placed his head into the rope harness. It slid to his shoulders. Together, they dragged the dome out of the culvert, past the shore line, and into the water. When the water was up to Eippy's knees, Pygmy hunters were twenty meters away.

One of them pointed a long sphere at Eippy and Spinach and excitedly yelled, "There they are!"

With the sound of feet pounding on the shore, Eippy tried to tip the dome upright.

It was too heavy.

He pulled the dome into deeper water. With the water making the dome lighter, Eippy easily tipped it upright and held up one end until Spinach ran under. Then Eippy ducked under, held out his hands, and lifted the dome a few inches. With Spinach at his side, and spears thunking on the outside of the dome, they walked on the sandy floor of the sea.

To get away, they pushed it into deeper water. Even though it was semi-dark under the dome, when the thunking stopped, Eippy knew he and Spinach were under water far enough that the spheres couldn't hurt them, and the angry pygmy hunters wouldn't follow. They didn't know how to swim. But they would be watching the shoreline. Eippy and Spinach would have to walk a long ways to get away from them. And Eippy didn't know how long he and Spinach could breathe the air trapped under the dome. As if in a deep sleep, they pushed the diving bell against the water, and in a cavernous silence, they continued walking.

After a while, a sickening stench from the bottom of the sea enveloped them. Fumes from the stench made Eippy cough and Spinach sneeze. Eippy knew he was walking through sludge from the river that had chocked the current and killed all the fish.

He turned away from the stench and walked toward shore until the water was knee deep. He tipped one side of the dome up and looked around. Along the edge of the river, moonlight revealed brown foam that seemed to thrive on the slime-covered water. To make the place even more uninviting, the area had the sour odor of a cesspool. But there were no pygmy hunters in sight.

In the past, after pig-people had ruined a section of land, they had moved to another area and never ventured back. If there were no pygmy hunters close by, Eippy and Spinach would be safe for a while.

With Spinach's paws plopping in the water, they walked out of the sea and pulled the dome behind them.

On land, Eippy surveyed the area beyond the shore. No green, lush foliage greeted his weary eyes. As if they were disgusted, tall blighted trees slanted back against the sky. Their growth, stunted by poison from the river, had caused the foliage to wither to a dark, dead-brown. As if cursed, smaller soot-dinged skeletal trees, denuded of leaves, clung to a grassless slope. The place was not a romantically lush and idyllic garden. It was dull and dead.

With the help of Spinach, Eippy dragged the dome over the grassless land until he was at a place where a line of leaf-filled trees stood above lush foliage. Here, he hid the dome and covered it with branches. When they walked further into the forest, they passed trees whose thriving boughs obscured the stars. But it didn't matter. Eippy could close his eyes and find his way to the little house he and his father had built.

Off to his right, the fog breath of a huge pig-person with a net jumped in front of Eippy.

It was a pygmy catcher.

If he caught Eippy, the pygmy catcher would place Eippy into a long line of Dinkies who were forced to carry buckets of sand up a long set of stairs. At the top, they would dump the sand into a huge hopper. The hopper had an opening controlled by a valve that allowed certain amounts of sand to fall onto a wheel with rectangular cups that caught the sand. Like water streaming onto a water wheel, the falling sand caused the wheel to turn and generate electricity. Pygmies would work on this line and live on a diet of mostly carrots until they turned orange. Then they would be killed, roasted, and eaten. Being a pie pygmy, Eippy didn't want to find out if the pygmy catcher would eat him or force him to haul sand up the stairs until he turned orange. If forced to haul sand, Eippy figured he would be on the sand wheel for the rest of his life. He had never heard of a pie pygmy changing color. He believed he would never turn orange. He jumped on Spinach's back, bent low, and hung on.

The pygmy catcher jumped up. His feet landed on two rocks, right in front of Eippy. With both legs spread, the pygmy catcher readied his net.

With Eippy clinging to his back, Spinach took off running and fearlessly zipped between the pygmy catcher's legs. Momentarily surprised, the pygmy hunter stood stunned.

After a second, he threw the net.

But he had not thrown it fast enough. It fell harmlessly onto the path.

The great speed at which Spinach ran was no match for the dim-witted, net-throwing pygmy catcher. Eippy looked back over his shoulder. The pygmy catcher seemed to be amazed at how easily Spinach zigzagged around wet depressions in the land, wove between trees, and leaped over a fallen tree trunk. But there would be more pygmy catchers on down the trail. They may not be so amazed.

At a place where the trail sloped upward, Spinach and Eippy veered around boulders where pygmy catchers hid with nets. But when the catchers stood up to cast their nets, the angle of the hill and being surprised at the speed of Spinach, they jumped up and lost their balance. Spewing cussing words, Eippy had never heard, they tumbled to the ground. They had not been amazed.

When the slope leveled off, Spinach panted, and his tongue lolled. Just as he slowed to a trot, lightning arced across the sky and reverberated off the damp limestone wall where overgrown vines crawled up the sides and strangled the entrance to a narrow opening that was further hidden with thick vegetation.

With Eippy clinging to his back, Spinach took off in a fast sprint. He slewed around obstacles, bounced over rocks, and ran into the opening. Twenty meters inside, a solid steel door blocked their progress into the tunnel. Eippy reached up, pulled a square rock from the wall, and pulled a rod. The door unlocked. As he shoved the door open, its hinges, badly in need of oiling, screeched a tooth-hurting pitch. Just before he and Spinach walked through the door opening, Eippy made a mental note to come back and oil the hinges. When he closed the door, its hinges let out one loud squawk. Hoping a pygmy catcher had not heard the noise, Eippy looked back to where he had come from. His peripheral vision glimpsed slight movement, but he figured it was a small animal. He turned, placed the square block back into the wall, and closed the steel door. The rod fell and locked the door.

No pygmy catcher or pygmy hunter had ever found or gotten through the solid steel door. Eippy wished he could stay on the safe side of the door forever, but he and his father had never found much gold on the safe side. Now that Eippy was on the safe side of the door, he was anxious to get to his house where his mother and sisters were waiting and worrying.

On his right, an unlit torch had been tucked into a crack in the tunnel wall. Standing on Spinach's back and bracing himself on the side of the tunnel, Eippy reached up, grabbed the torch, and held it against the wall. Then he took a piece of steel from the crack and scraped it across a flint stone in the wall. Sparks erupted onto the torch. It ignited into an orange glow. With the torch lighting their way, Eippy rode Spinach into a shallow pool of water. When he walked through the water, like tiny explosions, silver crowns of glistening water splashed up around his paws. After they made their way around three bends and finally out the other side, Eippy extinguished the torch and placed it into a holder for future use.

Just before the sky was about to opened up and release a downpour of black rain, they made it to Eippy's house.

Eippy inserted the key in the door lock. But it wasn't locked. He turned the knob. A strong gust of wind snatched the knob out of his hand. The door slammed against the wall. He stepped inside, but Spanish hesitated.

Encouraging Spinach to come in, Eippy patted his thigh. "Come on in, Spinach, you'll get wet and dirty."

Spinach reluctantly walked into the house. Eippy began to close the door, but the pressure of the wind caused him to dig his little heels into the dirt floor and struggle to close the stubborn door. When it locked shut, the dark sky let loose. As if trying to break into the house, rushing, filth-filled rain pounded against the door.

Eippy had expected to be welcomed by his mother, his two sisters, and a warm meal. But all that greeted him was a faint odor of garlic and wind whistling around the corners of the dark house.

As he stood inside the darkness of the house, outside, the wild, moaning wind lashed at the trees and rain rattled on the roof. The storm was growing worse. The rain was getting cleaner. But that didn't matter. If the wind knocked down the trees, the roof would cave in on him and Spinach. In the darkness, Eippy and Spinach made their way across the room. The wind hammered on the door. Rain splattered on the windows. Clear water raced off the edge off the roof and thudded onto the ground. Not moving and afraid, they huddled into a corner.

The storm held its breath for a moment. In the brief silence, movement at the window caught Eippy's eye. He froze and listened. Outside, footsteps sloshed on the path. A bright light cut through the window and illuminated the inside of the house. In the darkness of the storm, Eippy had not seen them before.

Now he did.

Seated before empty plates, his sister's arms had been tied behind their backs. His mother sat slumped over the table. The heads of big metal spikes protruded through her bloody forearms. She had been nailed to the wooden table. Not only had his father been murdered, now, Eippy's whole family was dead, and he knew why the house smelled like garlic.

When heated, arsenic doesn't liquefy but transforms into a gas and gives off a garlic odor. Someone had turned the house Eippy and his father had built into a gas chamber. And the man or people responsible were behind that light, right outside the window.

Eippy slumped over and cradled his head between his hands. Waves of defeat surged into his very being. He wondered if this were the final reward of his life. He wanted to give up, just sit at the table, let the revealing light shine on him, and let whoever killed his mother and sisters kill him, too. And he was going to do just that, but Spinach nudged his arm.

Eippy looked toward him.

As if to say, "Don't abandon me," Spinach looked at him with sad pleading eyes.

Eippy reached over, wrapped his arms around Spinach's neck, and embraced him. Eippy wanted to cry, but he was thankful Spinach and he were still alive. If he wanted to stay that way, he couldn't whimper about the cruelty of it all. His father's wise words entered his mind. "Life's nothing but a game. You win, you lose. The game goes on. The Orange Man of death circles overhead."

Even though he didn't know if he could win, Eippy knew he could play the game. He felt his eyes narrow into slits of determination.

The light beamed through the window and bathed him in brightness.

A voice filled with excitement bellowed through the window. "There's one still alive!"

Another voice boomed through the window. "It's a pie pygmy. I'm hungry. We can chop it up and make a pie. Get that little bugger."

Bam! The door flew wide open. With their lights fixed on Eippy and Spinach, two pygmy catchers bent over and peered into the house. With wet clothes clinging to their bodies, they blocked escape.

"Well, well, look what we have here." One pygmy catcher said and pushed up the bill of his soaking-wet, blue baseball cap. "Pie pygmy and dog meat."

Smiling with a mouthful of rotten and pointed teeth and water dripping off the tip of his pig nose, the other pygmy catcher nodded with satisfaction. "After he tells us where the gold is, we'll be eating in luxury." He placed his hand on his filthy-shirt-covered stomach and patted it. "We'll be eating up town."

Keeping the light fixed on Eippy and Spinach, the baseball-capped pygmy catcher squatted, low waddled under the top of the door frame, and duck-walked inside the hut. Staring at Eippy, he held his hand out behind himself and whispered to Rotten Tooth, "Give me the net."

Squatting in the doorway, Rotten Tooth handed him a long handled net.

Stalking toward Eippy, the baseball-capped pygmy catcher told Rotten Tooth, "Make sure they don't come out the door. We'll get both of them."

Rotten Tooth spread his arms wide and blocked the doorway.

The top of Eippy's head was only as tall as the pygmy catcher's knees. He didn't know what he was going to do. His silky black tail formed a threatening S and flared out, making him look larger than he really was.

Sensing danger, Spinach hunched low and let out a deep throated grow.

Before Eippy knew what was happening, the long handled net came swooshing down. It harmlessly nipped the side of his flared out tail and, Splat! The net hit the floor. Eippy ran under the table. Spinach let out a single yelp, leaped through the air, and landed behind Eippy. The baseball-capped pygmy catcher reached out and jerked the table up. For a moment, the weight of Eippy's dead mother nailed to the table caused it to tilt up on two legs. Then it crashed onto its side.

The net swooshed down.

Splat! It hit the floor right between Eippy and Spinach.

Growling, Spinach charged forward, bit into the back of the baseball-capped pygmy catcher's pants leg, and hung on.

Struggling to free his leg, the baseball-capped pygmy catcher began to stand up. Bam! His head bashed into the ceiling. He tried to kick Spinach. But Spinach stayed clamped on the back of the pants leg and out of the baseball-capped pygmy catcher's limited kicking range. The pygmy catcher bent over and frantically yelled at Rotten Tooth. "Get him off me!"

"Get the pie pygmy first," Rotten Tooth ordered and duck-walked away from the doorway.

The baseball-capped pygmy catcher used one hand to hold the top of his head that had hit the ceiling. With his other hand, he lifted the net to capture Eippy. But Eippy was too close to the baseball-capped pygmy catcher. The net on the end of the long handle was too far away to capture him.

Rotten Tooth tried to duck-walk to the doorway and block Eippy's escape. Figuring he was moving too slowly to catch him, Eippy ran along the wall and made it to the unprotected doorway. But Rotten Tooth grabbed Eippy's tail. Eippy came to a sudden stop. Pain ran from his tail and up his spine. He jerked to break free. But Rotten Tooth had gripped the sticks Eippy had been using for a splint on his broken tail. Eippy dug his feet into the dirt and pulled with all his might. Zip! The splint slid up his tail and off its end. Rotten Tooth stared at the sticks in his hand.

Eippy ran to freedom.

Outside, Eippy picked up a rock and stood in the doorway. Rotten Tooth lifted his thick-booted foot to kick Spinach away from the back of the baseball-capped pygmy catcher's pants leg. Eippy reared back and threw the rock. Thunk! It landed in the center of Rotten Tooth's back. In instant pain, he grabbed his back, and stomped his thick-booted foot on the ground.

Eippy called out, "Spinach!"

Spinach let loose of the baseball-capped pygmy catcher's pants leg, ran out the door, and leaped through the air. He landed running. At the edge of the tree line, he disappeared behind a bush.

Eippy rushed after him.

Seconds later, while Eippy stopped to catch his breath, Spinach crouched next to him, panting. Eippy looked back to where he had run from. He hadn't noticed it in the rain, but his garden and the green forest and fields that had led to the back of his house had been replaced with an endless expanse of black fields and withered trees with bare branches forlornly hanging over the scorched land. He turned and looked off into the distance. A few boards and a pile of smoldering ashes was all that was left of the barn. The pygmy catchers had burnt it down. As if it were a final parting gesture, the wind sighed, and a little whirlwind formed in the hot gray dust from the barn and merrily danced away.

Eippy didn't know if the pygmy catchers had broken though the solid steel door or had found another way into the safe zone. But as long as they were after him, it would never be safe for him to come back home. He would have to go to a place he had never been before. He would have to go deep into the unknown forest. Although he was afraid, the thought of something new seemed to fill him with elation.

CHAPTER 8

As the nip of the cold night fell, Ivan Law was once again in the dank cellar of the abandoned ramshackle building on Main Street, and he couldn't believe a little pie pygmy, with a broken tail, had managed to take a dog right out from under his nose.

After the dog had been taken, someone had said, "Law can't even keep a little pie pygmy from stealing a dog. What kind of leader is this?"

Although no one else had complained, it seemed as if the pig-people no longer felt Law could lead them to do anything. If he were going to control the pig-people, he would need more advice from the man he was waiting on: Derrick, the mysterious person who had gotten him out of jail early.

Derrick was never really interested in fighting for a good cause, but he was out for the lust of a battle and the rewards that came after. He loved to destroy, and when he did, it made him feel powerful. He liked to stand in front of a crowd and have them cheer for him. After all, his name was, Derrick which meant "people's ruler". And Derrick was good at writing speeches, but his ears had been burned off, and where his nose had been bitten off, two leather-brown holes remained. A single strip of hair ran down one side of his skin-tight skull, and his deformed hand resembled a crab's claw. Not only was he too ugly to be accepted as a leader, his mouth protruded into an obscene hog snout and was accented with a fat tong that stuck out and usually flowed with an uncontrollable, continuous stream of clear, snot-like slobber. If he were able to wipe the slobber from his mouth, he may have been presentable. But some of the coordination in his good hand was gone. He could only use a cloth to dab at his slobbering mouth. Each time he dabbed, yellow slobber stuck to the cloth. When he pulled the cloth away, he created sickening strings of rubber-like slobber. And an odor of glue surrounded his muscular body.

Therefore, he had asked Law to take his place. At first Law had refused. But after the purple pygmies had burned down his house, he had spent time in jail, wanted unlimited revenge, and a chance to get the Dinkies to return to Blue Town and make himself a hero, he had told Derrick he would think about it. When Derrick reminded him that he had gotten him out of jail early, Law felt that he owed Derrick. He accepted Derrick's invitation.

Next to the blanket-covered cellar window, Derrick sidled up to Law. "How did the speech go?"

Law smiled big. "The speech went just fine. Using your technique of protective rationalization, I can lie about anything and feel good about it."

Derrick patted Law on the back. "In civilian life it's called lying, but in our kind of politics it's called disinformation."

Law nodded in understanding. "Anything we have to do to gain control, I'll do it."

"It's good that you understand that," Derrick said and dabbed a string of slobber streaming from the leather brown holes where his nose used to be. "Did Peep give you the notebook?"

"Yes, he did. The map will be very helpful."

"Did you do anything to get rid of the Chief Earth Officer?"

"He's just about gone." Law chuckled. "We got a bunch of whores to say he raped them. And to make it even worse, we paid a bunch of kids to testify that he molested them."

"I'm proud of you," Derrick said. "Everybody believes a kid. For years, ambitious flunkies have grabbed a hold of that kind of disinformation and completely ruined innocent people's lives. It works every time."

"Thank you, but what should I do about the pie pygmy who took the dog?"

"I heard about that." Derrick grinned manically. "All you have to do is catch the pie pygmy and bring him and the dog back."

"I would, but those pie pygmies are hard to find. What if I can't find him?"

"Simple. You get any pygmy. Claim he is the one who told the pie pygmy to steal the dog. Then kill that pygmy."

Even though Law had killed pygmies from a distance, he had never killed one up close. He was going to ask Derrick about it, but sickening slobber began to string from Derrick's mouth.

Law turned from the sight. "I don't believe I could do that."

"You have to do it, and quick." Derrick placed the cloth over his mouth, and his voice came out muffled. "You've already let the incident go on much too long."

"But where am I going to get a pygmy?"

Derrick stepped away from the blanket-covered window. "Let's go outside. I'll show you."

After they went through the trap door and walked onto the street, two pygmy hunters were leading an orange pygmy down the street. When the pygmy saw Derrick, he reared back and pulled at the rope around the pygmy's neck. The pygmy hunters jerked the rope so hard that the pygmy fell to his knees. Wanting to know what their next meal looked like, hungry pig-people were coming out of buildings to watch.

After taking the cloth from his ugly mouth, Derrick lifted his hand, pointed to the pygmy hunters, and shouted, "That's them!"

The pygmy hunters stopped. The expressions on their faces took on a look of bewilderment. One of the pygmy hunters was grinning. He was a carefree, playful youngster who was just beginning to learn how to hunt.

He stepped forward.

Enraged and frustrated, his rubbery lips obscenely flapped. "While you were doing nothing, we caught a pygmy." Getting ready for a fight, he clinched his fist. "What do you mean that's *them?*"

Derrick jerked his finger at the youngster and yelled, "This is the trouble maker we have been looking for."

Bewildered, the youngster unclenched his fist and stood speechless.

Derrick jerked his finger again. "He is the one responsible for advising the purple pygmies. He is the one who helped the pie pygmy steal a dog."

Derrick's booming voice had managed to arouse the curiosity of other pig-people. They began to gather around. Derrick was going to have an audience.

He whispered to Law. "Go ahead. Kill the kid and the hunter, too."

Law shook his head. "I can't. He's just a kid."

Annoyed, Derrick talked though gritted teeth. "All you have to do is stand there and announce that the penalty for dog stealing is death."

Law nodded and turned toward the gathered crowd. "Friends of Blue Town, the penalty for stealing a dog is death." To place emphasis, he raised his voice. "Not only that!" He pointed to the youngster. "Here is the person who has been stirring up trouble. He will be severely dealt with."

The older pygmy hunter held up his hand in protest. Wait!" He reached into his back pocket. "We have a paper from the Friends of the Earth that gives us the right to kill or take any dog or pygmy we want to."

Derrick stepped next the pygmy hunter and yelled into his face. "If you have such a document, show me."

The pygmy hunter turned away from Derrick's ugly face and pulled a folded piece of paper out of his pocket. With his multiple chins quivering, he unfolded the paper and pointed to a sentence. "Look! It's right here."

Derrick snatched the paper from the pygmy hunter's hands. He and Law looked at it. It did, indeed, authorize the hunters to take any dog or pygmy. Derrick looked at the pygmy hunter. "It looks like you never gave this paper to anyone who could read."

Realizing he was being lied to, the pygmy hunter's eyes grew wide with alarm. "I can—"

Derrick jerked his hand up into a sudden halting motion. "Shut up!" He shook the paper at the pygmy hunter. "This paper is nothing but a reminder to keep your spears and machetes sharp." As if crazed, Derrick's upper lip narrowed and he bared his teeth. While he used his good hand to place the paper into his pocket, he jerked his claw hand toward the pygmy hunter. "Give me your machete!"

Puzzled, the pygmy-hunter gave Derrick his machete.

With the machete raised, Derrick stepped to the kneeling orange pygmy at the end of the rope. "We'll see if you have been keeping this sharp." He swooshed the machete down. It sliced into the pygmy's neck. With blood spurting sideways, the pygmy's head tilted to the side, but it did not fall from his shoulders. It hadn't been cut completely off. The pygmy fell face forward and flopped onto the pavement.

As blood gushed out of the pygmy's severed neck, Derrick examined the bloody blade of the machete and cast a mean stare at the pygmy hunter. "You haven't kept your weapon sharp." He pointed the machete at the fallen pygmy. "If you had that pygmy's head would be off."

For a moment the pygmy hunter sank down dumbfounded, but then he bucked up. "What did you kill it for? We were walking it to the pit. Now, you're going to drag it to the pit."

Derrick laughed with malicious defiance. "Just who are you to tell me what to do?"

The youngster boldly stepped in front of Derrick. "We're pygmy hunters. Give me that machete. I'll show what I can make *you* do."

Derrick handed him the machete.

Using the machete, the youngster pointed to Derrick. "We can tell people want we what them to do and when to do it." He shook the machete at the dead pygmy. "You killed it. You drag it to the pit."

Faster than Law could blink, Derrick reached up with his claw hand, pulled a Bowie knife from the center of his back, and swung it down. It sliced deep into the youngster's neck. It wasn't a complete slice. The youngster's head lolled to one side. Blood from severed arteries shot into the air. Derrick swished the knife again. The youngster's head fell off his shoulders and thunked onto the pavement. Then the youngster's body sagged and dropped.

Enraged, the older pygmy hunter stepped forward. "What did you do that for?"

"I wanted to show you what a sharp knife can do." Derrick lifted the knife. "I'll show you again." He slashed the pig nose right off the older pygmy hunter's face. The pygmy hunter grabbed his blood-spurting, nose-less face. Derrick's snot-spewing face contorted into what might have been a smile. He lifted the knife and sank it deep into the pygmy hunter's stomach, then he turned it up and twisted it until it cut the heart. Gasping for breath, the pygmy hunter fell to the blue pavement.

Stunned, Law staggered back. A person couldn't kill someone like Derrick had just done unless he had done it before. Law wondered if Derrick would kill anyone who got in his way.

Bending over and wiping the blade off on the pygmy's shirt, Derrick motioned for Law to bend over next to him.

Law crouched down. Derrick whispered to him, "If you want to be counted in this world, you have to find the courage to do what needs to be done."

Law looked to the youngster's severed head. Pain and guilt from being party to the murder of an innocent child caused tears to well up. Bleary-eyed, he turned to Derrick. "What should I do now?"

After Derrick told him want needed to be done, Law straightened up, wiped the tears from his eyes, and prepared to do what Derrick had told him to do: He addressed the gathered crowd.

"My friend has just shown us how to deal with trouble makers. As you can see these trouble makers will no longer be advising the pygmies." He looked down at the bodies. "And they will no longer be showing their pygmy friends how to steal dogs we can use for food."

Gullible heads, full of ignorance, nodded, and grunts of approval filled the crowd.

91

Law continued. "I could have done away with these traitors myself. But today, we have learned a valuable lesson. We have learned that a single person does not have to do everything." He gestured to Derrick. "My friend has done what was necessary. When all of us superior pig-people of Blue Town ban together, we can, too."

Peep seemed to come out of nowhere. "We'll crush them like cockroaches." He raised both of his short arms. "Ivan Law is the kind of a man we need to lead us."

A roaring cheer of enthusiasm reverberated down the street.

Law had gained back his respectability. The pig-people were behind him, again. He realized killing the youngster and the pygmy hunter was an amazing flash of genius. The pygmy hunter was dead, and the grinning, previously carefree youngster who had seemed so naïve in comparison to his obvious superior was no longer alive. With the help of Derrick, Law had, in a matter of seconds, become the leader of the pig-people. Although he felt he wasn't yet qualified to be the new Chief Earth Officer, he would be okay as long as he had Derrick's help.

Derrick turned to Law. "Are you hungry?"

"Ever since I was in jail I've always been hungry."

Derrick rubbed his flat stomach. "I could eat a nice piece of dog meat."

Law didn't particularly want to eat dog meat. "I'm not too fond of dog meat."

"That's okay," Derrick said. "We'll go after the pie pygmy, too."

CHAPTER 9

Eippy and Spinach evaded capture by weaving their way, but to do so they had to slog their way through the wet forest. When they finally came to the edge of a small clearing, Eippy brought Spinach to a stop and slid off his back. Standing perfectly still, Eippy watched Spinach. His ears did not point in the direction of something out of the ordinary, and he didn't growl a warning. There were no signs of anyone following them. Relieved, Eippy walked at Spinach's side and continued across the clearing.

At the end of the clearing, a slope in the land led to a stream. Eippy figured he could walk a ways up the stream and make it difficult for anyone to follow.

Wading through the stream at a relaxing pace, he suddenly realized they could be in the enemy territory of pygmies of another race. They could be cannibals. The former welcome change from familiar surroundings to unfamiliar surroundings had become an unwelcome and sudden shock.

His elation fizzled.

He and Spinach waded ashore and stopped at a patch of grass surrounded by bushes and trees. Eippy turned to Spinach. "Quiet!"

Spinach quizzically cocked his head to the side and stood still.

Standing motionless, Eippy listened. Nothing was moving about. Not a single threatening sound came from the forest. He relaxed, but then he remembered that it wasn't what a person hears or sees that got them captured and eaten. It was what they couldn't see or hear.

He waited a few moments.

Still, nothing threatening.

He gave Spinach a reassuring pat. Spinach wagged his tail, sat on his haunches, and watched.

Eippy stacked a bundle of dry moss under a stack of sticks, pulled out his metal fire starter, and struck it. The sparks flew into the dry moss. He cupped his hands around the moss to keep the embers glowing and blew into the moss. It burst into flame. He placed it under the sticks. The flame crawled around the sticks and grew into a little fire. As he warmed his tiny body, Spinach lay tight against his side.

Suddenly, Spinach perked up. Sensing danger, he lowered his tail and looked to the right. Eippy looked in that direction. At first, a poisonous water moccasin looked to be dead. But the heat from the fire had thawed it out just enough for it to find out where it was, but not enough for it to be quick enough to strike. Eippy thought about killing it, eating it, and getting some rest, but fear filled his body. He didn't know if the newness of the surroundings was causing it, but something wasn't right.

Voices drifted through the bushes. Spinach ignored the moccasin and looked toward the sound of the voices. Now, Eippy and Spinach could not sleep. Eippy kicked over the fire and smothered it with dirt. The moccasin slowly slithered away. But that wouldn't be the end of the problem. Just beyond the bushes, something was happening.

Eippy needed to know who or what was talking. Mesmerized, he crouched down. As Spinach's paws padded silently, they crept forward. For a brief, terrible moment Eippy's mind took him back to where his father had been murdered. Fear filled his entire being. He held his breath. The swish of the spears cutting through his father's body and the sight of him clawing to be free, invaded his mind. But he knew if he were going to stay alive, he couldn't dwell on the past. He forced his mind back to the immediate present.

He stood up, breathed again, and looked over the bushes. A few brown pygmies with wet clothes crouched around a small fire roasting something on stick. They were tough-looking, unshaven, and dirty, and they had rat tails like his father and mother had had. If he went up to the pygmies and they were not friendly, he may be eaten. But if they were friendly, he wanted to know where their village was. He decided to wait for them to break camp and follow.

According to pygmy custom, upon entering a village, Eippy would need an offering, a sort of gift, to present to the leader of the village. Before his father had been murdered, they had been chasing one of the few remaining rabbits on earth. It would have made an excellent quick-producing addition to his father's species-saving project. A rabbit would be a gift fit for a king. But Eippy didn't have a rabbit. Except for the moccasin, he hadn't seen a living animal in days. He decided to go back to the stream. Maybe his gold magnet could collect some gold. That would be a fitting gift for anyone.

At the stream, the gold magnet only picked up a small amount of gold dust.

If he only found gold dust, Eippy would have to use his coin mold. But before he could do that he would have to build or find a suitable vessel to put the gold dust into. Then he would have to build a bellows and melt the gold over an air-forced fire. After the impurities floated to the top he could pour the liquid gold into the mold. The resulting gold coin would still have some impurities but would be good enough for a gift. And his mold only had one coin cavity. It would take a long time to make enough coins for a gift.

He waded upstream and stopped at a bend where black sand had converged for a long stretch. Here, the magnet picked up enough gold nuggets to half-fill his little leather pouch. Satisfied that he had enough for a gift, he made his way back to the brown pygmies huddled around the fire. But when he got there all he found was smoking embers.

He surveyed the area around the fire pit. No broken branches, no tramped on weeds, and no small plants had been disturbed by feet. The brown pygmies had left no trail for him to follow.

Carefully walking in an expanding circle around the campsite, he searched for any sign that would lead him in the direction the brown pygmies had gone. On the seventh go around he found one tramped down spot of grass. Walking in the direction of the broken grass, he found disturbed foliage. The pygmies were no longer hiding their trail. It had become a well beaten path. Eippy and Spinach caught up with them so fast that they almost showed themselves. But his small size and Spinach's ability to lay flat enabled them to quickly avoid the brown pygmies' searching eyes.

Hours later, Eippy and Spinach came to a fork in the path and stopped. Trying to decide which way to go, Eippy turned to the right. Through the foliage, he watched the brown pygmies. Wearing wooden clogs, they clomped over a wooden bridge and stopped at a wall with an iron-grilled gate. They unlocked the gate, opened it, walked through, and locked it behind them. As they entered their village, Eippy wondered what kind of pygmies inhabited the place. Judging from the spill of light that washed over the land, inside the wall, the brown pygmies seemed to have electric lights. But more important, they seemed to be friendly. But Eippy needed to be sure. He decided to watch before he went to the gate.

The first thing he noticed was that some of the brown pygmies in the village were a little smaller than the pygmies he had followed. He hoped a few pie pygmies lived there, too. Next to a green and white building, pygmy children were building sand castles in a yellow sand box. Off to the right, a tree spread its lush branches over a lone chicken roosting on a canted plow. Indicating that someone had been working on the plow, small tools haphazardly lay around it. In the distance, the faint crack of a fire caught his attention. He crept around to where the sound had come from and peered through a decorative round hole in the wall. There, brown pygmy men with pointed spears surrounded brown pygmy women. While a bandanna-headed pygmy woman, wielding a straw broom, chased a child, knife blades flashed, and steel points winked in the sun light. A circle of brown pygmy women were slicing celery, chopping onions, breaking chicken eggs, and shredding lettuce. They were preparing dinner.

Although enchanted by the pygmy women skillfully handling of the scintillating blades and their flourishes that looked as if a mortal injury could occur with a single slip, it was a sign that they could be civilized.

With Spinach at his side and smiling encouragingly, Eippy walked toward to the iron-grilled gate and stopped. A stout pygmy woman with an armful of wood gathered into the crook of her elbows, stood on the other side of the gate.

She called through the gate. "Are you the one we have been waiting for?"

Eippy didn't know how to answer. He placed his hand on the pouch that held the gold. "I have a gift for your leader."

The woman straightened her elbows and let the wood fall to the ground. Then she nervously unlocked the iron-grilled gate and opened it. As if before a shrine, she bowed and backed away. "Follow me."

Eippy stepped toward the woman. Another pygmy ran up, closed the iron-grilled gate, and locked it.

Following the woman, Eippy passed brown pygmies who were flying orange and white kites. As if giving thanks, they held the strings of the kites and fell to their knees. A few steps away from the kite flyers, a family was having a picnic. The children were sneaking bits of food under the table, where a red rooster waited. When Eippy walked further into the village, a pygmy woman with a basket balanced on her head, hurried past. He walked past brown pygmy children with wet clothes dried on them sitting outside a tent and looking up in awe. Near the tent, the pygmy woman leading him motioned for a half dozen pygmies to get out of the way and muttered apologies all the way to a tent.

Inside the hot and quiet tent, bugs swirled around a lantern hung on a pole. Except for the lantern and a tree stump, the tent was empty. The pygmy woman turned the flame on the lantern so low that it sputtered on the wick. In the dim light, a brown pygmy dressed in a flowing purple robe appeared. Compared to Eippy's pared-down half-meter-high height this pygmy was twice as tall. His forehead slopped into large emerald eyes, and his double chin sunk into his chest.

The pygmy woman bowed and gestured to the brown pygmy. "Here is the leader of our village." Facing the leader, she backed out of the tent.

The leader stepped forward and sat on the stump. Although dressed in fine silk clothes, the leader didn't look like a happy pygmy. Apparently immobilized by his own bulk, he sat in silence. As if waiting for someone to trigger a malevolence that seemed to hang in tent like humidity, he cast an aura of oppressiveness.

Wondering if he had been lured into a trap, Eippy cringed and waited for the worst.

Wagging his tail, Spinach walked up to the leader and sniffed his hand. Patting Spinach on the head, the leader broke into a happy smile. "No need for formalities." In friendship, he offered his hand to Eippy. "My name's Eustis McCoy."

Eippy took Eustis' hand and gestured to Spinach. "That is Spinach, and I'm Eippy, Eippy Vanko. I have a gift for you."

Eustis lifted his hand. "Ahh, Vanko, your name signifies a gracious gift, but I am not the one who receives gifts." He heaved himself from the stump, stood up, and took one step toward the tent flap. "I must take you to Kaput." He walked through the tent opening.

Eippy wondered what kind of a person would have a name like Kaput, but he and Spinach followed.

After they came down the side of a rugged hill, they looked up. Above the waters of a pond, the sun beamed down on the remains of a once majestic estate. The exterior stonework was unbroken and seemed to have been built to stand for centuries. As they slogged through an overgrown and barely visible path that led to the great house, it became apparent that the insides of various structures had been gutted by fire but were being rebuilt.

Eustis stopped and held his hand toward the estate. "Welcome to Shangri-la, another magnificent and irreplaceable glory of our planet that the pig-people have tried to destroy."

Spinach backed up and growled.

Eippy looked off to the right. The limbs of low hanging branches parted. Searching eyes stared at him.

Eustis waved his hand down. "Pay them no mind. It's only curious villagers wanting to get a glimpse of Kaput. They mean you no harm."

Eustis ushered Eippy and Spinach up a set of marble steps and across a courtyard where a few scraggily weeds struggled to survive in a floor of hard-packed stone dust.

When they walked through the opening of a second wall, Eippy stopped and peered ahead. Little huts, arranged in a circle, created a little pygmy village. Nothing was loud in the village. Only the penetrating cacophony of a single cricket and a faint crackling of a fire broke the stillness. If these pygmies were unfriendly their intentions were buried beneath a peaceful exterior.

Eustis led Eippy and Spinach around the village and through various pathways. After he opened two white, wooden gates they were under the arches of red climbing roses. In front of them, flower gardens and fountains graced white marble statutes that lined red stone steps. Two pygmies, holding shields and spheres, stood at the top of the steps. They seemed to be guarding the entrance to an unsurpassed monument of extravagance. The tallest, unshaven, bleary-eyed pygmy looked out of place.

Walking up the steps, Eustis turned to the side and superstitiously flashed the pygmies a sign. The pygmies shifted uneasily and stepped aside. The bleary-eyed pygmy reached over, unlocked the carved wooden door, and opened it. Spinach stopped in his tracks and cocked his head to the side. A whiff of the sour ripeness of unwashed flesh and rotten teeth, from the bleary-eyed pygmy, filled the air in front of Eippy's face.

Eustis stepped to one side. "Go on in. Kaput is waiting for you."

After Eippy took a few fetid breaths, he and Spinach entered the room. Carved friezes formed a decorative band all along the upper part of the walls and framed the high ornately-painted ceilings, where crystal chandeliers hung down, glowing with warm and friendly light. Red velour curtains graced the sides of one of the enormous windows that looked out at ground level onto a flat grass lawn. Coming from poor pygmies Eippy felt that the room seemed embarrassingly luxurious.

Off to the left, maroon velvet drapes, with gold fringes, framed an entire wall of a detailed map of Blue Town. Directly across from the map, six elegantly curved white marble steps led to a huge elevated throne. Here, Kaput sat cross-legged on a high-backed, golden chair, thickly padded with red velvet. Consisting of smooth, red felt, with white trim, his pressed uniform broadcasted royalty. Although the many medals attached to his chest suggested greatness, there were too many to be believable. His chiseled chin sat under a smiling mouth topped with a mustache that was clipped and narrow, and his blue eyes were clear and steady. At the top of the chair, a gold crest with jewels reflected light so bright it hurt Eippy's eyes. He wondered if his gift of gold nuggets would be good enough for Kaput.

As Eippy creased his eyes to repel the glinting sunlight, Kaput rose majestically in front of his massive gold throne and pointed to a window. Eustis stepped to it and closed the red velour curtains. The brightness stopped.

Kaput placed his hands on the arms of his throne and spoke directly to Eippy. "Come forward."

While Spinach waited at the bottom of the steps, Eippy walked up the marble steps and stopped a meter away from Kaput. Kaput nodded with approval. "We know why you are here."

Eippy lifted his pouch of gold nuggets. "Yes, I have a gift of gold for you."

Kaput reached out. Eippy poured the gold nuggets into Kaput's hand.

"These are very nice." Kaput leaned over and placed the nuggets on the small table sitting next to the throne. Shaking his head, he straightened up and smiled. "We thank you. But gold is not the reason you are here."

Eippy had no idea why he was where he was. "Are you sure you have the right person?"

"That's just what a modest person would say." Kaput gestured to Eustis. "Get the lad a chair. We have much to talk about."

Eustis dragged a chair over the floor, carried it up the steps, and placed it next to Kaput's throne.

Eippy sat down and Kaput began.

"From your experience, you know most people are not used to figuring things out for themselves."

"How do you know I know that?"

Kaput chuckled. "You figured out how to get here without being led. Most people like to follow. They like to be led."

Eippy already knew very few people would volunteer or wanted to lead anyone. He nodded. "Yes, most people need a guide."

"Not only a guide. They need a messenger, a prophet. They always have and they always will."

"This is true. But what does that have to do with me?"

"Think about it, Eippy. We have a chance to create our own prophet. Can you imagine the possibilities?"

Eippy couldn't think what a prophet would do, and he didn't know of any possibilities. "I don't understand."

A discouraged look flashed from Kaput's face. "Don't you realize what we can make the little people do?"

Eippy figured he knew what Kaput was talking about. "Your people are too little to fight, and I'm even smaller."

Kaput frowned but a curious light shone in his eyes. "If my people weren't little, how would you expect them to fight?"

"My father said that there are only two ways to get people to do what you want them to do. You have to overpower them and make them do it. Or you let them know Orange Man wants them to do it."

"Yes, Orange Man wants them to do it, Orange Man or a prophet."

Eippy continued to listen.

"The little people will fight," Kaput said. "But only if someone shows them how. We want you to show them how."

Flabbergasted, Eippy stepped back. "What?"

"The people already believe you are a prophet come to save them."

Eustis broke in. "Because of your small size and black fur they most definitely believe you are the prophet they have been waiting for. Let's not disappoint them. Be our prophet."

Eippy was beginning to believe Kaput was some kind of idiot. Before he could say anything, in a harsh voice, the tall bleary-eyed guard yelled from the doorway. "But I was supposed to be the prophet."

Kaput held up his hand. "We're sorry, Clarence, but you know you are too tall, and you lose your temper too quickly."

"But I've been working on my temper."

Kaput shook his finger at Clarence. "It does not matter. The little people do not trust you."

Although Clarence was behind him, Eippy was conscious of Spinach watching him.

Clarence screamed in a high-pitch voice that resembled a baby's whining. "If I can't be the prophet, then no one will be the prophet." In a sudden rage, the disappointed Clarence raised his spear, aimed it at Eippy, and rushed toward him. Spinach growled a warning. Eippy jumped out of the path of the sphere. With his free arm grasping for Eippy, Clarence zipped past Spinach, but Spinach snagged his pants leg. Clarence stumbled, causing the spear to just miss Kaput's head and swoosh into the back of the red velvet of the chair.

With Spinach tugging at his pants leg, Clarence jerked his finger toward the gold nuggets setting on the table. "That gold should be mine!" He vigorously shook his pants leg. It ripped free of Spinach's grip. Squealing, Clarence ran up the steps and lunged toward Kaput and the gold on the table.

Amazingly agile, Kaput sprang up from his cross-legged position and deflected Clarence's attack. He grabbed Clarence's hand and elbow and twisted his arm sideways. Just as Clarence turned to catch his balance, Kaput kicked his leg out from under him. Clunk! Clunk! Clunk! Two at a time, Clarence tumbled down the six hard marble steps. In one final Clunk! His head slammed against the stone floor. Dazed, Clarence struggled to his hands and knees and shook his head.

As he tried to claw up the steps, Kaput shook his finger at him. "Out of kindness I never told you. But I'm telling you now! For years, your caustic laughter and your constant complaining have irritated me and others around you. We let you get away with it because we felt sorry for you. But it is over. You have become nothing but a debauched ugly man."

As if the words had just shot him, Clarence collapsed onto the floor. With his chest heaving, he breathed deeply.

Eippy didn't know if it were a delayed reaction from hitting his head on the floor or what Kaput had said, but Clarence was out.

Kaput turned his back to the fallen Clarence and gestured to Eippy. "We tried to help him. But he came from a society of vastly undereducated people who believe wealth is knowledge."

Eustis bent over, grabbed Clarence by the arms, and lifted him. "This poor excuse of a man has no sense of morality. I'll take this waste of life out." He grabbed Clarence by his rat tail, dragged him to the wall, and stopped. Then he lifted his foot, placed it on a block in the wall, and pushed. A trap door opened and revealed a set of wooden stairs. Eustis pulled Clarence to the top of the stairs, let him slide down, and closed the door.

Not wanting to have Clarence throw another spear at him, Eippy asked, "After he comes to, can he come back up the stairs?"

"Except for the main entrance, all exits are one way," Kaput said, and, as if he had never asked Eippy to be a prophet, he gestured toward an exit next to the curtain. "Let's go outside for a moment."

Walking to the curtain, Eippy wondered if Kaput had used the prophet conversation to get rid of Clearance. And he was beginning to think there was something wrong with Kaput's mind.

Outside, Eippy and Kaput slipped into the white archway of a veranda. It gave them an excellent view of the pygmy village. All around them, enthralled pygmies produced a muted buzz of conversation.

"At first, Shangri-la hadn't been much of a place," Kaput said. "There were only dim orange lights in places where tiny thatched huts had been

108

set up around our burned out estate. It had looked like a temporary camping place for travelers on the run." He pointed to his left. "Now we have flat roofed buildings and stone foot paths." He pointed to the side of what looked to be a storage house. "Inside, there are wagons we use for hauling produce from the growing fields."

As Eippy surveyed the land beyond the storage house, it seemed to be a secluded hideaway, and he felt it possessed great beauty and peacefulness.

He turned toward Kaput. "The people are at peace. Why would we want to change them?"

"We don't." Kaput's eyes grew wide and large and he flared up. "But we have to. The pygmy hunters and the pig-people want to eliminate our entire race."

"Why? We do them no harm."

Kaput sharply glanced at Eippy. "They have no accountability."

"But what about right and wrong?" Eippy wanted to know. "Shouldn't the pig police be doing something about it?"

Kaput grunted with what seemed to be merriment. "The pig police used to have instructional meetings to keep abreast of how to handle things. But when they had those meetings the only pig police permitted to ask questions were the ones who never did. The Friends of the Earth decided that pig police who never questioned anything already knew everything. So it wasn't necessary to educate them. They canceled the meetings."

"That's just plain ignorance."

Kaput's head bobbed with sardonic laughter. "No, that's pig-people politics." He stopped bobbing his head and took on a serious look. "Now, uneducated pig police blame us for all their troubles. They won't help. Before they replaced decent police with pig-people they used to keep violence to a minimum. Now, pig police rule with fear and punishment." He paused. "You passed through the solid steel door that keeps them out of our safety zone. If they somehow get through that, we have built the iron-grilled gate to keep them out of Shangri-la."

Eippy felt his dark, brown eyes fill with tears. "There is no one who can break the laws better than the corrupt pig police." Remembering the pygmy hunters who had killed his mother and sisters, he gasped with realization. "The pig-people may have broken through the solid steel door."

Kaput sadly shook his head. "A few probably found another way into the safe zone. I don't think they have found the door. I don't want to do it, but we have to fight back while we're still able."

"But how?" You and most of your people are twice the size of me, and we're all too small."

"Our small size is our advantage," Kaput said with his voice accelerating with emotion. "We have many things we can do."

"Name a few."

"I don't see why you haven't figured that out," Kaput said and an injured look formed on face. "We can hide under stairs, crouch under tables, lurk behind curtains, squeeze into crawl spaces, and ambush people. Any place a little pygmy can hide,

110

with something sharp, will be a place to create terror."

Eippy didn't consider himself a guerilla fighter. He and his father had done things they hadn't wanted to do because it was the only way they could have survived. Their only motive had been survival. Eippy had never killed anyone.

He blurted out, "But why do we have to kill so many?"

"We don't have to kill them, but we can stab them.'

"Isn't that a little drastic?"

"Not any more. We've tried to be friendly, but every time we did, they used us as slaves, fed us carrots until we turned orange, and ate us. It just doesn't work. Degenerate pig-people who eat their fellow man have no business living an easy, carefree life. We have to make them fear us more than we fear them."

Eippy stiffened angrily. "We can't build anything or grow anything when there are pig-people ready to take it from us. But what good will stabbing them do?"

With a trace of aloofness in his voice Kaput replied, "We'll shift the balance of horror to our favor. We'll use all the means we can to reach a crescendo of terror so great that no one will even think about hunting or eating us."

Eippy thought about how the pygmy hunter had taken a bite out of his father's arm. Eippy didn't want to lower himself to the level of a pygmy hunter. And because of the prophet conversation, he didn't know if Kaput had adequate leadership

111

abilities. "I'll do anything you want me to do," he said. "But I won't kill anyone."

CHAPTER 10

After Law and his entourage failed to capture Eippy and his dog, they decided to go back to Blue Town and get some much needed rest.

While sleeping, a stinging sensation in his rear end awoke Law. In total darkness, he reached down. His hand felt warm and wet. Wondering what it was, he reached over and lit a candle. The yellow light revealed blood on his hand. He let his gaze fix on the straw mat he had been sleeping on. It was stained with blood. It was as if he had sat on a shard of glass. He lifted the straw mat. The canvas bottom of his cot had been slit open. Someone had stabbed him from under his cot. It had to have been someone small. It had to have been a pygmy. Maybe it was still there. Or worse yet, maybe there were more than one of them. Law tensed with fear. If there were five or six of them and they all had something razor sharp, he could be cut to shreds. With his heart thundering with fear, he cautiously bent over and looked under his bed.

No pygmies were there.

Outside, a full-fledged, terrified cry ripped out from the base of a huge stomach. Law leaped to his feet, threw the curtains aside, and looked out the window. A pig-person, wearing blood-soaked underwear, was running like he had been hit by lightning. With his chubby legs scrambling frantically, he zipped past the window. As if his cry had been a signal to collectively panic, squealing and the thudding feet of hysterical pig-people filled the air.

Law cautiously looked to his left. Standing next to smoke puffing from the holes in a manhole cover, about twenty pig-people had their hands clamped over their rear ends. Dripping fresh blood, more pig-people squealed in pain and ran up and down the street.

Holding a cloth over his bleeding rear end, Law managed to pull his clothes on and step outside.

Outside, standing on the sidewalk and with his hand behind his back holding the cloth, Law straightened his jacket, adjusted his tie, and tried to assume the image of a man who knew what he was doing.

In the center of the street, as if awaiting orders, a pig-person held his blood-covered hand to the side of his head and looked to Law. When Law didn't give him any orders, the pig-person lifted his hand from the side of his head. "Look what they did."

His ear had been sliced off. He placed his hand back over the side of his head and gave Law a pleading look. "Sir, you have to save us."

Before Law could reply, another pig-person came up to Law and fixed him with an adoring look. "Thank you for coming out at this late hour," he murmured through lips that seemed to be in pain. "I am privileged, sir. You are a good man. Could you do something to help us?"

Huffing and grunting, six more pig-people came hobbling down the street.

"There he is," one shouted and gasped for breath.

"A good Chief Earth Officer wouldn't let this happen," another pig-person chimed in.

Using a thick stick to support himself, an unshaven pig-person, wearing a checkered shirt, limped toward Law. "Look what they did." He pointed to his foot. "They burnt my foot. Now my house smells like bacon."

Belching, doorways spewed out wheezing and grunting pig-people holding their rear ends. And more pig-people flowed down the street. When they stopped in front of Law, their criticism avalanched down on him.

"If you were the Chief Earth Officer, would you let this happen?"

"How can we sleep?"

"We didn't see anything until it was too late."

"I can hardly walk."

"We need protection."

"You're supposed to be a man of authority.

"Call out the pygmy hunters."

"Yeah, call out the pygmy hunters."

Law held up his hand and shouted, "Gentleman! Gentleman!"

With expectation, the pig-people looked to Law and stood silent.

Law lowered his voice. "Gentleman, calm down. There has to be a reasonable explanation."

"There is an explanation," Peep said and rubbed his rear end. "Little purple pygmies snuck under our beds and stabbed us."

Law surveyed the crowd. "Did you catch any?"

"They stabbed us when we were sleeping," Peep said and pointed to the stab wound on his rear end. "It was one stab, and they were gone. If I wouldn't have seen them, I wouldn't have believed purple pygmies existed."

"You are not alone." Law turned and revealed his hand holding the blood-soaked cloth over his rear end. "Purple pygmies have also stabbed me."

As if they couldn't believe a person like Law could be stabbed, in unison, the pig-people gasped.

"Don't be surprised," Law said. "I'm just as vulnerable as all of you."

Peep flashed a perplexed and worried look in Law's direction. "Who would dare to do such an act?"

"Only pygmies would do such a cowardly act. I've seen purple pygmies before."

Peep looked in the direction of the pig-police building. "Can't we get the pig-police to protect us?"

"I wouldn't count on it. Not only did the police not believe I saw purple pygmies, they threw me in jail. You can go and try to wake them, but they'll get angry and throw you in jail, too."

"What can we do?" Peep wanted to know.

"I'll get the pygmy hunters. We'll set up guards."

"But that's only a temporary measure," the pig-person with the missing ear quickly added.

Law placed his hand on shoulder of the pig-person with the missing ear. "This man is absolutely right." Trying to instill more fear into the pig-people, Law warily looked to his right, then to his left. "If we want to defeat them, we have to fight back. We have to organize. We're going to

116

need an overwhelming force and the element of surprise."

"That's right," Peep added. "We have to build an army and wipe those cowards off the face of the earth."

"Where are you going to get men for an army," The pig-person with the missing ear asked with pleading concern.

Law hooded his eyes with his hand, drew his cheeks taut, and surveyed the crowd. "A good start is right in front of me."

As if he had just come to life, a thin-faced pig-person who had been leaning against the corner of a building and nervously looking around. pointed to a pig-person sitting on the ground. With blood seeping between his fingers, the pig-person held his head in both hands. "Many of us are too weak to fight."

Law let a radiant grin of self-satisfaction form on his face. "We don't have to fight. All we will have to do is kill pygmies."

The pig-person dropped his blood-covered hands from his face. "What if I don't want to?"

Law took an arrogant stance. "I'm declaring martial law. Everyone here has just been drafted into the army."

In frightened surprise, the thin-faced pig-person's jaw gaped open, and his face took on an appearance of shocked disbelief. "You are not the Chief Earth Officer. You have no authority."

Law complacently leaned back. "The Chief Earth Officer is not here. He hasn't been here for months. Apparently he is too busy raping helpless women and molesting little children."

"That doesn't mean you can be the Chief Earth Officer."

Law puffed up with self-importance. "Oh, my friend, but it does. When the Chief Earth Officer has been absent for thirty days, and we have basic intelligence that can stop a global holocaust, the principle of law, right here in Blue Town, gives anyone the power to protect the health, moral, and general welfare of its citizens."

As if he didn't understand what Law was talking about, the pig-person shook his head. "Don't give us a bunch of double talk."

"It's not double talk," Law shot back. "It's the law. And the law states: 'And that person may assume command as temporary Chief Earth Officer and declare what activities are a nuisance and may prohibit or limit such activities." He lifted his hand for emphasis. "And that person may declare martial law and create an army.'"

A sullen contemplative appearance formed on the face of the pig-person. "You may be right."

"I am right," Law pointed to himself. "Until the Friends of the Earth Corporation approves the use of Blue Town's Emergency Powers Act and holds an election, I *am* the Chief Earth Officer."

A mild mannered pig-person with a bald dome held up his hand. "Now wait a minute. It doesn't matter who the Chief Earth Officer is. Just because a few mischievous pygmies tried to scare us, it doesn't mean we have to go to war and die."

Using wary glances to instill more fear and control, Law nervously looked around. "Purple pygmies could be anywhere. Are you saying that purple pygmies sneaking around stabbing people does not disturb or unreasonably interfere with the health and comfort of the fine people of Blue Town?"

"I'm not sure."

"For you information, you and everybody else, has the right to the enjoyment of their property?"

"I didn't know that," the bald dome person timidly said and looked behind his back.

Law continued to badger the pig-person. "Do you believe in defending your right to live peacefully and be free of fear?"

"Everybody does," the pig-person agreed. "But believing in something doesn't mean you have to die for it."

"Getting stabbed is only the beginning." Law tapped the pig-person's bald dome. "Think about it. The pygmies already know how easy it is to attack us in our sleep. They will be back. Like an army of ants they will overwhelm us. When they do, none of us will have to worry about dying for any cause. We'll all be dead."

Reduced to a whimpering hulk, the bald dome pig-person nodded in understanding.

Law continued. "We need to do something besides cry about it, and you need me to show you how to do it. And besides" — he squinted his dark eyes and scowled at the group — "who is going to stop me?"

The gathered group of demoralized pig-people cowered under the threat.

"All right!" Law barked. "Everybody line up."

The pig-people formed a crooked line.

"Okay count off."

The eyes of the pig-person with the missing ear became steady, cruel, and unblinking. "What?"

Law dismissed him with a wave of his hand and looked to Peep. "Peep, count these people off."

Peep came to attention and saluted. "Yes, sir!" He went down the line, and with each count, he tapped each pig-person on the chest.

When he came back and stood next to Law, Law shouted, "Those of you that have an odd number will be on guard duty for the first two hours."

A collective groaning and grunts waved over the line.

Law raised his eyebrow in disapproval. "Don't act like you can't or won't accept a simple command," he said. "It's not that complicated."

The thin-faced pig-person flashed Law a concerned look. "But we need our sleep."

"Don't worry," Law said reassuringly. "You'll get your sleep. "After two hours, those of you with the even numbers relieve the people with odd numbers."

"Oh," the thin-faced pig-person said with realization.

"And stay awake!" Law barked loud and clear. "Those purple devils will come back."

The thin-faced pig-person's jaw dropped in astonishment. "Are you sure?"

"We can't be sure of anything. When you sleep, sleep well. Tomorrow we're going to build an army. And I won't tolerate unsatisfactory performance.

CHAPTER 11

Walking toward the gray archway of the veranda in the complex of Shangri-la, Kaput led Eippy down a white graveled path. At the base of one of the spotless, gray columns that were enhanced with circular, pink rose gardens, they stopped. Eippy looked off to the side. Even though hedges obscured little huts, he could see a circle of women sitting on a circular bench that surrounded a small fire.

Pretending to be warming themselves, the women held ceramic tea cups in their hands and looked toward Eippy. Peaceful expressions filled their faces.

Eippy turned toward Kaput. "Pygmies usually live in the forest. Why do they live inside the walls?"

Kaput raised an eyebrow. "It's safer." He paused and patted his well-fed stomach. "Before we came here, every chance they got, the pig-people hunted us down and stole all the food we could grow. Back then they had no ambition to learn to grow their own crops, and they still don't. They claim farming is beneath their dignity. It never crossed their Neanderthal minds that farming could give them an easy life." He gestured to the walls that surrounded the village and the estate. "Being high on the mountain, we can watch for the pig-people to come. If there are only a few pig-people, we can hurl rocks down upon them. But if there are many, we have no effective weapons to fight against an out and out onslaught. But the walls will give us a little protection and time to get away."

"That's strange," Eippy said. "At one time all the pig-people wanted to do was lie around with their hands out and their mouths open, whining, 'Give me food!'"

"That was before the Dinkies escaped and the pig-people attempted to replace them with pygmy slaves. And that plan failed."

Eippy looked up at Kaput. "So that's when the pig-people began killing and eating pygmies?"

"That's right. They can't kill enough pygmies to support their bloated stomachs. So we have to hide our gardens and our food."

Eippy remembered what his father had said: "Control a people's food supply and you control those people."

"That is correct," Kaput said. "We cannot let the pygmy hunters and pig-people control our food supply."

It didn't matter how much malfeasance the pig-people had allowed to happen, Eippy still didn't want anybody killed. He breathed a sigh of relief. "Then we won't have to kill anybody. All we'll have to do is keep our food away from them." He paused to let his point sink in. "Eventually our problems will be over."

As if in thought, Kaput's forehead creased. "That's the general idea. If the pig-people can no longer kill pygmies and they cannot steal our food" — Sorrow and anger filled his voice — "eventually they will starve on the very land that could give them life."

A female pygmy as tall as Eippy, with a silky-black tail, like his, walked to the bench and began talking to the other pygmy women. As she talked, Eippy couldn't help but noticed she was a pie pygmy. It was the first time he had seen another pygmy like himself. He wanted to meet her.

He turned toward Kaput, cautiously lifted his hand, and pointed to the girl. "Is she married?"

Kaput sadly shook his head. "Because she is a pie pygmy, and does not have a rat tail, she had not been able to find a mate." His eyes opened wide. "Hey!" With stark realization, he looked toward Eippy. "You're a pie pygmy, too. Are you interested in her?"

Eippy could hardly control his excitement. "You bet I am!"

Four bass beats of a drum echoed through the village.

Kaput turned to go but turned back toward Eippy. "I have to go. I'm sure the girl will talk to you." He took off walking at a fast pace.

One of the girls sitting on the bench whispered into the pie pygmy girl's ear. All the other pygmy girls placed their hands over their smiling mouths and stood up. Giggling like school girls, they walked away. But the pie pygmy girl stayed.

A clean and pressed denim work shirt seemed to be molded to her tremendous breasts, and her short, white shorts showed off her long, shapely legs that she had stretched in front of herself. Her fine hair trailed to her shoulders and lay like a shawl, and her silken tail curled next to her small waist. She was not only gorgeous, she was a ravishing beauty.

When Eippy stepped away from the gray archway of the veranda, throngs of pygmies flowed in and out of the village's entrance. Busy with a muted buzz of conversation, they seemed to be studying him. As if they were brightly colored peacocks, a few girl pygmies strutted past while others smiled and nodded but quickly walked away. A knot of pygmies stopped and gaped at Eippy, then turned their heads toward the pie pygmy girl, nodded, and smiled.

The pygmies seemed to be amazed at Eippy's resemblance to the girl. One pygmy girl gasped and turned to the pygmy walking next her. "Could he be her long awaited lover?"

Eippy sauntered toward the pie pygmy girl with the silken tail and stopped ten meters in front of her.

She turned her cute head and looked in Eippy's direction. As if in a trance, her eyes locked with his. Swaying her body as if romantic music were playing, she walked up to him.

Her presence seemed unreal. A dazzling aura enveloped her pure black silken hair. Elegantly long, it accented her unlined face. Just like Eippy's, her body was graced with silken-black fur. And a sharp intelligence seemed to beam from her blue-green eyes. Her short, white shorts had been perfectly tailored to her small but slender figure. Eippy couldn't believe he was standing next to another pie pygmy. A strange warm feeling filled his heart. He had never felt anything like this. For a moment, he could not breathe.

The girl turned to Eippy. "Hello," she said and laughed.

Right away, Eippy felt her delightful laugh warm his entire body. It was the laugh of a girl who loved life and felt good about herself.

Smiling, again, she said, "Hello." Her voice was music.

Eippy stood open-mouthed.

The girl continued smiling.

Eippy didn't speak. He couldn't.

Slowly moving her silky-black tail, the girl leaned forward, looked directly into Eippy's eyes, and waved her hand in front of his face. "Hello. Is anybody home in there?"

Eippy's didn't answer.

Waiting for him to answer, the girl leaned back and inhaled a deep yawn. Her breasts swelled against her soft denim work shirt.

Eippy managed to blurt out, "Hello."

"My name's Trinket." She inquisitively tilted here cute head. "What's yours?"

My name's—" Eippy began to say, but his throat constricted. All he could do was watch her exquisitely delicate beauty, her fluid movement, and her perfectly proportioned body. Trinket was the perfect name for this raven-haired beauty. Although her name was Trinket, she was not a trinket. She was a precious jewel. If Eippy managed to win her heart, he would have something much more valuable than anything he could find with his gold magnet.

126

He cleared his throat. "I'm sorry," he said and regained his composure. "My Name's Eippy, Eippy Vanko."

She flashed a coy smile.

Eippy slipped next to her and looked into her eyes. A mild sunburn caused the black skin on her face to glow to an almost pink color. Her hands were hard and scratched like a man's who worked, but her inner beauty emanated from deep in her blue-green eyes.

A serious look filled her face. "We have to talk."

"Go ahead. I'm all ears."

She nervously looked around. "Not here." She turned. Putting roll-and-sway into her walk, she said, "Follow me."

As they excitedly swished their silky-black tails back and forth, and Spinach trailed behind, Eippy followed her to a little hut at the end of a line of huts. He walked past a willow tree, stopped at the hut, and opened the straw door. Instinctively trying to shield her from harm, he barred her with his arm. "Let me make sure everything is all right."

Trinket stood outside the door and waited. Eippy stepped through the doorway and lit a candle that was sitting on a little shelf. The candle's light gave the room an amber glow, and the lingering aroma of oil and garlic from something cooking in a small pot reminded him that he hadn't eaten in a long while. Except for the small pot, a few dishes, and a small cot, the shadowed room was empty. But the expectation of food and the low amber light was inviting.

When he stepped back into the doorway, Trinket pressed her body against him and whispered in his ear. "I'm impressed."

Eippy felt his knees go weak. To keep from falling, he placed his hand on the doorframe which caused his arm to bar Trinket from entering. Trinket playfully rested her chin on Eippy's outstretched arm.

Eippy dropped his arm, delicately took her hand, and kissed it. He dropped her hand and turned toward Spinach. Cupping Spinach's head in both of his hands, Eippy looked into his eyes. "Stay here."

Spinach hungrily looked toward the small pot and lay down.

Trinket reached over and patted the top of Spinach's head. "Let me get you something to eat."

She scoped some sort of stew from the pot, placed it onto a plate, and set it in front of Spinach.

As if to say, "Thank you," Spinach wagged his tail and began eating.

Eippy glanced at the cooking pot and walked to the cot.

Trinket stood in the doorway and stared at him for what seemed too long of a time. Then with a sensual sway, she walked deliberately to him. "Do you know I wanted to be with you since the first time I saw you?" She leaned forward and kissed him on the lips.

Again, Eippy felt his knees sag. This time, to keep from falling, he sat on the cot. It gave out a strange squeak. The noise made them both smile. Looking into her beautiful face, he gently urged her to sit next to him. Comfort overwhelmed him. Her warm glow excited him. He completely forgot about being hungry. The feeling in his chest was nothing like anything he had ever felt before. It was a special thing. Their lips, as soft as the pedals of a flower, touched. At first, gently and softly, then their mouths moistly explored, pressed, and widened. Eippy's and Trinket's long delayed hunger for companionship and love overwhelmed them. They were both trembling. Trinket held him with an intensity that was more than a desire to be taken. Hesitancy did not slow their actions. Anxiety erased all holding back.

Trinket unbuttoned her denim work shirt, placed her hand on his, and gently guided his hand to her waiting breasts.

In a loving embrace they lowered themselves to the cot.

He caressed her and whispered. "This is so sudden. Do you think we should wait?"

"I don't think I can. I'm falling in love." She withdrew her hand from his and caressed the flatness of his stomach and then his thighs.

Eippy knew they could not wait. He pulled her to him. She pulled back. "I want to be close to you. She stood up and quickly slid off her clothes. Eippy did the same. Embracing each other fiercely, they fell onto the cot. Staring into Eippy's eyes, she lowered her head onto the pillow. Her dark hair fanned out on either side, framing her beautiful face. As they kissed their silky tails entwined and formed a loving heart.

Hours later, after they had eaten and continued to do what they had already done three times, they lay beside each other, naked, and under the soft covers. Trinket rose on her elbow, her silken tail cascading over her shoulder.

Eippy lay with his chin supported on his crossed arms, peering out the window. The friendly shadow of the mountain moved out across the village and twilight fell over the land.

This was the happiest moment of their lives. It would be the day from which all good things would begin. Eippy finally felt safe. Tomorrow, with Trinket at his side, he could begin a new day with hope. He wanted to stay with her forever, but he pulled back.

Confusion and sadness filled her face. "Did I do something wrong?"

"You could never do anything wrong. I have to check on Spinach. Will you wait for me?"

"I'll always be here for you."

A sharp rap on the doorframe vibrated the hut. Fear filled Trinket's eyes. She tried to conceal it, but she could not. Her beautiful smile became taut.

"Eippy," a voice called out. "Something has happened. You have to come, right away."

"I'll be right there."

After they quickly jumped back into their clothes, Trinket led Eippy to the door. While a throng of pygmies impatiently waited, Eippy and Trinket stood in the doorway.

"Kaput isn't a very good leader," she said. "If he happens to go kaput, we'll meet again near the green hills in another place and a much better time."

130

They kissed.

As tears spilled from Trinket's eyes, a unit of pygmies formed a protective circled around Eippy and glided him and Spinach noiselessly through the village.

When they arrived at Kaput's palace, no one was there. Feeling safe within a circle of guards and with Spinach at his feet, Eippy sat down and placed his head on his folded arms. He had only wanted to take a short rest but he fell asleep. When he opened his eyes, a pygmy panting to catch his breath rushed through a mist-filled light, ran to the circle of guards, and stopped.

It was the leader of the Freedom Fighters. He could not control his maniacal frenzy. "Eustis McCoy is dead."

As if exhausted, Kaput squeezed through the circle of guards and wearily sat in the chair next to Eippy. "Perhaps it is best," he said, showing no emotion. He would have destroyed us all." He looked down at the table top and shook his head. "I knew we couldn't trust a man who sat on a stump when luxuries were available."

Kaput's remark bothered Eippy. Kaput's wanting him to be a prophet, Trinket saying, 'if he goes kaput,' and now, Kaput not trusting Eustis because he sat on a stump, gave Eippy more doubts about Kaput's leadership abilities. But then he realized that it didn't matter whether it was pig-people or pygmies, incompetence always rose to the top. He would just have to make the best of it.

He had had a good feeling about Eustis. Wondering why Kaput hadn't trusted Eustis, he turned toward Kaput. "If we couldn't trust a man like Eustis, how can we trust anyone?"

Kaput leaned forward and rested his forearms on his knees. "When Eustis went through the tunnel he never made sure the pig-people were not watching, and he never oiled it. If the pygmy hunters have found the steel door, and have broken through it, our way of life will change for the worst."

Eippy remembered the screeching of the steel door. A pygmy hunter could have easily heard it. A pang of fear entered Eippy's chest. "How do you know the pygmy hunters haven't already found the door?"

"We don't. But someone had to kill Eustis."

"How can you be sure it wasn't the pygmy hunters?"

"We have teams of pygmies on the sand wheels. They are under the leadership of experts in intelligence, infiltration, and sabotage. With their help we will find the killer. If he isn't a pygmy hunter, then we can look forward to a brighter day."

"Who leads these experts?"

"A man called Turk. He is a human from ancient times. He is a man not to be messed with. It is time for Turk to come back and create an army. We need him."

"Will you send someone to get him?"

"Eustis was the only person who knew a safe route to Turk Town. In the past, people who have tried to go there have never returned."

Trinket was a pie pygmy. If the pygmy hunters invaded Shangri-la, she would be immediately killed and eaten. Eippy felt a dark hand clinch his heart. He couldn't let Trinket be killed. He could travel through the forest and avoid detection better than anyone. If he got into trouble, Spinach would provide him a quick escape.

He lunged to his feet. "Spinach and I will go into the forest. I will find Turk. We will go to the sand wheels. We will gather all the pygmies we can and bring them back. Together, we will fight the pygmy hunters."

Eippy slowly turned and stalked off. Although his heart was filled with love for Trinket, a mixture of elation and sadness overwhelmed him.

When he looked to his right, the last of the sunlight was giving the overgrown slopes of the nearby mountains one last spray of golden light and causing the valley to be in shadow. On the left, sky and dark trees met the horizon. There, the black battalions of the forest would be an excellent place for red pygmies to hide and jump out. That was where Eippy had to go.

With his knees stiff and his short legs kicking out, and Spinach trotting alongside him, Eippy walked toward the forest. Desperately looking back, he caught the last wave of Trinket's hand. Although she was smiling and waving a friendly good-by, her silky-black tail had formed a sad curl.

CHAPTER 12

Ivan Law's tall frame was clad in muscle, but he knew his physical strength wouldn't be enough. If he were going to lead an army of pig-people, he would have to make a lasting impression. His first trick was when he walked toward the gathered pig-people and made sure the bright-yellow sun threw his black shadow ahead of him. That way, he appeared to be like some kind of an Orange Man coming out of a spiritual light. And he dressed the part: His military-looking coat had been tailor-made with years-old high-grade wool that had hollow fibers with superior insulating ability, even when wet. Pygmy bone buttons and pygmy-skin elbow patches showed he was a man unafraid to kill. His knife-pressed slacks broke perfectly over spit-shined boots. Although his black shirt was frayed along the rim of the collar, his red hair covered that. And a Windsor knot hid the fabric erosion in the center of his orange tie.

He looked like a leader.

But his favorite thing was what was on his arm: An orange arm band that matched his orange tie. The armband had a Black Sun design based on a sun wheel with twelve L-shaped spokes leading to a smaller center circle. The band matched the flags that pig-people held at an angle and created an arch for him to walk under and stand in front of.

Standing in front of the mass of the sorriest-looking pig-people he had ever seen in his life, Law restlessly waved his hand. "All right, gentleman, recess is over."

As if trying to be funny, a pig-person, with stick-like arms and a long neck, deliberately let out a guttural grunt.

The disrespectful act caught Law's attention. He turned toward the pig-person.

Waving his stick-like arm, the pig-person spoke up. "Who put you in charge?"

Law walked up to him. "Are you a clown who would like to take charge?"

Stick Arms cringed and turned his face away.

Trying to continue the comedy, a pig-person with big ears placed his hand over his smiling mouth and mumbled, "What? I can't hear you."

Law deliberately walked slowly to the pig-person and stopped. Then he screamed in the pig-person's big ears. "Are you another clown who would like to take charge?"

Shaking his head and rubbing his ear, the pig-person lamely replied, "I'm not qualified to take charge." With each negative shake of his head, his plump torso sagged.

"You don't have to take that from him," Stick Arms said. "He's not the Chief Earth Officer."

"Hold it!" Peep roared. Waving his short arms and stepping forward, he excitedly repeated, "Hold it! Hold it, right there!" He turned and faced the group. "Let me tell you how it is." He lowered his voice. "Due to the fact that our former Chief Earth Officer decided it was more important to rape defenseless women and abuse little children, he is too worn out to do his job properly. Therefore,

135

under emergency powers, the Friends of the Earth voted last night. The man standing before you *is* your new Chief Earth Officer."

Stick Arms slumped and looked down. "Oh."

Like most leaders, Law knew he would have to spice up his importance and cover his lack of knowledge with morsels of reality. It could be unimportant stuff, but it would keep the pig-people under control. He walked to the front of the formation, turned, and pointed to the line of buildings on his left. He knew the buildings were empty, but the pig-people didn't. He was going to use their lack of knowledge to his advantage.

"Gentleman," he said and stared at the empty buildings. "They are out of sight. But if you could see behind those walls, you would see idiots cowering in the shadows. You would see brain-dead cowards afraid to come out into the light and join our formation." He shouted at the empty buildings, "What's the matter, losers? Doesn't our formation have a shade of daylight you like?"

The pig-people's eyes expanded to cartoon proportions. It showed Law that he was now in charge. And more important, he knew he could go into the store that had stolen the things from his house and force the smug owners to give everything back and more. He savored the thought, but decided to do it later.

"Gentleman," he said loudly to get the pig-people's attention.

They all looked toward him.

He continued. "We can't run an army on empty stomachs, and we can't let worrying about

136

our families going hungry interrupt our training. We are going to confiscate all the food in Blue Town. Anyone who doesn't join us will not eat."

The formation of pig-people cheered in approval, but from far in the back someone spoke up. "What if they won't give us their food?"

"Yeah!" another pig-person spoke up. "What if the pig police try to stop us?"

In a show of importance, Law puffed up his chest. "We're under martial law. If they don't give us their food, we'll take it by force." Although the thought of the pig-police caused him to stiffen with resentment and grizzle with anger, Law continued. "As for the pig-police, they're too lazy to do anything out of the ordinary."

"But we're just weak pig-people," the pig-person whined. "We're no match for some of the people who hoard food."

The whining pig-person was correct. Being pampered all their lives and neglecting the land around them had made them listless beings who had lost most of their pride and ambition. The least bit of manual work or exercise exhausted their lethargic bodies. It would be a challenge, but Law had no one else to train.

"We're going to train," he said. "When you have finished your training, you will be warriors." He pointed to the black sun on the orange arm band on his arm. "You will have earned the right to wear the Black Sun insignia. No one will say, 'No!' to any of you fine men."

A stooped-shouldered pig-person with thick glasses and an unruly thatch of white hair held up his hand and shouted, "Wait!"

All eyes turned toward him.

"We should not be doing this. It is not right. A power greater than all of us will come down and put a stop to this foolishness."

Law's eyes searched the crowd for the person who had spoken. He caught movement and directed his voice toward it. "It is not foolish to fight for what rightfully belongs to us."

The hidden person replied, "The world has had enough wars."

"No it hasn't." Law shot back. "This will be the final war. It will end all wars."

The pig-person stepped out of the formation and allowed himself to be seen. "If you persist, Orange Man will return and take what you fight for away."

Law knew if he verbally tore the pig-person down, he could reduce his credibility. He jerked his finger at the pig-person and talked to the formation. "Look at that crooked smile on his face."

All eyes turned toward the pig-person.

"And look at those beady little eyes. You can't believe a thing he says."

"But you should believe me," the pig-person said and pointed to his own chest. "First there were the humans. They had money and businesses. But that wasn't enough. They had to fight with the uncivilized people. When they both almost eliminated their races, we pig-people emerged as the dominate ones."

A pig-person with mud-caked hair shouted at the pig-person, "Shut that rotten mouth, Benny. You're not going to ruin our chance to wear the Black Sun arm bands."

Benny defiantly shook his finger at the mud-caked pig-person. "I'll talk if I want to."

"We don't have to listen to this." Mud Cake pushed Benny.

Benny hit the hard-packed dirt, twisted into a fetal position, and whimpered in pain.

A pig-person bent over to comfort the fallen Benny.

"Let him lie," Law commanded. "Warriors have no time for petty interruptions."

Stick Arms spoke up. "But what if we have questions?"

"I would love to answer all your questions, but the purple pygmies will be back. We have no time to explain why things must be done the way they are. We must train quickly and efficiently. It will not be an easy task, but in the end, we will all be warriors. Then, and only then, will we be ready for another pygmy attack."

Mud Cake spoke up. "When are we going to start our training?"

"Right now!" Law turned to Peep. "Peep, take charge."

Peep snapped to attention. "Future warriors! Attention!"

The pig-people's attempt to stand at attention resembled a bunch of circus clowns trying to make people laugh.

Peep looked to Law. Law looked to Peep. They both knew it was going to be a long day.

After a week of the pig-people in the formation attempting to do push-ups and only managing to plop to the ground like soft lard, a few could do five.

For seven weeks Law and Peep drilled and trained the pig-people. And because of the free food, more and more joined. And more and more pygmies were killed and eaten. Pygmy gardens were found and raided. Law showed pig-people, who were able, how to cook and serve balanced meals, which greatly enhanced the pig-people's physical shape, but they needed more incentive.

So, Law held a torch rally next to the river where uniform straight lines of newly trained pig-people, held one hand on their hearts, and with their other hand they held torches above their heads. Although the river was polluted, at night, the orange glimmering reflections of the torch-lit water, created a majestic sight, and the beating of drums made the event seem more important and significant than it really was.

With the knowledge that everyone wants to feel important and everyone needs to feel needed, Law stood in front of vast hordes of pig-people and used the created ambient atmosphere to present medals and armbands to undeserving pig-people. The medals and armbands not only made the pig-people feel important, it gave them something they had never had before: confidence in themselves and the respected and feared titles of warriors.

After the presentation ceremonies, pig-people warriors wore their orange Black Sun armbands and were enjoying a great feast, spiced with wild women, skilled prostitutes, voluptuous belly dancers, and all the beer they could drink.

The hand shaking and patting of backs of pig-people warriors, gloating in the phony fame of receiving their arm bands and medals, wound down, but the celebratory mood continued. Law stood on an orange-and-Black-Sun flag-draped plastic platform and held up his hands. "Warriors, gather around."

After much mumbling and random fits of laughter, the warriors gathered around him.

"Are you enjoying yourselves?"

A great cheer of drunken approval rang over the water of the river and echoed up the valley.

Law turned serious. "We have it pretty nice now."

Stick Arms held up his arms that had been transformed into muscle. "It's a lot better than it was before. But will it last?"

Knowing that pig-people filled with greed could become a very powerful force, Law held a chicken drumstick into the air and shouted, "After we wipe out Shangri-la, we will no longer go hungry. We will no longer have to fear the purple pygmies."

A cheer rose up.

Law took a bite out of the drumstick and held it high.

The cheering died down.

He lowered the drumstick and continued, "Warriors, after we wipe out the pygmies and the Dinkies come back, good times, just like this, and all the food we can eat" — he took another bite of the drumstick — "will be our future."

A roar of approval filled the night, and the pig people began chanting, "Law! Law! Law!"

Like an angry lynch mob, the fired-up troops were ready to go into battle. But Law needed more pig-people. He was going to break the prisoners out of jail. Although they wouldn't be trained, he could have them lead the charge. Untrained, they would likely to be killed or wounded in combat. But they wouldn't be as valuable as the pig-people he had trained. It wouldn't matter if they were used as cannon fodder.

CHAPTER 13

With Spinach leading the way, Eippy traveled far into the forest. When a screeching sand wheel caused Eippy's teeth to hurt, he stopped. He didn't want to go near the sand wheel. If he did and were caught, he could spend the rest of eternity hauling buckets of sand to feed the conveyor belt. But he needed to get close enough to see if Turk's team of pygmies were there. If they were, he could secretly talk to one of them and find out where Turk was.

With Spinach leading the way, Eippy crept toward the screeching sand wheel. When he got close enough to take a look, he crouched down, made his way to a pile of broken sand wheel parts, hid behind them, and listened. Spinach's ears did not point forward, and he didn't whine a warning. Eippy looked through a space in the pile of broken parts. The sand wheel had been deserted. The screeching was coming from a windmill that needed oiled. There were no pig-people or pygmies. He walked around the pile of broken parts.

And there they were: About thirty pig-people and pygmies in exactly the same nightmarish state: The fluid from their melted eyes had run down their cheeks, and their hollow eye sockets grotesquely started out from their burnt faces. Their mouths had become swollen, pus-covered wounds which stopped them from talking or eating or drinking. One fallen pygmy whose face was scarcely a face anymore sat up. His face was covered with pus and blood, and his eyes swollen shut.

At the edge of a clearing, children with red burnt faces looked to be cheerfully playing, but their actions were deceiving. They occasionally stopped playing and began to cry for their mothers.

Eippy figured that the pig-people had stumbled upon a stretch of vegetation-free sand, and because they would not have to go through the trouble of clearing the land to get to the sand, they thought it would be a good place to set up a sand wheel. What they did not know was that the reason there was no vegetation growing on the sand was because it was a radiation dump. They must have dug into the sand and exposed an extremely strong source of radiation. Except for the crying children, those left living, sat and lay on the ground, vomiting and waiting for death.

Knowing he could do nothing to help, Eippy sadly walked into the forest and continued his search for Turk.

In the distant forest, great plumes of steam rose toward the sky. Eippy and Spinach headed toward it. Where a light mist filled the air, Spinach stopped. Then he turned around, trotted back, and stood next to Eippy. With wind whistling through skeletal trees, Eippy cautiously walked forward. Ahead, densely-packed rotting grasses and nameless, mutated, brown weeds, interspersed with skeletons of dead animals, choked the scenery before him, and a maze of aboveground, rusting pipes zigzagged through a sickening pond of oil-tinged water. On the left side of the water, steam streamed from a hole in the ground. Looking like ghosts in a spooky land, corroded cones containing burp valves for methane gas seemed to hover over the pipes. As if wanting an answer as to why gas companies had ruined the land, Spinach looked to Eippy. He looked as if he were about to cry.

Eippy looked into Spinach's face. "Don't worry, we'll find a better place to rest."

They continued walking.

A ways later, the broken promise of methane's clean energy was left behind and replaced with a much better place.

This place was void of pig-people's interference. As if it were background music, the rising and falling of birds chirping and all kinds of hidden life-forms became a soothing sound. Although he longed for Trinket to be by his side, the sounds calmed Eippy's very soul, and he wondered if the insects and animals were aware of the askew world creeping up on them.

After the red sun had set, Eippy and Spinach continued to walk until they came to a soft patch of grass. Exhausted, Eippy sat on the grass. Under a star-studded sky, Spinach nuzzled next to him.

Eippy slowly ran his hand along the fur on Spinach's head. "Ready for bed time?"

Spinach curled up, arranged his tail neatly over Eippy's feet, and laid his chin delicately on Eippy's lap.

For a few moments, Eippy stroked the fur on Spinach's back. Then he rested his head on Spinach's side and fell asleep.

As if it were a dream, a stabbing pain in Eippy's rear jerked him awake. He sprang to a sitting position. Momentarily bewildered, he blinked his bleary eyes. Right in front of his face, a purple pygmy with a wide smiling mouth, displaying rows of sharp, pointed teeth, was tapping on his butt with the toe of his foot. At first Eippy thought it was a nightmare. He closed his bleary eyes, rubbed them, and looked again. The purple face was still there, much clearer, and real.

He jerked back and felt for Spinach.

Spinach was not there.

Laughter filled the air.

More purple pygmies surround him, all with wide open mouths, displaying pointed-teeth.

A thick-necked, barrel-chested human wearing a military uniform seemed to materialize from nowhere.

"Gentleman," he said to the purple pygmies and smiled. "Are you planning on eating a pie pygmy today?"

The purple pygmy standing in front of Eippy smiled an ear-to-ear smile and pointed to Eippy. "Is he on the menu?"

While everybody laughed, Eippy studied the barrel-chested human. Silver highlighted the human's razor-cut, black hair. Deep crow's feet accented the corners of his brown eyes, and he stood strong and rigid. Just the way he stood told Eippy this was the man in charge. If he said to go ahead and eat Eippy, no one would argue. Eippy figured his only hope was to call Spinach. When Spinach got close enough, Eippy would jump on his back and make a quick getaway.

Hoping Spinach would be near, Eippy called out, "Spinach!"

No reply.

"Spinach!"

A playful bark came from the edge of the brush. Eippy looked toward the sound. With his tongue lolling and his eyes bright, Spinach trotted up to Eippy and sat beside him.

"That's a healthy looking pooch," the barrel-chested human said and patted Spinach's rock-solid flank.

Eippy shifted his eyes toward the human. "Do you eat dogs, too?"

A ferret like expression filled the human's face. He was only five meters away, then one. He stopped in front of Eippy.

"We don't eat dogs," the human said, towering over Eippy. "But if things get worse we're going to try eating pig-people. They should taste like pork."

In unison, the purple pygmies' foreheads wrinkled with confusion. Apparently they weren't cannibals.

The human extended his hand in friendship. "I'm Turk. Sorry we had to meet under undesirable circumstances." He gestured to one of the purple pygmies with pointed teeth. "He didn't scare you, did he?"

Although Eippy was glad he had found Turk, he wondered if the purple pygmies would eat him. "Anything with pointed teeth scares me."

"Then you have seen purple pygmies turn red?"

Eippy shook his head.

"It's a good thing you haven't. It's not safe to be sashayin' around the forest. If they had caught you, they would have gone into an eating frenzy and gobbled you alive."

Wondering how he made it as far as he had, Eippy was suddenly filled with fear. He shook it off and nonchalantly replied, "That's nice to hear."

"Unlike my friends here" — Turk gestured to the gathered purple pygmies — "there is another incredible race of purple pygmies. Their cannibalistic habits have caused them to be infested with a wasting disease called Kura. It has invaded and mutated their bodies and minds. They have become eating machines. When they are angry they turn red. Like wild animals, they get down on all fours and swarm their adversaries. Their pointed teeth can chew down a field of corn in a few minutes."

"See," the pointed-toothed pygmy said and bared his pointed teeth. "I told you our pointed teeth would scare people."

Turk smiled. "I don't think we have to scare everyone we meet."

Another pygmy ran his hand through his stringy hair. "Yeah," he said, "as long as we have a safe place to live, I'm not filing my teeth into points." He smiled a full set of straight non-pointed teeth.

Eippy breathed a huge sigh of relief and stood up. "I'm Eippy Vanko. Kaput sent me to find you."

"Is there trouble at Shangri-la?" Turk asked with a sense of immediacy.

"Eustis McCoy has been killed."

Turk gasped and violently shook his head. "It is difficult to believe Eustis is dead. Sometimes he could be dim-witted, but I always liked Eustis."

"Kaput believes there will be more killing. He needs your help."

With the back of his fist, Turk wiped a tear from the corner of his eye. "When Eustis wasn't around, Kaput never could keep anything going for an extend period of time." He looked away and sighed.

"Is that why they call him Kaput?"

Turk turned back. "You got it. Sooner or later, just about everything he does, goes kaput."

Skepticism crept into Eippy's mind. "If that's so, then why is he the leader?"

"Kaput was once a bold fighter. But he has grown fat and weary. Instead of tending to the safety of Shangri-la, he has become obsessed with meaningless details. He has become a functionary leader."

"Why hasn't he been replaced?"

"He is old and forgetful, and they should replace him. But his past accomplishments make the pygmies feel indebted to him. Although he holds the title, Eustis was the real leader. Eustis used to be subtle, sly, and treacherous. And he was also harmless as a dove. Kaput is as harmless as a dove, but he is no longer sly, subtle, or treacherous." Turk held up a finger. "And, he is no longer knows how our enemies operate."

"Do you think the people of Shangri-la will be all right?"

"The place usually runs itself. For a short while, the people should be just fine." Turk paused. "Why do you ask?"

"Kaput says that the pygmy hunters may have found the solid steel door and are going through the tunnel."

Turk's features contorted with irritation. "Are you sure?"

"They ambushed me a few times. Maybe they have found another way in. If it weren't for my dog, they would have me for supper."

Tensing for action and looking warily around, Turk's eyes swiveled suspiciously. "Because of the radiation dumps, there is no other safe way around the solid steel door. The pig-people have found the door. They have broken though." Smoldering with resentment, he looked away. As if he had just thought of something, he looked back. "Did they follow you here?"

"I hope not. But if they did" — he gestured to Spinach — "my dog would have warned me."

"That should give us a little time," Turk said. "But we're still in trouble. After the Dinkies left and the pygmies wouldn't be their slaves, the pig-people became angry. Over the years they have suppressed that anger. Now, Derrick is causing their long repressed anger to surface. They have become consumed with hate for people who don't look like pigs. The worst part is that greed will prevail. Derrick's forces will outreach his control. They'll destroy everything just to destroy." Turk relaxed his stance, but a worried look filled his face.

"I can see why Kaput wants me to come to Shangri-la."

Above, leaves on the trees rustled. All heads turned toward the sound. A billow of dust danced through the trees and was gone.

Eippy turned toward Turk. "What are you going to do?"

"To do anything we have to have strength. We'll have to have many. We'll go to Turk Town, gather our forces, and go to Shangri-la. If it's not too late, we'll join forces. Then led by a very strong, militant few, we'll make our world safe again."

"That sounds like a good plan, but the people of Shangri-la seemed docile. How will you get them to fight?"

"When people are fighting for their own land and what they need to live, no one fights better." He turned and started walking. "Follow me."

As if seeking approval, Eippy looked to Spinach. Wagging his tail and ready for whatever was to come, Spinach took a step toward Turk.

Eippy, Spinach, and the band of purple pygmies followed.

A while later, Eippy walked under sky-reaching trees that soared out of sight. Dark-green, almost black, creeping vines climbed and gracefully curved into elongated, tenacious shapes and obscured the tops of the trees. In front of Eippy, thatch, moss, fungi, and plants he had never seen, battled to coexist in the strange forest.

Like treacherous traps, under his feet, ensnarling spreads of gluey tentacles of ground-crawling plants spread across a sponge-like ground. Further down a winding trail, pools of swamp-like mud hid in thick sprays of fibrous brush. After they had made their way around that, hills seemed to rise out of nowhere, and the walking became difficult. Eippy didn't think a pygmy hunter would exert the effort to follow. But he couldn't be sure.

They crossed a small stream and approached an area encased with a single wire. Following close behind, like a crowd of tourists, more and more purple pygmies joined the migration, swelling into an army flowing toward the wire. Turk stopped at the wire and shook it five times. Then he lifted the wire and held it up. Eippy and the pygmies marched under the wire and stopped at a plank that extended across a deep crevasse. Turk walked to the plank, lifted its end, and moved it to a flat rock.

"What did you do that for?" Eippy wanted to know.

Turk placed the toe of his boot on the spot where the end of the plank had been. The ground was soft and gave easily. "If we don't move the plank and a pygmy hunter steps on it, it gives away. Then the pygmy hunter trying to cross will have a non-stop flight all the way to the bottom."

Eippy nodded in understanding.

One by one they all crossed the plank. The last pygmy across repositioned the end of the plank onto the soft ground on his side of the crevasse.

A ways from the crevasse, three bass-toned whistles filled the air. In reply, Turk whistled once and signified that they were about to enter Turk Town.

Spinach's ears perked up. Eippy patted him on the head. "It's okay." He turned toward Turk. "You have strict security here."

Eippy's statement caused Turk cheeks to grow tight with determination. "We are not fools," he said. "We are not like the crude uneducated bullies who are managing the affairs of Blue Town right into disaster."

With the remnants of Turk's determination filling the air, they kept on walking.

In the distance, a gray riverbank, with strange streaks of deep green, blue, and yellow, lay beyond a stretch of untamed grassland.

As if a warning, the sounds of a screeching bat filled the air.

Turk held up his hand. "Stop!"

Everyone stopped.

Eippy opened his mouth to speak.

Turk jerked his hand toward him. "Quiet! Someone may be sneaking through the forest."

Eippy nodded, held his cupped had to his ear, and listened. The soft thrashing of a rat's feet, engaged in a game of life and death, faded. Every now and then a wild pig squealed. Eippy figured the pig was chasing something or running to stay alive.

Turk dropped his hand. "Okay, let's keep moving."

Around the bend, at the end of a foot-beaten path, Turk Town appeared. As they walked forward, white gravel wove a path around a colossal fountain. A few meters away, circular floral gardens fronted white spotless columns that

153

supported a moss-covered, round roof. Off to the side, small outdoor tables peeked out from behind tall hedges.

Amazed that something this nice still existed for common people, Eippy stared in wonder.

"There's something wrong," Turk said and quickly made his way to the tables.

When he got to the tables no one was there. But a human scampered to the side of a tall hedge and stopped.

Turk walked up to the man. "Security is something we do not take lightly. Where were you?"

"I only stepped out for a moment," the man said and smiled.

Turk grabbed the man by the front the shirt and slammed his frail body into the stone wall. "Your little break could have cost many people their lives."

Squirming under the grip of Turk, the man defensively replied, "I was only gone for a few minutes."

"The pygmy hunters have broken through the steel door and have come through the tunnel"

The man's face paled to a deathly white. His voice strained. "I'm sorry. I didn't know. It will never happen again."

Turk released his grip. "I'm sorry, too. Our little bit of safety and freedom has come to an end."

"Are you saying we are going to get ready for war?"

Turk cussed under his breath. "We don't have a choice. If the pig-people takeover Shangri-la, they'll have the food they need to grow strong."

Nodding sadly, the man said, "Then they'll be too powerful to fight."

"Damn, damn, another war," Turk said, his anger clearly rising. "Sound the alarm," he cried. "Everyone is going to Shangri-la."

CHAPTER 14

Most of the pig-people Law had been trying to train weren't ready to help break the prisoners out of jail, but he managed to find thirty who considered themselves warriors and would do as he told them to do without question.

Knowing that first impressions can be an advantage to an aggressor, Law made sure his thirty followers had scabbard swords at their sides, they were dressed in clean pressed uniforms, their dull-black helmets were perfectly aligned, and their boots were spit-shined. Using a strict military formation, and marching to the loud, threatening beating of war drums, he and his best-dressed warriors advanced toward the Friends of the Earth Corporation building. When they were within viewing range of the building, the drummers rattled out long drum rolls. The second they stopped, Law gave the command to goose step. Then with each high step, the drums beat a fear-provoking pace.

The warriors' spit-shined boots clomped on the pavement in precise exaggerated steps. Not only did their dull-black helmets project a message of doom, their marching as a disciplined unit broadcasted total domination.

Marching next to his warriors Law gave the command, "Warriors! Halt!"

The warriors took two clomps and stopped in front of the entrance of the Friends of the Earth Corporation building. Standing motionless and at strict attention they waited for further orders.

Law placed the right toe of his boot behind his left heel and shouted, "About-face!"

He and his warriors performed a perfect about-face. With his warriors standing behind him at strict attention, Law aimed to make himself all powerful. As if he were an unstoppable force, he walked slow and erect and stopped at the entrance to the Friends of the Earth Corporation building.

Bam! The judge, who had sentenced Law to jail, kicked the doors of the building wide open. "Who is making that noise?" he roared and stomped toward the formation.

But when he saw Law, he stopped. He struggled to not show fear, but his eyes betrayed him. "What is the meaning of this?" he wanted to know.

Law wanted to beat the judge to idiocy, but he if he did, the judge would never know what was happening to him. Law decided to prolong the agony. "Your Honor!" His voice boomed through the air. "We are here to release the prisoners."

Keeping a stone face, the judge defiantly held his ground. "You'll have to go through the proper channels." He jerked his finger in the direction of the jail that was part of the building. "Until that time, your filthy friends will be inside looking out."

With a look of murderous antagonism, Law stared at the judge and stated. "As of right now, we *are* not only the proper channels, we *are* the only channels."

The judge jerked his head to the right and then to the left. There were no pig police to help. He began to tremble.

Law didn't let up. With a long, hateful stare, he continued to sadistically intimidate the judge.

The prisoners must have been listening. A buzzing of nervous anticipation came from inside the jail.

Two pig policemen came through the doors and stood next to the judge.

Looking at Law, one of the pig policemen with an ill-fitting jacket snubbed his nose at Law and arrogantly asked the Judge. "Is that troublemaker back again?"

It was the pig policeman who had slammed Law against the wall.

"I'm back again," Law said. "Do as you're told or you'll be the one slammed against the wall."

A band of pig police rounded the corner and approached the formation. The pig policeman let out a loud horse laugh. "If you think you can come in here with a bunch of dolled-up vagrants and tell us what to do. Just try it."

"Ask and you shall receive." Law did another perfect about-face and faced his warriors. "Warriors! Draw your sabers."

In one smooth motion, the warriors reached across their bodies, grasp the handles of their long sabers, and pulled them from their scabbards. As the long sharp blades blazed in the sun, in unison the warriors shouted, "Ready to do battle, sir!"

The band of pig police stopped a safe distance from the formation and looked to the Judge.

Law did another about-face and looked toward the pig policeman. "Do you want to do this the easy way or the hard way?"

"I don't care how many—" the pig policeman began but was cut off by the judge.

"Do whatever you want," the judge said. "After the Chief Earth Officer hears about this, I'm sure you'll all be behind bars. Then we'll be the only ones in control."

Law jerked his thumb toward the pig policeman in the ill-fitting jacket. "You should have him wear a sign signifying his ignorance."

Enraged, the pig policeman's face turned purple. He took a furious step toward Law but stopped.

After the pig policeman and the judge backed off, Law rounded up the band of pig police. While some of his warriors held them at bay with their sabers, he led a squad of warriors into the jail.

Inside, the buzzing of nervous anticipation of the prisoners grew to a swelling roar. As the warrior squad inched through the prison looking for lurking pig police guards, the shabby, half-starved prisoners with constant weariness and fear in their eyes came to their feet and anxiously waited to be released.

When Law had been a prisoner, he had lost fifty pounds in weight and had become a sorry, weak specimen of a living person. From the looks of the prisoners, nothing had changed. The jail authorities had kept them in a constant state of fatigue, imposed by brutality and constant hunger.

With the pig police reluctantly helping unlock the cells, Law and his squad released one hundred and thirty prisoners. As a parting gesture, he marched the bewildered jail guards out into the street for all the gathered pig-people to see that they had been handcuffed with their own handcuffs. While the pig people watched, Law slammed the pig policeman with the ill-fitting jacket against the wall of the building. After he locked him, the jail guards, and the judge into cells, he went to the police station, gathered up all the pig police, and locked them in the jail, too. Then his warriors looted the station, taking clubs, blackjacks, machetes, and swords.

Marching home, Law halted the warriors and ceremoniously threw the keys to the cells into the polluted river. Now, he and his warriors were the new and only law of Blue Town.

After a few weeks of eating regular meals, being humanly treated, and given somewhat new uniforms, the prisoners easily acclimated. Although they were not qualified, they were given the Black Sun armbands and proclaimed warriors. Now, Law could go to Patagonia, convince those pig-people to join up, and use them for cannon fodder, too.

Marching down the dirt road to Patagonia, Law looked to his left. Someone had pulled a leafed branch to the side. To his surprise, a barrel of beer sat in a cold-water stream. Peep, who had been watching for purple pygmies, saw it, too. He drifted back until he was at the end of the marching formation. Believing no one was watching, he slipped into the brush and ran to the barrel.

But Law had been watching. He looked to Derrick. "Peep just ran into the brush."

Nodding, Derrick lifted his arm in a halting gesture and shouted, "Company!" He paused. The warriors took notice. "Company! Halt!"

The warriors took two steps and halted.

"Take a water break. Smoke em' if you got em.'"

The warriors broke ranks and meandered around. Some sat on the ground under the shade of trees, and others lit cigarettes or cigars and blew smoke into each other's faces.

Law and Derrick superstitiously weaved their way through the brush and stopped at the beer barrel sitting in the stream.

Law leaned forward and inspected the barrel. It had not been touched.

"That's weird, "he said. "Peep would have taken a least one drink."

As if he were about to smile, Derrick's eyes wrinkled at the corners. "Maybe he already had too much beer and had the runs."

With the odor of death all around, Law looked right then left. The air became still and lifeless. As if an omen, a black cloud covered the sun. Then somewhere off in the mountains, thunder rolled and grumbled.

A "terp, nerp, tnep" sickening sound came from deep in Derrick's throat. Yellow strings of snot, with the odor of glue, crawled from the two leather holes, where his nose used to be, and curled onto the front of his uniform jacket.

Law turned from the sickening sight.

Using his claw hand to scrape the snot off his jacket, Derrick lifted his good hand and pointed to a place just beyond a bend in the stream. Peep's foot stuck out from a stand of tall grass.

Law let out a sigh of relief. "Maybe he came to get a drink and passed out from heat exhaustion." He ran over to Peep and stopped at his outstretched body.

The tips of the fingers of Peep's short arms were directed to a thin line of blood that had formed a perfect circle around his neck. His extended tongue and his blank, bulging eyes indicated that he had been swiftly garroted.

Derrick pointed to the circle around Peep's neck. "That's something a purple pygmy would do."

Enraged, Law whirled on Derrick. "How many times do they have to kill people before the stupid pig-people will do anything about it?"

As if getting ready to fight, Derrick clinched his fist and claw hand. "We'll do something about it right now." He turned, rushed through the brush, and stopped in front of the warriors. "Warriors! Listen up!"

As Law walked into view, the warriors jerked their heads in Derrick's direction.

"The pygmies have killed one of your leaders." Derrick said with sadness in his voice. "They have killed Peep."

Amazed, the warriors goggled at Derrick.

"They couldn't do it on a field of battle," Derrick said frantically. "They had to sneak up on him." He remorsefully lowered his head. "They garroted him when he wasn't looking." He looked up. "It just goes to show what cowards they are."

A warrior who had been lounging next to a tree stood up. With great dignity he turned toward Law. "Sir, what are we going to do now?"

Law sent a sharp angry stare toward the warrior. "Are you going to just let Peep lay on the ground and rot? Show respect for your dead comrade."

"What do you want us to do with him?" the warrior asked with a fear-filled voice.

Law sensed the fear the warrior held for him and Derrick. He was sure that the rest of the warriors could smell that fear, too. He counted on it. It gave him power over them. They would do as he told them to do.

He pointed to the warrior and to four others. "I don't care what you have to do. Use your bare hands if you have to. Dig a hole." His words stamped out. "We will give Peep a proper burial?"

After Peep was gently lowered into a hand-dug hole and covered with dirt, Law stood over the fresh grave and lied. "Peep's last dying request," he said, swallowed, and began again, "Peep's last dying request was that we eliminate Shangri-la before someone else gets murdered."

Wiping the tears from his eyes, Law stood in front of the warriors. When they stood up and waited for orders, he regained his tough composure and shouted, "From now on, we'll post guards, and everyone will keep an eye out for those sneaky pygmies. They could be hiding under a bush, behind a tree, or in a stand of grass. They will be everywhere just waiting to spring out and kill any one of us."

Derrick ordered the warriors to attention. The company formation reformed, and they marched toward Patagonia, revenge uppermost in their minds.

CHAPTER 15

The sagging sign on the red-brick bar in Patagonia read "THE ZOO". Above that, a huge orange canvas canopy was snagged on the corner of the flat roof. Other than the flapping and whipping of the canopy in the wind, there was no evidence of life until a cacophony of band music blared across the broken road, flowed past ragged, limply-waving plastic bags snagged on the black branches of a dead tree, and invaded the air above the polluted Shenango River. And the rattle of poker chips, the clink of glasses, and celebrant's overjoyed clamor occasionally made its way through the jumble of booms and bangs of annoying music.

Law and Derrick let the warriors stand in the road, walked up to the door, and stopped. Although operational, the dirty footprints on the once white door showed that it had been kicked down numerous times. The hinges and the door knob and been moved to places on the door that had not been broken or splintered.

Staring at the door, Derrick stepped back. "Be careful. Patagonia is supposed to be a place where gangs of thugs beat and murder people."

"I'm not worried," Law said. "I've heard they're just a bunch of braggarts, boasters, and liars. We'll control them just like we control everybody else."

Law reached out to place his hand on the door knob. Before he could grasp it, the door opened. A pig-person who looked like he had just jumped out of the window of a nut house stood in the doorway.

He tilted his dented head to one side and asked, "Are you here for psychotherapy or commitment?"

As Law stood speechless, the pig-person reached behind his back, pulled out a black top hat, and placed it on Law's head. "That's better," he said. "Now you don't look like a waste of space."

Before Law could reply, the pig-person swished past and trotted on down the broken road and past a jumble of ramshackle shacks.

Law took the top hat off his head, stepped just inside the door, and looked around. The air reeked of mud, beer, and the odor of bacon. A weaving pig-person, with a look of a deceptive sewer rat, made his way to a chair and plopped down. Staring at the top hat in Law's hand, he stood up, leaned on the back of the chair in front of him, and held out his hand. At the top of his lungs he yelled, "Give me my hat back!"

The bartender roared at him. "Keep it down, Canyon Mouth."

Canyon Mouth jerked his extended hand toward Law.

Law handed him the top hat. Canyon Mouth placed it on his head, smiled a missing-tooth smile, and sat back down.

Along the wall, on the right side of the bar, muscular pig-people, with angry contorted faces and thick arms bulging with veins, blinked their tiny pink eyes. Eenforcers from the nefarious past of Patagonia, they sat silently around square tables, playing cards and nursing expensive mugs of beer.

Once in a while, as if they were bothersome fleas, they stoically reacted to blabbering of the vacuous-looking, plump pig-women at their sides.

Law started toward the bar. Red bar stools, with nicotine-yellowed legs, curved around its U-shape. A crudely painted paper sign on the wall read "Seating Capacity: Seventy People, if Sixty-nine People Stand Up".

In front of the bar, various lengths of cigarette butts lay on a floor that stretched to another door. On that door, brush-painted, red letters read "Emergency Restroom".

Law wondered what an emergency restroom was until the door opened and reveled a pig-person with a silver crew cut and washed-out blue eyes. As he zipped up his fly, it was apparent that he had just been outside peeing against the side of the building or some other convenient place.

Before Law sat at the bar, he couldn't help noticing what was suspended above his head. Rows of plastic beer cups, crudely painted with names, hung on a taut wire. He had seen this before. The bar was using a gimmick to attract patrons. Pig-people would line up at the bar. Bets would be made. The pig-person who could make his stomach expand the most by drinking huge amounts of beer before they passed out gave that pig-person immortality in the form of having his name crudely printed onto a plastic beer cup and hung in an ever expanding line.

Hiding his ugly face behind a cloth, Derrick walked behind Law and stepped up to the bar. As the bartender turned his head, the cloth fell from

Derrick's face. When the bartender got a good look at Derrick's face, one of the bartender's three chins quivered, and his face paled.

A muscular, half breed pig-person, called Hog, called out to the bartender, "What's the matter, Jack? You think he's the boggy man?"

Jack smiled in Hog's direction. "No, but I still think you're an asshole."

Giving Jack a thumbs-up, Hog chuckled. "Good come back." He took a sip of beer from the mug he had clutched in his powerful hand.

After Derrick placed the cloth back over his mouth and covered the two leather brown holes where his nose used to be, Jack stared at Derrick with interest.

"We'll need to make an important announcement," Derrick said through his cloth-covered mouth.

Jack's fat middle finger pointed to an empty glass.

Law knew Jack wanted them to buy him a drink. Law gestured to Jack. "Give yourself a drink. We're buying."

A smile formed in the rolls of fat on Jack's face. "Thanks." He poured himself a full glass of whisky, lifted it to his lips, and threw it down. Then he exhaled with satisfaction and leaned forward, causing rolls of fat on the back of his neck and shoulders to look like an extra mouth.

"Make your announcement," he said in a low voice. "But use as few words as possible." With a tilt of his head, he gestured to the back room.

Law looked toward the room. While the band played completely out of tune and created a poor facsimile of music, a skinny pig-person with a pony tail stood on a plastic crate and brayed through a nonfunctioning microphone.

"I have to pay the band," Jack said. "Make your announcement quick. I don't want them standing around doing nothing." He drew back and motioned to the long-haired pig-person standing in the doorway that led to the band.

The long-haired pig-person did not respond.

Derrick turned and sat on the bar. He cupped his un-claw hand to his mouth. At the top of his lungs, he yelled, "May I have your attention?"

The music continued to blast from the doorway, only louder. While the eenforcers from the nefarious past of Patagonia reached behind their backs for their knives, the hostile black eyes of pig-people sitting at the bar stared at Derrick and seemed to bore right to his very soul.

From the left, someone yelled out. "Get your dumb ass off the bar. Gold payin' customers have to drink off of that."

Another pig-person joined in. "Yeah! If you don't get your ugly ass off that bar, we'll throw you off."

In the doorway that led to the band, black-skinned pig-people leaned forward, their ears cocked, ready to listen. In front of them, a row of pale-yellow pig-people with strong hands and wide backs seemed to be bodyguards.

Closer to the bar, pig-people of various colors and builds mingled and formed a tight knot, but not one paid any attention to Derrick.

A short, big-bottomed pig-woman, wearing ridiculous bright-green slacks, squeezed her way through the knot of pig-people and waddled over to Derrick. As if seeking sin, she placed her hand on his thigh.

Derrick looked down at her grease-stained hand and dirt-filled fingernails.

She squeezed his thigh and cooed, "Honey, you have to give that long haired person a tip."

Derrick made a move to slip off the bar.

Keeping her had on his thigh, the pig-woman held out her other hand. "I'll take it to him."

Derrick jerked his thigh away from her filthy hand. As she hid her displeasure by lowering her eyes, he reached into his pocket, took out a small piece of gold, held it with two fingers, and dropped it into her hand. She pointed above his head. "You have to ring the bell."

With one quick, graceful movement, Derrick sprang into a standing position on the bar and rang the brass bell that hung from the ceiling.

Nothing happened.

Canyon Mouth roared, "Shut up!"

The music stopped.

All eyes turned toward Derrick. When the pig-people saw the ugly holes where his ears had been burned off, the one strip of hair that ran down one side of his skin-tight skull, and his deformed hand that resembled a crab's claw, it was if they had seen a ghost. The women shrieked in horror and others turned away.

But as there is in every crowd, a jokester laughed, pointed to Derrick, and said, "That guy ain't got no ears."

Hog butted in. "Yeah, we know. He can't wear glasses."

A pig-person with a red bandanna wrapped around his head, tipped his glass of beer toward Hog. "You tell 'em, Hog."

Derrick cast Hog a jaundice eye.and pointed to his own face. "Take a good look at me."

Hog, defiantly stared into Derrick's face. "With a little more disfigurement, your face could pass for a Patagonia person's."

The pig-people around the bar let out a muffled chuckle.

"This is no laughing matter." Derrick pulled the cloth away from his slobber-spewing mouth. "The pygmies have just murdered our friend, Peep." All eyes cautiously turned toward him. "There is danger at your doorstep." He leaned forward. For all to see, he slowly turned his ugly face from right to left. "This is what the pygmies have done to me."

A gasp of horror came from a woman sitting at a table.

"Don't get excited, Lady," Hog said. "We've seen things worse than that. We let you in."

The lady smiled and bobbed her middle finger in Hog's direction.

Derrick stopped turning his head, but his eyes went right then left. The door that read "Emergency

Restroom" opened. A long line of sober pig-people streamed inside. Anxious to quickly remedy their condition, they stampeded to the bar.

Derrick waited unit the pig-people had drinks in their hands and continued. "Tonight, a new leader is with us." As Peep had done in Blue Town, Derrick clapped his hands and began walking backwards. "Give a rousing welcome to the man with a different kind of intelligence. A man with new techniques. A man with a new approach. A man who is going to turn Patagonia around."

Hog shrugged. "I didn't know we were going the wrong way."

Derrick ignored Hog, quit walking, and held out his arms in a welcoming gesture. "Our new Chief Earth Officer, Ivan Law!"

In a show of excited support, Derrick applauded and vigorously nodded.

Law hopped up onto the bar and turned to the people. "I'm here to help you. What would you like me to do?"

Hog lifted his hand. "Sir! You don't owe us anything, and we don't owe you anything."

"I know that, but I would still like to do something for you."

As if in earnest, Hog leaned forward. "I've been to places you can't pronounce and don't know anything about. I don't think you can do anything for me."

"I wouldn't be too sure of that. Go ahead. Tell me what you would like me to do."

A grin began to form on Hog's lips. Then he proudly stated, "I would like you to go fuck yourself." He topped it off with a nonchalant flick of his hand, leaned back, laced his fingers across his stomach, and smiled. "How do you like me now?"

Stunned with amazement, Law goggled at Hog and wished he didn't have to be nice. He was thinking about kicking Hog right in his smart mouth, but, Jack, the bartender, pointed to Hog. "Come on, Hog, this is Patagonia. Everybody gets to speak. Give him a chance."

Hog waved his hand down and looked to Law. "Okay, bright boy, you're on."

As Law's face screwed up with excruciating irritability, a pig-person with his shoulders against the wall stepped forward. "We didn't vote you in. Why are you claiming to be our new Chief Earth Officer?"

The eyes of a pig-person sitting astride a chair with his arms resting on the back, flared. "He just wants the job so he can sit in the shade and avoid work."

"I did not want this job," Law said with a taut strain of nervous tension. "But because our old Chief Earth Officer cannot be found, and I want to save our land, the Friends of the Earth voted. I am your new Chief Earth Officer."

"The price of beer here in Patagonia had risen sharply," a pig-person with a friendly smile said. "But we don't need any help. The Friends of the Earth Corporation are coming. They have guaranteed us that everything is going to be just fine."

"Yeah," Hog said to the Law. "What's the matter? Don't you trust your government?"

"I'm sorry, my friend," Law said and faked a sad, concerned look. "The Friends of the Earth are not coming."

"That's nothing new," Hog said. "The Friends of the Earth Corporation is just a sham, run by a bunch of puffed-up assholes living the high life in their corporation-protected mansions, while everybody else starves and murders each other."

Law ticked his finger at Hog. "That man is correct. And everything is not going to be just fine. Our struggle is not only against the price of beer. It is also against the powers of the dark and secretive world of the pygmies and their forces of evil."

Hog opened his mouth to reply, but Frog, a lone pig-person with Indian-like features and a humped back that resembled a frog's back, walked up and whispered in Hog's ear.

Hog didn't speak.

Frog turned and flashed a friendly smile in the direction of the crowd.

Heads turned to each other. A plethora of whispers traveled through the crowd.

The friendly smile on Frog's face faded. "We have had troubles with the pygmies," he said. "But we have been waiting for the Friends of the Earth to come and fix that. Now that you say they are not coming and that you are the new Chief Earth Officer, just what are you going to do about the pygmy problem?"

Law didn't' hesitate. "I'm going to show you that we cannot sell out whole-heartedly to these pygmy forces and become part of conspiracies against ourselves. I am going show all of you how to defeat these evil forces." He paused and raised his voice. "If necessary, we'll battle them to the death."

Heads of concerned faces turned toward Law.

A pig-person, lounging against the bar, took off his baseball cap and stepped forward. "But we don't want war."

"No one wants war." Law's eyes swept the bar. "'Peace! Peace!' the pygmies say.'" He slowly shook his head. "But there is no peace. And when there is no peace, there is war."

The pig-person nervously held his baseball cap in his hands. "We should be thankful for the freedoms we have."

Law leaned toward the pig-person. "If you believe a pig-person trying to stop a bleeding artery and pretending it is not life threatening is telling you the truth, then you will believe the pygmies when they tell you that there is peace when there is no peace."

Frog walked up to the pig-person and whispered in his ear. With a faint grin on his face, the pig-person nodded, placed his baseball cap on his head, and leaned back against the bar. Although he scarcely could be heard, he muttered, "We should still be thankful."

Law heard him.

"Let's tell it like it is," he thundered. "The pygmies are really telling us to be thankful for the freedoms that we have left!"

A lean man with crossed eyes lifted his hand. "What do you mean, freedoms that we have left?"

As if getting advice from above, Law lifted his head toward the ceiling and looked back toward the crowd. "Let me explain." He paused for effect. "If the pygmies took one of my arms, should I be thankful that they allowed me to keep my other arm?" He waited for the words to sink in.

Hushed, the crowd sat in thought.

Law continued. "If I took half of your wages, throughout your entire life, would you be thankful for what remained? Or would you come after me for what was rightfully yours?"

A broad-shouldered pig-person, sitting directly below Law, stood up, made a fist, and talked though his clinched teeth. "I would be after you in a second."

Law cast the person an uneasy look. "Sure you would," he said and kept a wary eye on the person. "We all would." He turned from the angry man, took a few steps down the bar, and turned back. "Let me take it to a pygmy level of greed. What if I confiscated half the earnings of ten of you?"

As Frog continued to whisper in people's ears, no one answered.

Law continued. "If I were allowed to do that, I would have ten times more wealth than any one of you. If I confiscated half the wages of one hundred people then I would have one hundred times more wealth than any one of you. If I continued to do this, a million would become ten million, then billions. It would go on and on. I would become dreadfully wealthy." He stopped and pointed at the crowd. "The pygmies already have most of the gold. Do you want them to have your gold, too?"

Led by Frog, the crowd let out a resounding "Noooo!" that overflowed the bar.

Law didn't know what Frog was telling the people, but whatever it was, it was working. As if he had been cuffed in slave irons, Law held out his hands. "If I wanted you to be my slaves, I could buy you all out and bring you under my submission. This is what the pygmies are trying to do. If I stole a few pieces of gold from you, you'd want it back. You would call the police. But when the pygmies take half of the fruits of your labors, you do nothing."

A pig-person, who appeared to be dozing, lifted his shaggy head and shouted, "No pig-person has ever escaped the pattern of his habits."

Law jerked his finger at the pig-person. "My friend, you are wrong. The only thing necessary for the evil pygmies to triumph is for you good men, here tonight, to do nothing."

After trying to adjust the crooked glasses on his face and failing, a pig-person raised his hand. "Now just wait a doggone minute." Apparently inebriated, he made a futile effort to rise, but sagged back into his chair. "I forgot what I was going to say."

Laughter filled the bar.

A voice from the back rang out. "Go ahead, Clyde, speak up."

Clyde regained his composure. "If we eliminate the pygmies, who is going to grow our food?"

"He may be drunk," a pig-person cried out."
"But he's right. What are you trying to pull off,
Law?"

A huge smile spread across Law's face. "We
know where the Dinkies are."

A collective gasp came from the crowd.

Rubbing his ear as if he weren't sure of what he
had heard, the pig-person said, "What?"

Law raised his voice. "We know where the
Dinkies have fled to. When we eliminate the
pygmies, the Dinkies will gladly come back.
Patagonia will be like it used it be."

In a super abundance of approval, the crowd
cheered.

Hidden somewhere in the back, Derrick
shouted, "What do you want us to do?"

"It is not what I want you to. It is what you can
do for yourselves and Patagonia."

Boom! Boom! Boom! Outside, the drums of
the Blue Town warriors began to thump.

Canyon Mouth stood up. "I don't care what
you do, but if those assholes don't stop pounding
those drums, I'm gonna shove them up their asses."

Frog lifted his hands and gestured for Canyon
Mouth to sit down.

Canyon Mouth snarled but sat back down.

Frog pointed to Law. "You're on."

Law continued. "We don't have time for
bureaucratic idiocy." He stretched his arm straight
out and pointed toward the exit that didn't read
"Emergency Restroom". "Our drummers are
signaling."

A few pig-people got up but timidity stood next their tables.

Moving his arm from right to left, Law pointed to the pig-people who hadn't stood up. "While you just sit there with your asses glued to the chairs, rich pygmies are buying up more of your world."

A pig-person stood up so fast that his chair toppled backwards and crashed to the floor. "We don't own any world," he bellowed. "Your great government—"

Shaking his head, Frog lifted his hand and cut him off.

The pig-person nodded and sat back down.

A pig-person with hate-filled eyes stood up. "I'm ready. Where should I go?"

Law jerked his finger to the exit. Two pig-people warriors stood in the doorway. One held a bundle of orange Black Sun armbands, and the other stood under an orange flag with a Black Sun insignia.

"Thank you," Law said. Join us at the door. You will be issued a Black Sun armband."

The pig-person hurried to the door. A bright orange armband with the Black Sun insignia was placed around his arm. He proudly turned and flashed the orange and black armband toward the other pig-people.

Law hoped the act of giving the armbands to the Patagonia pig-people would give them disdain for anyone not wearing one. And that it would boost their sense of superiority and encourage other Patagonia pig-people to join. He leaped from the bar, ran to the exit, and held up a fistful or orange

179

Black Sun armbands. "Place these on your arms. When you do, our powerful force will be even more powerful."

As if the armbands were free gold, pig-people rushed to the door. Hog went through the line three times and sat back at the bar.

Law stood on a chair and shouted over the commotion. "With you at our sides, we are going to Shangri-la. When we get there, we will stop the evil pygmies once and for all."

Frog, who appeared to be dozing, stood up. "We don't want a long drawn out war. How long will it take us to destroy Shangri-la?"

"With your help, we'll be back before sunset."

As if he were exhausted, Frog slumped. "After a long battle we're going to be hungry. What will we eat?"

Law swung his arm in the direction of Jack, the bartender. "Get the drinks and free hot dogs ready. We'll be back to celebrate." He jumped down from the chair and started for the door.

Jack roared, "I'm not getting anything ready until I'm paid."

Law turned back. "No problem." He reached into the breast pocket on his uniform jacket, pulled out a small bar of gold, and dropped it on the bar. "Will that be enough?"

Smiling, Jack scooped up the gold bar. "Hurry back. We'll be waiting on you."

With pig-people patting him on the back, Law led most of the bar people outside. Proudly wearing the Black Sun armbands, they joined the tail end of the warrior formation standing on the broken road.

Inside the bar, Hog called to the bartender. "Hey, Jack, give me another beer. Those have to be the dumbest people I ever saw in my life."

Jack disgustedly leaned over the bar. "A thirsty man is easy to lead, but that asshole took most of my customers away. If they get killed, there go my profits."

"Yeah, some people will do anything for a free drink." Hog took a fist full of Black Sun armbands from his pocket and started wiping spilt beer from the bar but stopped. "Hey, I just thought of something."

"What?"

With a big ear-to-ear grin Hog held out his hand. "You wanna bet your customers won't go to Shangri-la?"

CHAPTER 16

The pig-people from the Patagonia bar stood at the tail end of the warrior formation. Instead standing at attention, in strict military lines, they huddled together like an unruly mob.

Law stood at the side of the formation and shouted. "Warriors! Attention! Forward, harch!"

The pig-people warriors in the front and center of the formation led off on their left foot and marched in precise precision to Law's cadence. The pig-people from the Patagonia bar stood in one place, tilted bottles of beer to their lips, and watched the warriors march away.

Frog shook his head. "Not yet! We have to make it look good."

The others reluctantly nodded. Intentionally not keeping step with Law's cadence they followed the formation Every now and then an empty beer bottle would fly from the rear of the formation and land in the land bordering the road.

A half hour later, Law held up his hand. "Warriors! Halt!"

Except for the Patagonia pig-people, the formation took two steps and came to an abrupt stop. The weary Patagonia pig-people took a few more steps and stood in a huddle.

Law's voice boomed over the formation. "Fifteen minute break. Smoke 'em if you got 'em."

While the Patagonia pig-people huddled around Frog, the warriors broke ranks, stood around talking or sat on the ground.

Frog stood inside the huddle and whispered to the others, "I think we've gone far enough."

A pig-person holding an empty beer bottle spoke up. "That ain't no lie." He turned the bottle upside down. "We're out of beer."

Frog smiled in agreement. "When that idiot gets his toy soldiers moving, again, we'll drop out, but only a few at a time."

The pig-person with the red bandanna wrapped around his head asked, "What will we say when we get back to the bar?"

"Say that everybody else got killed, and that we need to get drunk to forget about how horrible it was."

"Will Jack believe us?"

"It doesn't really matter. He's already been paid."

Adjusting his red bandanna, the pig-person looked into the forest. "In that case, I'm going back now." He slipped into the forest, made a half circle, came out on the road, and began running back to the Zoo.

Before Law and the warriors got to Shangri-la, Canyon Mouth was surreptitiously placing free hot dogs under his top hat, and all the other Patagonia pig-people were back at the bar doubling over with raucous laughter, enjoying free hot dogs and free beer.

Jack, the bartender, stood in front of Hog and placed his hands on the bar. "How did you know they would come back?"

Hog responded with a benign smile. "Old books I have read tell about the causes and effects

183

of war. They tell of phony heroes and fighting for Orange Man and their country, but when it comes right down to it, wars were invented so a few people could get rich off of a bunch of dumb asses' ignorance."

"Yeah, but how did you know they were coming back?" Jack demanded with defiant mistrust.

"No one knows war rules better than Patagonia people do. We wrote them." Hog jerked his thumb toward Frog. "And besides, Frog told me to let Law talk all he wants, said, 'He's getting rich off a war. And since all battles are based on deception, let's fool him into spending some of his wealth on us.' Everybody knew nobody from Patagonia was going to go fight in that half-wit's stupid war."

Jack conceded defeat. "You want that bet paid off in beer or gold."

"Aren't they the same things?"

CHAPTER 17

While Shangri-la lay sprawled in the sleepy comfort of sunlit streets, Law slithered through a field where long grass rippled into long waves of green. When he got to the wall around Shangri-la, he stopped and studied the iron-grilled gate. It was closed but it hadn't been locked. He crouched down, crept to a decorative round hole in the wall, and looked through. Next to the other side of the wall, sacks of gold sat in a wheel barrow next to a flat marble circle of truth.

Apparently counterfeit gold had been showing up. It was time to determine which coins were real gold. Three listeners stood ready. Kaput tossed the first coin. It hit the circular marble surface and rang. The three listeners nodded. The coin had rung true. It was real gold. Kaput tossed another coin. It hit the marble and made a different sound. The listeners shook their heads. They coin had not rung true. It was counterfeit.

Kaput let out a resigned sigh. Apparently it was going to be a long day of sorting coins. While he was busy listening to the coins and the iron-grilled gate was unlocked, Law could easily attack. As a red rooster walked proudly down the dusty street, Law went back to begin the attack.

At the edge of the concealing forest, Law patted Derrick's massive, boulder-like shoulders. "We should have an easy go of it, but they may have a secret weapon."

"I totally agree with you," Derrick replied, and the fold in his truncated neck tensed. "Presumptions and assumptions are dangerous. We'll let the prisoners we broke out of jail lead the charge."

Law knew there would be killing. He didn't want to do it, but Derrick had convinced him that it was a necessary evil. Still angry at himself because he had gotten so engrossed with the main goal that he had missed the Patagonia pig-people's obvious rouse and that they had dropped out of the formation without him noticing them, he wished he could put them at the front of the charge to absorb the brunt of the initial attack. That would have taught Hog and the other Patagonia people to tell him to go fuck himself. But it was too late now. And he suddenly realized he had done just what Hog had told him to do. He had fucked himself out of the gold he had paid the bartender. For a moment, he entertained the thought of going back to the bar and getting his gold back. But the Patagonia people could be a sneaky bunch. When it came to warfare, they didn't play by the rules. They never attacked as a group. They always separated and slowly and methodically eliminated their enemies one by one. Amazed at how gullible he had been, Law stared bleakly ahead. Ready to vent his anger on the pygmies of Shangri-la, he looked to Derrick. "Are you ready?"

Standing next to the orange flags with the Black Sun insignia, Derrick placed a folded red cloth into a triangle and placed it over his slobbering mouth. Then he tied the ends of the cloth behind his head, and held up his hand.

The warriors took notice.

Derrick pointed to Law.

All heads snapped toward Law.

Law shouted, "Let the drum beats begin."

As the drummers pounded a slow steady cadence, similar to a funereal march, Law thought it fitting. The released prisoners were headed to their deaths.

When they got to the wall around Shangri-la, a wooden draw bridge that was usually up was down. When the released prisoners walked across it, faint unthreatening foot falls could scarcely be heard. When the trained warriors marched across it, loose boards thundered with the pounding of their high goose-stepping boots.

Waiting to see who or what was coming into Shangri-la, defiantly pounding drums and stomping their feet, Kaput directed his eyes toward iron-grilled gate. The wind no longer rippled the grass into long waves of green. Now it was being tramped flat by the lumbering steps of pig-people wearing arm bands, followed by the goose-stepping feet of warriors.

The expression on Kaput's face indicated that he realized he had not locked the gate. Pig-people carrying spears, rocks, shields, and weapons of war, were streaming through it. He turned to run. But he was too late. Masses of pig-people blocked every avenue of escape. Whatever was going to happen was going to end in a welter of gore.

A stone whipped past Kaput's face. Taken aback by the unprovoked attack, as if mesmerized, he only stared.

Another stone zoomed out of nowhere. Klunk! It hit Kaput in the mouth.

An advancing pig-person chuckled.

Kaput quit staring. His bloody lips parted over broken teeth. He let out a snarl of rage. "Why you!"

Another rock hit the wall behind him, bounced off, and struck him in the back of the head. Clutching his head, he fell back against the wall. A pig-person with a goatee and a raging face came swinging a sword. When he was right in front of Kaput, he kept right on swinging the sword. It came down and sliced into Kaput's shoulder. Kaput fell to his knees.

The warrior squealed with delight and lifted the sword for another strike.

With an artery spurting blood into the air, Kaput swore and defiantly spat into the dust.

With both hands, the warrior brought the sword down and chopped Kaput's head clean off. As if it were the only thing the warrior had done right in his entire life, he jumped for joy. Extremely excited, he grabbed the hair on Kaput's severed head, picked up the head, proudly ran down the dusty street, tripped over the red rooster, and got back up. Standing there looking for someone to blame for his tripping, he looked around. His eyes fixed on the door of a hut. Being that the hut was only as tall as his waist, the pig-person deliberately walked up to the door and kicked it down. Inside, pygmies huddled in fright, but he didn't care. Laughing, he kicked the side of the hut until it canted to the side, fell over.

Still laughing, the warrior jumped onto the side of the knocked over house and jumped up and down.

The trapped pygmies cried in pain until they were smashed dead.

An old pygmy with extremely thick glasses walked up to the warrior and squinted in his direction. "What did you do that for?"

The warrior jumped off the house, stepped behind the almost blind pygmy, and kicked the back of his knees. The pygmy's knees buckled. He fell to a kneeling position. The warrior lifted Kaput's severed head and used it to continually bash in the skull of the pygmy. After the pygmy's head was nothing but a bloody mess, the warrior turned around. As if he were expecting applause and approval from his fellow pig-people warriors, he stood still. But no other pig-people warriors were near. Still holding Kaput's bashed and severed head, the warrior laughed and continued running down the street.

Other pig-people warriors leaped over the bodies of fallen pygmies, knocked down other pygmies, smashed blackjacks against their protesting mouths, and kicked them to death.

A warrior with a torch ran along a line of waist-high huts and set them ablaze. A pygmy staggered to the doorway of the first hut, crying out in angry yells. A rock hit him in the center of the chest. He fell to the ground, struggled for a moment, half

189

arose, turned, and slumped back into his burning hut.

In the heat of the burning huts, continuous beads of sweat rolled down the perspiring faces of a group of brown pygmies, but they didn't bother to wipe the sweat away. It was as if they were in a trance.

A ways from the group, unseen before, grotesque features, formed on the faces of husbands, wives, and children. With frenzied eyes looking all around and wondering what was happening to their docile world, they stretched their necks and forced their bewildered faces out of shape. Before they realized what was happening, a band of warriors with broad blade axes wound up and chopped the heads from the outstretched necks.

Other pygmies ran out of the burning huts, hands raised. Not a single warrior paid attention to their surrender. Knives, rocks, swords, and hatchets chopped the surrendering pygmies to the ground. Then the warriors began chopping off pygmies' arms and legs, taking bites out of them, and throwing them into the burning huts.

"We'll eat good today," a warrior with a lopsided head announced through his blood-coated mouth and rubbed his bloated stomach. He took a few steps and stopped. A woman pygmy stood before him. With her face bright-red and tears raging in her pleading eyes, she crossed her arm over her shoulder and clutched at her oozing wound. But the warrior had no pity. He wound up and slammed his heavy club into the side of her head. After the loud crack of her skull breaking shot through pandemonium of the continuing slaughter, she hit the ground.

The warrior was joined by twenty laughing warriors. Together, they danced down the street swinging their swords. Constantly swishing the swords, like machines on high speed, they diced brown pygmies into lifeless hunks of flesh and bone.

After all of Shangri-la had been destroyed and most of the pygmies had been slaughtered, Derrick used a body that had jagged holes torn into its side as a foot stool and proudly stood in an ankle-deep mire of bloody body parts.

Turning from Derrick and the gore, Law looked to the smoldering remains of a hut. A few meters away, the scorched limbs of a weeping willow wept into the wind-blown ashes of desolation.

A pie pygmy, with smoke curling from its black fluffy tail, scampered around the trunk of the willow and hid behind it.

A lopsided-headed warrior's eyes grew wide. He screamed, "A pie pygmy ran behind that tree!"

Other warriors looked in the direction of the tree.

With a smoking tail, trailing behind, the pie pygmy fled down the gravel path. The warriors ran after it.

CHAPTER 18

Just before the red-tinted setting sun blinked to black, a cold wind from the north, dispelled the last warmth of the day, and replaced it with a faint scent of smoke. With the dark, eerie stillness settling over the land leading to Shangri-la, Eippy sensed something was wrong. He hoped and prayed that Trinket's little village he loved and wanted to live in for the rest of his days had not been destroyed. He jumped onto Spinach's back, followed Turk and the others, and hoped for the best.

When they were close enough to Shangri-la that Eippy could throw a stone and hit the wide-open, iron-grilled gate, the acrid smell of burning bodies and smoldering ruins filled the night. As he rode Spinach through the gate, a thousand tiny flames erratically blinked. It seemed as if the tiny flames were signaling for help that would never come. Eippy realized that all semblances of dignity and moral codes of a civilized world had vanished in the smoke that hovered over Shangri-la.

A few paces past the iron-grilled gate, Eippy and everyone around him stared at the horror before them. The gruesome sight held them immobile for long seconds. Then as if it were a delayed reaction, the coppery smell of blood greeted Eippy. He rode on. The stench of excrement, expelled from traumatized sphincter muscles during death, covered him like an unwanted, humid blanket. Misery wallowed everywhere.

While Turk and his pygmy friends searched for survivors, Eippy slid off Spinach's back, lit a torch, and searched for Trinket. When he stopped at a mound of splintered wood and crumbed brick, feeble voices came from deep in the mound. He stepped closer and looked into a dark opening. Yellow teeth and flashing red eyes erupted into an explosion of activity. Black rats, as big as cats, ran out of the opening and shot off in all directions. Squeaking and scurrying, they raced across his feet, made a quick right turn, and ran around the mound. Watching for more rats to follow, Eippy froze in place. But the pack of rats had been replaced with a swarm of purple pygmies. They were chasing the rats. As if he and Spinach weren't there, the purple pygmies ran right past him, made a quick right turn, and were gone.

Eippy walked around the mound and stopped. His torch light revealed a pile of bodies. They had been chopped and piled like bloody firewood, but one body demanded his attention. What was left of its face stared upward, its mouth gaping in a silent rictus of startled alarm. The aroma of parboiled flesh suspended over the body pile and would not go away. Eippy placed his hand over his nose and mouth and turned from the sight. In the past, he had occasionally encountered natural and accidental deaths, but the deaths of Shangri-la were different. He hoped and prayed that the flickering orange torch light hovering over the bodies wouldn't haunt him in his dreams. But he knew it would.

Trying not to throw up, he stepped around a stack of arms and legs that had been chopped from pygmies. Holding the torch, he turned from the gruesome sight, placed his hand on his knee, bent over, and threw up.

When he lifted his head, he stared at a place where a door had been on a burnt down hut. A trail from someone who had dragged themselves away from the flames led to the lower part of a charred body. As if the person had been crawling from the flames before dying, the body lay stretched out on the ground. From the waist down, blackened ends of broken femur bones trailed behind. The fingers of its grotesquely twisted hands still clawed into the dirt. As if they were tiny flags honoring the person's one last effort to survive, tendrils of flesh on the body's turned up face delicately waved in the death-filled air. Visualizing the agony of being burnt to death, Eippy tried to shake off the monstrous image. But as if it were tattooed onto his brain, it remained.

He turned from the scary sight and jumped on Spinach's back. He rode past the curled, black leaves of scorched hedges, and stopped where he had first seen Trinket sitting with a circle of women on a circular bench. The bench had been broken into three pieces. Black, greasy soot covered the jagged pieces, and ashes, from what used to be a small fire, had been kicked into an ugly array. A ways from the pieces, orange light from fires revealed the remains of smoldering huts and other debris that threw sad shadows against the ash-covered ground.

Eippy gasp. Next to the wall, a tiny figure, the size of Trinket, was curled into a fetal position. A broken stick, with a bloody rock tied to its end, lay next to the figure. Eippy swung his legs over Spinach, hesitated for a moment, and then slid off. With great trepidation, he slowly stepped to the body and held the torch over it. Where blood had coagulated, the body's skin was ashen and dark red. The tail had been burnt crusty black. Eippy hoped and prayed it wasn't Trinket. But it could be. The body's head was turned toward the ground. Trembling, he reached over and turned the head up. With the odor of putrefaction permeating the air, the lifeless eyes of the horrified face of a child stared back at him.

He turned from the sight. With Spinach at his side, he walked through the devastation. At a section of a wall, where it had been broken, he picked his way to the top and Spinach followed. Walking on the top of the wall, he held the torch and searched for Trinket. After he had walked a few meters, he stopped and held the torch over an area on the inside of the wall. Although he couldn't be sure, off in the distance, it looked like purple pygmies were standing around a fire and eating a pig-person. He dismissed the sight and continued looking for Trinket. He didn't see her, but at the base of the wall, a small, bare-footed boy stood in a pool of blood. Eippy bent over and looked into the wide, brown eyes of his freckled face. The boy's face screwed up in a grimace. Eippy jumped off the wall. With his knees bent to absorb the shock, he hit the ground, staggered and almost dropped the torch, but recovered enough to place a comforting hand on the boy's shoulder. "It's over now."

The boy only stared at Eippy.

Spinach jumped off the wall and landed in front of the boy. The boy reached out and stroked the fur on Spinach's back.

"See," Eippy said. "Everything's going to be all right."

But Eippy knew everything wasn't going to be all right. He had found a home. Now it had been destroyed. He had found a girl he loved. Although his heart was filled with pain, he still had a glimmer of hope. Trinket had said they would meet again near the green hills in another place and a much better time. He thought he was only thinking it, but he heard himself crying into the darkness, "Trinket! Where are you?"

As if he were about to be attacked, the boy cringed.

Not wanting to upset the boy more than he already had been, Eippy shook his head and recovered from his sudden panic attack. Then he guided the bewildered boy around the end of the wall and stopped. The boy's mother limped toward her son. He ran into her waiting arms. As Spinach wagged his tail, she gratefully thanked Eippy and hobbled away.

Hoping to see at least a flash of Trinket's silky-black tail, Eippy looked toward her hut. The hut where their hearts and tails had become entwined in an unending love was gone. It had been replaced with ashes created with ignorance and hate. The few shards of the broken cooking pot they had eaten from brought tears to his eyes. Where the door to the hut had been, a dead lady lay. A few meters from her, a pygmy with a bleeding wrist cried out in pain.

With the odor of stench and excrement filling the air, Eippy cut strips of cloth from the dead lady's dress and stanched the blood flow at the pygmy's wrist.

With a background of hacking men and women trying to clear their smoke-inflamed throats, Clarence the guard, crawled out from under a pile of rubble. His body was a sea of welts and mottled bruises. When he finally struggled to a standing position, he looked like he should be dead. Small pieces of rubble and dust fell from his body. He coughed up dense wads of phlegm and spit it in Eippy's direction.

"I told you I should have been the prophet," he whined. "You didn't get back in time."

He held up a spear. It fell from his arthritic-like hand. In addition to his limited dexterity, Clarence looked tired and strained. His eyes seemed to be lost behind a feeble mind. He would be no threat.

As Eippy watched Turk survey the devastation, he couldn't believe that only a few days ago Shangri-la had been alive with picnics, soaring kites, and a red rooster. Now it was riddled with pygmy carcasses bleeding in the sun. Some had had their noses grotesquely hacked from their faces. Even though the pig-people could have used the pygmies for meat, they had left bodies everywhere. Swarming maggots would soon be having picnics on them. Animals and birds would be eating the dead. It was apparent that the pygmy hunters not only wanted the pygmies for food, they wanted to eliminate them. The odor of death hovered and would not dissipate. Many of Turk's purple pygmies vomited and others fainted.

As if possessed, Turk slowly turned from side to side and stated, "I want them. I want all the rotten pig-people to pay for this."

He opened his mouth to continue speaking, but when he looked at what had become of Shangri-la, words failed him. Tears of rage and frustration filled his eyes. He struggled to control his emotions, but he couldn't. "Damn, damn them all to hell," he cussed. "I hate war. Now, there will be no rules. We'll use all means necessary to fight those uncivilized pig-people."

Eippy waited for a few minutes for Turk to calm down. Then he cautiously approached him. "Have you seen Trinket?"

Turk ran his forearm across his sweating forehead and seemed to calm down. "Maybe she has gone into Kaput's throne room and is safe."

Eippy and Spinach quickly weaved their way through ashes and debris. But a badly burned woman crying for help blocked their path. Eippy reached down and took her by the hands. Her skin slipped off in huge glove-like pieces. Her watery eyes filled with horror. She fell over, dead. Eippy became so sickened that for a moment, he had to lean against Spinach.

When he and Spinach got to the throne room, the velvet curtains had been torn open. Behind them, dying pygmies lay. Although trying to look cheerful and resigned to their discomfort, they were clearly scared to death. Everything that was not tied down had been knocked to the floor. The carpet was a litter of plastic books, spectacles, dressing gowns, broken teeth, and other things Kaput had kept inside. For a moment, Eippy figured that everything in Kaput's rich and glamorous world had come to an end. But when he looked to his left, the six white marble steps that led to the huge elevated throne were spotless. The high-backed, golden, thickly-red-velvet-padded chair with the gold crest and the jewels reflecting light had not been touched. It was as if the throne had been preserved for a new king.

Eippy wondered if all this could have been stopped if he and Turk had gotten back in time. He felt an agonizing stab of guilt.

After he had searched the throne room and didn't find Trinket, Eippy accepted the fact that she had been killed. Since she was a pie pygmy, she probably had been one of the first ones eaten. Disappointed and heartbroken, he sauntered outside. Subduing another urge to vomit, he stared at the carnage.

Wavering, Turk stood in the aftermath of the massacre. Stench from body gasses coming from spear holes and bowels that had voided in death spasms soured the air.

Looking over the devastation, Turk's features stiffened with determination. "The plight of the pig-people is now in our hands. They have chosen to doom themselves."

Eippy wasn't sure that they could ever defeat the pig-people, but it seemed Turk knew something he didn't know. With his mouth open in astonishment, Eippy starred at Turk. "What can we do that we haven't done already?"

"In the past, I've tried to be civilized," Turk said and waved his hand in the air. "But you can't be civil with people who do this." He pointed to the devastation. "The time has come. Now we are going to do more than poke spheres through the bottoms of beds and chairs. Anywhere we can hide, we are going to spread terror. We are going to set bombs in their homes. In the dead of night, we'll sneak under their beds. This time, it won't be a little stab. We'll poke knives and spheres into their sleeping bodies until their blood freely flows. We'll hide in storm drains, reach out, and slash the ankles of pig-people walking past. They'll never walk without fear again. They'll be forced to sleep on floors and check under chairs. When we get them to chase us, we'll set off Molotov cocktails."

A purple pygmy, leaning on a stick, broke out into uncontrolled sporadic laughter.

All turned in his direction. He quit laughing long enough to blurt out, "I have something better."

Eippy wondered if the purple pygmy was in the second stage of Kura disease. He hoped not and asked, "Are you talking about the secret brown soap formula?"

As his hand trembled, the purple pygmy nodded.

"That's even better," Turk said ignoring the pygmy's sighs of Kura disease. "We'll create napalm and burn holes through their bodies right down to their very black souls."

200

A purple pygmy stood on a block of stone that had been knocked from the wall. "We'll all file our teeth to points and get more than revenge. We'll wipe the pig-people off the face of the earth."

For a moment there was only silence. Then the sky became an angry, swirling, black mass of clouds. It was as if some obscene hell had broken loose. The dark air filled with screams and shrieks. As if they were being chased, a flock of ash-dusted, clucking chickens beat their wings and ran for cover. The wings of frightened crows flapped, and black feathers fell from a black sky. After the swirling black mass of clouds raced across Shangri-la, the revealing light of a bright moon broke through. Eippy looked outside the open iron-grilled gate. Seven purple pygmies raised their bloody mouths from a feast of dead pygmies. The eyes of the purple pygmies standing next to Turk opened wide with panic.

Right behind the seven purple pygmies, thousands of mouth-snapping, pointed-toothed, red pygmies, on all fours, swarmed across the wooden bridge. With their stringy hair caked with dried blood and their rat tails curving behind them like snakes, they rushed through the wide-open iron-grilled gate, and crawled over the walls. They were invading Shangri-la. Clacking their mouths like machines, they were devouring everything living and dead thing in their paths.

Turk turned to run. The advancing red pygmies blocked every direction he turned. His purple pygmy friends huddled and looked to him for advice.

"They can't kill us all." Turk charged into the red pygmies.

Most of his purple pygmies blindly followed.

But there were too many red pygmies. It was no use. As Eippy and Spinach backed away, Eippy could see that Kura disease had driven some of Turk's purple pygmies mad. They had turned red and dropped to all fours, too. One held a half a bleeding heart in his mouth. Now most of Turks purple pygmies were four-legged, mindless eating mechanisms. Eippy figured that the sights and sounds were going to be wiped from Turk's world. The red pygmies would easily chop him and his sane purple pygmies to shreds and gobbled up their remains.

Standing next to Spinach, Eippy spotted an empty place at the top of the wall. But it was too high for him to reach. He looked at the block that the purple pygmy had stood on. If Spinach could run to the block and bound off it, they might be able to land on the empty place on top of the wall.

But if they were going to try it, they had to do it quickly. The red pygmies were gobbling up Turk's remaining purple pygmies before they could fall to the ground. The menacing clacking of their snapping mouths, followed by sounds of strong, sharp teeth scraping on bone, amplified and filled his ears with horror. The red pygmies were only a few meters away.

Spanish whined in fright.

Eippy swung onto Spinach's back, reached down, and talked to him. "Come on, boy. We can make it."

Eippy guided Spinach to a spot just in front of the advancing pygmies. Getting a running start, Spinach gained full speed and bounded off the rock. He landed on the empty place on the wall. Excited, at an easy target trapped on the wall, a mass of red pygmies began to crawl up the wall. They gnashed their teeth in anticipation and became so excited that they bunched up and created an empty lane. Before they realized what was happening, Spinach jumped off the wall, flew over their snapping heads, and landed in the empty lane.

With red pygmies snapping and snorting all around them, Eippy hoped Spinach could run fast enough to escape from Shangri-La.

CHAPTER 19

In midafternoon, at the edge of a lake, fed by a flowing spring, Tommy, the Dinky, sat in his wooden reclining chair with his feet propped on a tree stump. Fishing to forget about life for a while, in blissful contentment, he closed his big eyes against the weak sunlight filtering through the pleasantly damp air that warmed his floppy ears and his short body. Off in the distance, healthy-green trees and grass stretched along the far shore and created a peaceful backdrop.

Content and relaxed in the pastoral setting, Tommy kept his hand on the end of his fishing pole and waited for a fish to jerk the line. A ways behind him, perfectly aligned stone sidewalks lined the fronts of well-kept buildings. Clean streets, with street lamps, led to houses just a little taller than a pig-person's waist. Just beyond the houses, windmills and solar panels generated electricity to trickle charge power to blue lights that illuminated the tallest structure in Dinky Land: A pyramid.

Beyond the pyramid, wildlife flourished, especially in the shallows of still ponds, where bass jumped, performing majestic leaps, causing snow-white trumpeter swans to lift their black bills from the water and watch in wonder. Even after years of harvesting, the water still teemed with delicious sunfish, and perfectly planned and planted forests were ideal habitats for small, white-spotted deer, gray and red squirrels, rabbits, and dozens of other woodland species. This section of Dinky Land was a model of Dinkies and nature working together in productive harmony.

The lake in front of Tommy should have been a desert. It existed because a thick rubber liner held in water that otherwise would be absorbed into the dry land and flow into a desert.

Oblivious of how their ancestors had struggled to obtain a comfortable way of life, the Dinky children inside Dinky Land made merry. But it was all right. Unlike the pig-people's purpose of education which was to confuse, so the child would become ignorant and enable the government to become a "nanny state" that took care of and controlled the ignorant pig populace, the children of Dinky Land were being correctly educated. And that education continued to improve the Dinkies' lifestyles.

It had taken huge amounts of education and a long time for tiny sections of the earth to recover from the magnetic pulse that had wiped out all electronic devices containing stored data. For ten years, the Dinkies had been using uninterrupted service of alternating current electricity. Three years ago, old electronic books had been found in the pyramid. Those books gave information about what had been long lost.

Through trial and error and using the ancient books, the Dinkies learned how to use 15 Megahertz transmitters and receivers to transfer electricity through the air that eliminated the need for wires to run from the pyramid. Although in an infancy stage, the system provided electricity to many places that did not have wires. It was a fragile system, but so far, it was working. Pig-people used coal-fired generators that produced direct current. The direct current only traveled through wires a few miles before the voltage drastically dropped. The direct current and the coal-fired generators were not only unreliable, their continued use constantly placed the earth's atmosphere in danger and placed many slave pygmies lives in danger as they mined the coal. Tommy hoped the pig-people wouldn't find Dinky Land and ruin the Dinkies' clean and renewable electrical system.

Sludge, the mining Dinky, stopped walking along the shore of the lake and stood next to Tommy. Tommy and Sludge not only could pass as identical twins of their great, great, great grandfathers, they had their mannerisms and characteristics, too. Like Tommy's, the top of Sludge's head only came up to the waist of a pig-person's, and his head was covered with thin reddish-blond hair and was just like his long line of ancestors. It did not add to his looks. He was not handsome. When he talked, his mouth looked like it had a fat night-crawler hanging down the side of his mustached mouth that moved and jerked with each word. His skin broadcasted age lines that were records of the many years he had spent drinking and fighting, and the top of his muscular back was bowed from a life of picking and shoveling in the mines. His eyes were watery-brown, set in a face that had worn out many a combatant's fists.

Although a rugged individual, Sludge was liked by all Dinkies: He and his Dinky race didn't maim or malign the earth. They didn't suck the life out it.

206

They didn't just live on the earth, they lived with the earth. They weren't like pig-people who destroyed what gave them life. And that was one reason all Dinkies had to guard their little piece of paradise.

Keeping the pig-people within the confines of the blue grass around Blue Town had worked for years and had been for their own good and for the good of the recovering earth. Pig-people should have never been told the truth about the fake virus. They were too ignorant. And now their ignorance was threatening the earth, again.

Before the Dinkies had made it safe for themselves to live on top of the earth, old hand-and-knee coal mines had been refurbished into thriving Dinky underground cities, complete with labyrinths of tunnels, cut by hand and continually expanded by the little mining Dinkies like Sludge. Back then, when solar flares increased, the electric from the Aurora Borealis crept down from the far north. It was a fantastic sight. But it wiped out electrical power for weeks and months at a time. When it receded and electricity was restored, radiation, magnetic fields, and earth shifts, interrupted electric motors and generators, causing their armatures to reverse and spin into bird nest tangles. But in the underground hide-a-ways, chemical batteries and hydrogen generators that fed electric lighting and heating technology had created a livable place for men Dinkies, women Dinkies, and children Dinkies. Although the tunnels were only about a meter high, they were not the hostile environments that would be expected in an underground environment. The city under Dinky Land was still there, but was only used during storms or when danger threatened.

With his muscular legs supporting his small, muscular frame, Sludge looked down at Tommy. "You know you ain't gonna catch nothin' lying back like that?"

Tommy slowly turned his head and looked up at Sludge. "What makes you think I'm fishing?"

Smiling, Sludge shook his head. "You're the only person I know that can fake fishing so they can do absolutely nothin'."

"You should try it while you can," Tommy replied and crossed his legs that were propped up on the stump. "If the pig-people find us, we may have to go back underground."

Sludge waved his hand down. "Those pig-people are too dumb to find us. And besides, I like diggin' in the tunnels."

"I don't think you would like it if you had to stay down there for years."

Sludge reached up and scratched the back of his head. "I don't know how our ancestors could a done it."

"If they wouldn't have, we wouldn't be here today."

Before the Dinkies had escaped from Blue Town, the pig-people had been forced to stay within the confines of the blue grass that surrounded Blue Town. During that time, if the pig-people went off the blue grass, touched any wood, green vegetation, or came into contact with unfiltered water, they had been led to believe that they would be infected with a virus that would cause them to shrink to half their height and begin to mutate into Dinkies. If they weren't given antidote shots, which usually killed them, they would continue to mutate and be fated to lead a substandard life of a Dinky. He or she would spend the rest of their lives as agricultural slaves or performing some other demeaning work, like pulling a rickshaw. This living lie had kept the pig-people on the blue grass, and their earth-destroying ways had been kept in check.

With his large round eyes peering from under the brim of his floppy hat, Tommy leaned back against the reed-woven back of his chair. "Hey, Sludge, don't you have something better to do?"

"I don't mean to spoil your day," Sludge said and pointed off in the distance. "But lookie over there."

Tommy looked.

A Dinky, called Scout, was guiding a blindfolded pie pygmy riding a dog. They were rushing toward them.

Tommy moaned. "Scout probably never saw a pie pygmy. He's probably bringing him here to show us what he found." He reached down, lifted his fishing pole, and reeled in his line. The hook was bare.

"No bait," Sludge said in amazement. "Did you really think you were gonna catch something with a bare hook?"

"Not really. Usually, I don't use a hook. I just throw the line in. The fish just tie themselves on and let me pull them in."

While Sludge shook his head in disbelief, Tommy got up, placed the fishing pole on the chair, and waited for Scout.

With the pie pygmy clinging to its fur, the dog and Scout ran along the beach until they stopped in front of Tommy and Sludge.

When Tommy had seen pie pygmies before, they had always had a friendly smile. This time the pie pygmy wasn't smiling.

Tommy spoke first. "Scout, your friend, doesn't look too happy. What's the big rush about?"

Scout took three deep breaths and managed to say, "I blindfolded him so he couldn't see how to get here. He says he has important information."

Scout was young and inexperienced. Tommy doubted he had brought him anything significant. "Are you sure it's important?"

With excitement in his voice, Scout said, "Take off his blindfold and ask him."

Tommy uncrossed his legs, dropped them from the stump, stood up, and lifted his hand. "Take it easy young fellow." He reached over and slipped the blindfold off of Eippy's face.

Eippy blinked at the light.

"What's your name?"

Eippy took a deep breath. "Eippy, Eippy Vanko."

"And what is this important information?"

A sense of emergency filled Eippy's face. "Purple pygmies are turning red and going insane. They swarmed Shangri-la and ate every living thing."

Tommy knew there were purple pygmies, but purple pygmies turning red? He found such a tale hard to believe. "Are you sure you haven't escaped from a nut house?"

A frown of disapproval formed on Eippy's face. "I can understand your doubt," he retorted with an injured look. "A first I thought I was seeing things. His voice quavered with frustration. "But the red pygmies *are* real."

Eippy was a little pie pygmy, but he seemed to be telling the truth. Tommy became interested. "Did they follow you?"

Eippy shook his head and looked around. "I don't think they can keep up with Spinach."

Tommy reached over and patted Spinach on the head. "He's a nice dog."

Eippy nodded and asked, "Do you know if the red pygmies are eating Dinkies and will come here?"

"I don't know if they are eating Dinkies, but when you're dealing with the results of what pig-people have done, you can't be sure of anything."

For emphasis, Sludge shook his finger at Eippy. "Pig-people want us to be their slaves. They just sit on their fat bacon rear ends and don't pay you nothin'. We tried to be friends with them but for what? The chance to associate with brainless half-wits?"

"Half-wits?" Eippy questioned. "On my way here, I spotted two pig-people. They may be headed this way."

"We ain't got nothin' to worry about," Sludge said. "Pig-people are too dumb to get through our defense systems."

"That may have been true in the past," Eippy said. "But the pig-people's food supplies are becoming scarce. They're getting desperate. They have resorted to killing and roasting slave pygmies."

"The purple pygmies used to be a superior race," Tommy said. "Too bad well-dressed tycoons and aristocrats said it was safe to dump chemicals into the air and water that caused them to mutate. From what you have told us they are nothing but purple cannibals who turn red and go mad."

Sludge flashed Eippy a concerned look. "How many red pygmies did you see?"

"Hundreds, maybe thousands. There were just too many to count."

"I hope you're wrong," Tommy said and felt discomfort. "Since Dinky Land has been shut off from the rest of the world, we have experienced and enjoyed continuous peace and the greatest advances in technology that do not harm the earth. We live in a paradise."

Eippy gazed around. "I can see that."

"If the Kura disease has infected a lot of pygmies and caused them to go mad, we'll have a war on our hands. A war could destroy Dinky Land."

"Maybe not," Eippy said with hope. "Not only are the pig-people eating slave pygmies, they are trying to eliminate all the pygmies. If they do, there will be no pygmies left to make war."

There was a long silent pause.

Tommy broke the silence. "If the pig-people eliminate the pygmies, then what are they going to eat?"

"Their self-appointed Chief Earth Officer claims that once the pygmies are gone, the Dinkies will gladly come back to Blue Town and grow their food." He looked to Sludge. "They want you to be slaves again."

Sludge's eyes filled with hate. "Those pig-people are too greedy to live like regular human beings, and they're too lazy to grow their own food. While our ancestors broke their backs plowin' and weedin' eighteen hours a day to build up a food supply, and sweated all day diggin' underground cities, the pig-people cheated and stole from them and lived the easy life. Now they want to beat us up and make us slaves again. Well, they ain't gonna make no slave out-ah me. They're just gonna haft to starve to death."

"If they do," Tommy said, "there will be no more pig-people and there will be no more wars."

"From what I have seen," Eippy said, "those pig-people are mean, but they aren't very smart."

"Maybe one of them mutated and has some form of intelligence." Tommy shot a peculiar look toward Eippy. "Just who is this self-appointed Chief Earth Officer?"

"Ivan Law is his name. He doesn't have all the characteristics of a pig-person. I think he's half human. He may be clever, but he is being told what to do by an ugly pig-person named Derrick."

"I know Derrick," Sludge said and made a face. "He comes from a long line of people users. Ain't no way he can be trusted. He's a manipulator."

Eippy climbed down off of Spinach's back. "Law and Derrick are the two pig-people headed this way."

Sludge looked to Tommy. "What are we going to do?"

Tommy shrugged. "We'll go beyond our defenses and see what they want."

"Do you think it is safe to go to the fake Dinky Land?"

"There's only two pig-people," Tommy said. "If they were going to fight they would have brought an army."

Sludge wildly looked about. "I hope you're right. But just in case, we'll activate the guards."

"Sounds good to me." Tommy looked to Sludge. "You ready?"

Sludge's voiced deepened with seriousness. "They'll probably want food. If we don't give it to them, they'll come back with an army try to take it." He disgustedly shook his head. "Why do they always have to rob what we'll have worked to get?"

"It's no use robbing the pig-people," Tommy said and chuckled. "They haven't got any food."

Sludge gave a disgusted shrug. "I've got better things to do than play around with ignorant pig-people. Let's get this thing over with." He looked toward Eippy. "Do you have a safe place to go?"

"I did but the red pygmies destroyed it."

"Hey, wait a minute." Sludge defiantly stared at Eippy. "What if you turn red?"

Eippy's fluffy tail curved downward. "Then you'll have to kill me."

"We won't have to do that," Tommy said. "Pie pygmies are not cannibals. They have never been infected with Kura disease." He looked to Eippy. "If you don't stay here, you'll be eaten."

"Okay," Sludge said and gestured to Scout. "Go with Scout. While we go to the fake Dinky Land, he'll show you around the real Dinky Land."

"What do you mean the fake Dinky Land?"

"We have a fake Dinky Land. In the past, when attackers believed they had won control of it, they have gone away. If Law and Derrick decide to attack, we have a surprise for them. But to make it work, we'll have to make the fake Dinky Land look like it is inhabited."

Scout led Eippy and Spinach along the beach.

Tommy and Sludge walked a ways from the lake and along a path that led to a little canoe. An iron plaque, poking above thick magenta-and-white-flowered bushes, read, 'Gas and toxic oil was Orange Man's way of keeping inhabitants away from what eons of people had poisoned the Earth with. May we never forget penalty for ignorance and greed'.

The canoe sat at the edge of a pool the size of a small pond. Fingers of fog hazed the surface that bubbled with green, greasy brine that had been created from the dumping of chemicals that had been used to force methane gas from horizontal wells deep in the ground. Although horizontal drilling caused massive earthquakes, it had been proclaimed a great engineering feat, but was nothing more than an extension of the pig-people's unending destruction of the planet for unearned wealth. The brine fouled the once clear cool water that came into the pool. The plaque always reminded Tommy of the distant past. Environmentalist had always blocked attempts to drill horizontally for gas. Even then the Chief Earth Officer knew that no matter how many precautions the gas companies took, the land would be destroyed forever. Stating that drilling was the lesser of two evils and that it was a small price to pay for a cleaner life for the world, the Chief Earth Officer had swept those concerns aside. Although the brine pool could have been drained and made beautiful, as a reminder of the past, it, and the iron plaque remained.

After Tommy and Sludge walked past the weeds that grew in the black ashes of the entrance to old Dinky Land, they tramped up over the hill and stopped at the entrance to the Grotto. Many years ago it had begun here. Underground, the Dinkies who had escaped from farms, rickshaw taxi companies, and the Wheelbarrow Buffet, lived in a secret society. Back then in the light of non-rainy days, the Friends of the Earth Corporation would send Dinky hunters, wearing protective plastic suits and facemasks, to search for the Dinkies who had escaped. At night or on rainy days the Dinkies would come up out of the ground, dance among the green grass, swim in the canals, and drink water that was forbidden to the pig-people. Tommy was glad things had changed. But he always worried that the pig-people would find Dinky Land, and they would have to return to their old underground cities.

Walking, Tommy turned to Sludge. "We're almost there. Did you ever see a purple pygmy turn red?"

"No, but with Kura disease anything can happen."

They stopped at the edge of the canyon that surrounded Dinky Land. At the bottom of the kilometer deep cliffs, even deeper water awaited any intruder who managed to scale the cliffs. Without the secret craft and the cable car, the natural barriers made it impossible to enter Dinky Land. And from a distance, Dinky Land looked like a lifeless desert.

Dinky ancestors claimed that a huge orange oval-shaped space craft had hovered over Dinky Land for six days. When it departed, Orange Man had created the canyon and the pyramid.

Tommy and Sludge walked through the entrance to the pyramid. Inside, an elevator that ran up and down an underground shaft, connected the top to the bottom of the canyon. At the bottom of the shaft, a tunnel snaked through the solid rock under the deep water of the canyon. This tunnel always had a few meters of water on its bottom. The water not only allowed a water craft to glide through the tunnel, it had been said that Orange Man had designed the water craft, and that it received its power from some weird blue solar panels on the outside of the pyramid. The tunnel also had an emergency valve that when pulled would flood the tunnel and trap any unwanted pig-person who had managed to be coming through.

Half way through the tunnel, as a contingency if anything went wrong, an air lock had been chiseled out of the solid rock. The water craft could be stopped and the occupants could lock themselves into the chamber until the problem had been eliminated.

After Tommy and Sludge exited the elevator, they stepped into the water craft. Similar to a submarine, its silver-skinned hull made it possible for the floating craft to glide across the water and go through the tunnel at a leisurely pace. For Dinkies who wanted to go faster, they traveled underwater and watched through a clear alloy plastic see-through shield.

Tommy gave the signal to the operator. The operator placed his hand on the lever. Tommy closed the dome. The operator pulled the lever. At the rear of the craft, a propeller thrashed the water. They were moving. The craft lunged forward. As Tommy felt the G force, water surged over the craft in a rushing roar. Spray flew in front of the window and hazed the view. In a few seconds, the spraying water reduced to a low shush. The craft stopped. Although it was a good five hundred meters, Tommy and Sludge were already on the other side of the tunnel.

Tommy lifted the dome. He and Sludge stepped out. They still had to get to the top of the other side of the canyon and walk to Fake Dinky Land.

Walking through a maze of tunnels, designed to confuse a pig-person's sense of direction, they took the correct path and came to a dizzying whirl of wires. Below the wires, an electrical dynamo softly whined. It was part of the machinery that enabled the cable car and the bridge beam to function.

Tommy and Sludge stepped onto the cable car.

Freddy, the operator, said, "We've been having trouble with the bridge beam."

A look of concern flashed in Sludge's face. "Does it work?"

"It works but it doesn't go all the way down to the platform. You'll have to jump off." He closed the doors and pushed the lever into the up position. As the car began its climb, Freddy warned, "Be careful. There are no safety railings."

The concerned look faded from Sludge's face. "Just as long as it can get us over the acid pit."

Freddy flashed a confident smile. "No problem. I should have it fixed by the time you get back."

Although not as elaborate as the elevator, on the other side of the canyon, the cable car was usually reliable, and its gears could be disengaged which would let the car run free until it crashed into the ground and kill any unwanted intruders. As an extra added security measure, the only way to exit the cable car once it arrived at the top of the canyon was to use a retractable bridge beam that Freddy would operate and extend over an acid pit that surrounded the cable car entrance.

When the cable car stopped at the top of the canyon, it was on a cement island in the center of the acid pit. Not only was the cable car island a secure way of entering and exiting Dinky Land, it was also surrounded by heavy boulders that rose fifty meters high and had no visible exit or entry points.

Tommy and Sludge stepped onto the bridge beam. While the odor of rotten eggs coming from the searing acid permeated the air, Freddy pushed the control lever. The beam extended over the acid pit. On the other side of the pit, Tommy and Sludge jumped down off the beam, landed on the platform, and signaled to Freddy.

Freddy retracted the beam and gave them a farewell wave.

Tommy and Sludge walked down the cement steps of the platform and stepped on the lifeless ground. As a deterrent, sharp, pointed stakes had been pounded into the steep ground around the pit. To scare intruders away, skulls and bones had been placed at various places. It made the place feel and look spooky. Tommy and Sludge jogged past the skulls and bones and pushed a rectangular rock to one side. A hidden trap door yawned open.

Sludge turned to Tommy. "Are you ready to manipulate the manipulators?"

"If we don't, it will be war."

On the other side of the high boulders, they walked into the forest. They were on their way to Fake Dinky Land.

CHAPTER 20

A ways from the canyon of the real Dinky Land, Law stopped and studied the map. With Derrick looking over his shoulder, he tapped his finger on a place marked with a red X. "This is where Dinky Land is supposed to be."

Derrick stared off into the distance. "Are you sure it's not on the other side of the canyon?"

Laughing lightly, Law said, "That canyon is over a kilometer deep. The lower part is steep with shattered rock and sharp, broken edges. And the water is supposed to be full of creatures that will eat you alive. No living man has ever gone there."

Derrick took a deep breath. As if he were going to attempt to climb down the side of the canyon, he braced himself. "That doesn't mean we can't go there."

In disbelief, Law stared at him. "Without a special rope or cable, it would take days to climb down the side of the canyon, swim across the water, and climb back up the other side."

Hooding his eyes against the sun, Derrick looked at the land on the other side of the canyon. "I don't see any signs of life. Maybe you're right. It looks like a desert."

Law folded the map and placed it in his shirt pocket. "The map doesn't lie. Dinky Land has to be somewhere close."

With the usual snot flowing out of the two leather-brown holes where his nose had been,

Derrick gestured with a tilt of his head. "Let's try that way."

After walking through a tangle of vines and shrubs, a small but well-beaten path appeared.

Law stepped onto it. "This path is narrow. It has to be a path the little Dinkies use."

After they followed the path a ways, they rounded a bend in a lush part of the path and stood in awe.

A wooden cabin, with a porch, covered with dark-green vines, sat among cherry trees. Nearby, a clear stream flowed under the shade of willows and ran past two walls that surrounded Dinky Land. The outer wall had been built with red bricks and had been topped with razor wire that circled the entire top. A sentry shanty sat between the outer chain-link gate and an iron-grilled gate that was the entrance of a second stone wall.

Outside the walls, fishing canoes, only big enough for Dinkies who may have guaranteed their owners would have something to eat lay on the shore of a broad estuary. Hard shell-like coatings covered the canoes, and braces in the center could support masks and lateen sails. Beyond that, old-wood-brown, abandoned cottages with screened-in porches hugged a poisoned desolate beach with old boat docks canting into the water. Where shell and algae could have been the home of Fiddler crabs bubbling and sputtering in their holes, weeds choked the dirty-white sand all the way to the water's edge. In the shallows, devoid of the usual crawling, swimming, and growing things, scrawny blades of grass stood rigid. No green algae waved in the gentle currents, and not one fish scampered around the smooth rocks that jutted out of the water. Beyond the beach, a weathered, white picket fence surrounded a clutch of cottages where dead flowers in window boxes wilted below sun-faded canvas awnings that struggled to hood windows.

Law walked toward the razor-wire-topped entrance to Dinky Land and peered through the outer chain-link gate. No children were playing anywhere. The town seemed to be slowly dying.

"Anybody in their right mind wouldn't want to stay in this place," Law said. "It looks too easy to attack." He took a step forward. "Let's go in."

Derrick grabbed Law's shirt sleeve and pulled him back. "Wait!"

"What for?"

"Let's scout the area around Dinky Land. That way, if we have to come back and fight, we'll have knowledge of the site of the battle."

"Good idea." Law said. "It's like you told me, 'Every battle is won before it is fought.'"

Expecting Dinky guards to be on the alert, they made a wide circle around Dinky Land and mentally took notes. After they familiarized themselves with the area, they headed toward the Dinky Land entrance.

At the entrance, they looked through both gates. A Dinky guard with buzzard-like shoulders sat on a chair tipped back against the guard shanty. His slack-jawed face tilted back, and his eyes were closed. He was sleeping.

Beyond the guard, little fishing nets covered canoes in front of little houses. The canoes seemed to be abandoned, no longer of use on a desolate beach. The area was nothing like the area around the cabin and the stream.

As Law and Derrick searched for signs of Dinky life, splashing water and the singing of caged birds met their ears, and the sweep, sweep of brooms on hard surfaces followed. Then the pleasant fragrance of eggs frying and blueberry pancakes on a griddle wafted through the iron bars and hovered at the entrance of the chain-link gate.

Law turned to Derrick. Because of Derrick's constant uncontrollable slobbering, Law hadn't given his appearance much thought. Now, he noticed that a really terrible suit hung on Derrick's muscular body. His mouth had a brutal look, and the strings of snot were beginning to flow from his nose.

"Don't look so mean," Law said. "We're here to convince them to come back. And they might give us something to eat."

Derrick lifted a brand new white triangular cloth to his slobbering face, covered his mouth and nose, and tied the ends of the cloth behind his neck.

"That's better," Law said, but keep your claw hand behind your back. We want to make a good impression."

Derrick grunted with resentment, but changed his demeanor. "You're right. Professional courtesy will suppress honest opinion every time." He placed his claw hand behind his back.

Law grasped the chain-link gate and shook it. It vibrated with metallic clinks. The Dinky guard's slack jaw closed. He opened his eyes. The two front legs of the tipped back chair, he had been sitting on, flew down and thunked onto the stone ground. Awake now, the guard stood up, picked up a shiny brass bell, and stepped across a cracked sidewalk. At the iron-grilled gate, he calmly talked through its bars and the chain-link gate. "Can I help you?"

"Yes," Law replied and bowed his head. "We're here to see your leader. I believe his name is Tommy."

The Dinky lifted the latch on the iron-grilled gate. As he swung it open, above his head, the razor wire jangled with spooky resonance. When he opened the outer chain-link gate, he rang the brass bell. Derrick and Law entered and Dinkies came out of little houses and stood, watching.

With Law and Derrick next to him, the Dinky guard closed the outer chain-link gate and then the iron-grilled gate. Hunching his buzzard-like shoulders, he started walking. "Follow me."

With the aroma of eggs frying and blueberry pancakes filling the air Law tried to put on a friendly face. But as they walked behind the Dinky guard, the dark eyes of the Dinkies standing in front of houses watching them were filled with hatred.

Law cringed under their glares.

"Don't let them bother you," Derrick said through his cloth-covered his mouth. "Once they know the pygmies are gone, they'll be thanking us and serving us eggs and blueberry pancakes."

"Sure we will," the Dinky guard whispered and chuckled.

He led them down a wind-swept street that resembled a desert. On both sides of the street, what once had been thriving with life was virtually dead. They walked past abandoned houses, a few shops, then over a weedy patch that once had been a flower garden and stopped in the front of the tallest structure in Dinky Land. It was large and lavish by neighborhood standards. A small knot of Dinkies stood near its set of white marble steps. Derrick and Law followed the Dinky guard up the steps, past the banister-and-spindle-enclosed porch, and stopped at the door.

The Dinky guard reached up and grabbed a string that was attached to a brass bell attached to the side of the wall and pulled. The bell rang with a pleasing brass tone.

The door opened.

The Dinky guard quit pulling the string and swung his arm into the opening. "Go on in. They're waiting on you."

Law and Derrick stepped into the house. Inside, thick carpets covered the floor. Misted lighting fell from the high ceiling and caused velvet fabrics, soothing colors, and deep upholstery to glow warm, soft, and inviting.

Off to the left, in a room that looked to be an old kitchen with a wood-burning stove, Tommy and Sludge sat at a table.

Law and Derrick walked over the thick carpet and stepped onto the granite floor of the kitchen.

Tommy and Sludge got up from the table and respectfully stood until Law and Derrick were at the table.

Standing over them, Derrick crossed his thick arms across his chest. The gesture was clearly meant to intimidate.

But Tommy ignored it. "Gentleman, welcome to our humble abode."

Expecting to see eggs frying and blueberry pancakes, Law looked around the lavish kitchen. "It doesn't look so humble to me."

"We made it bigger for visitors like you two," Sludge said and gestured to the two chairs on the opposite side of the table. "Please be seated."

As if disappointed that his intimidating gesture had failed, and there were no eggs and pancakes, Derrick uncrossed his arms.

He and Law sat down.

Tommy and Sludge sat down, too, but on higher chairs than Law and Derrick were sitting on.

Tommy leaned toward Derrick. As if Derrick's odor of glue had wafted into Tommy's face, Tommy leaned back. "What can we do for you?"

"It's not what you can do for us," Derrick said. "It's what we can do for you."

Confusion filled Tommy's face. "Just what is it that you can do for us?"

"We can take you away from all this. We have made it possible for you to return to Blue Town. You have the opportunity to live the easy life again."

A burst of laughter erupted from Sludge's face. "What are you, some kind of nut house thing?"

"No, I'm no nut house thing," Derrick calmly replied. "We want you to return to the fields and become slaves again. After all, Dinkies are inferior.

They should be eager to accept their rightful place in society."

Tommy pointed to the cloth Derrick was holding over his mouth and nose. "You have your mouth and nose covered," he said. "Do you think us inferior Dinkies have a disease you might catch?"

Derrick reached up and began to pull the cloth from his face. "I'll show you—"

Not wanting Tommy and Sludge to see Derrick's ugly face, Law held up his hand. "Don't do it."

Derrick stopped pulling the cloth.

"It's nothing like that," Law said. "My friend has a very unsightly wound. He does not wish to offend you. So he keeps it covered."

Derrick nodded. "Although you are inferior, we still have compassionate feelings for you. And our compassion is the main reason we would appreciate your returning to Blue Town." He reached down, took a pouch from his pocket, opened it, and dumped the contents onto the table. Thirty small nuggets of gold formed a haphazard array. "We hope you'll find it in your heart to like us. We have brought gold to make your move as comfortable as possible."

"Comfortable?" Tommy questioned. "When we were slaves, pig-people ate the food we Dinkies grew. But not one cared about the Dinkies who grew it."

"We can't eat gold," Sludge broke in and seemed to instantly sizzle with anger. "And what if we ain't gonna go?"

228

"If you resist," Law said with authority. "The penalties will be stiff."

"You may try and inflict all the penalties you like," Tommy said. "You may not know it, but we have guardians throughout the land."

Law began to speak, but Derrick cut him short. "You may have guardians, but I don't think you realize just how powerful we have become."

Tommy rolled his hand in an encouraging gesture. "Enlighten me."

"We have had such an easy victory over the pygmies of Shangri-la that our warriors have no doubt that they can do the same with Dinky Land. But a slaughter can be avoided." He pushed the gold toward Tommy. "Of course, you two won't have to be slaves. All you have to do is take the gold, get your people to surrender, and tell them to go back to working the fields like before."

Law leaned back, spread his arms in a welcoming gesture, and smiled. "Then we can all be happy again."

His eyes blazing, Sludge sprang to his feet. "If you think we're going to let anyone treat our people like that again, you better get right back to the nut house."

Derrick looked regretfully at Sludge. "We're sorry about how you and your friends have been treated in the past."

As if trying desperately to stay calm, Tommy's lips tightened. "It's easy to say you're sorry and do nothing about the problem."

"We didn't have time to do anything about it," Law whined. "We were too busy trying to survive."

The glue odor coming from Derrick was beginning to fill the room. Sludge started to back away, but he aggressively leaned toward Law. "If pig-people are dumb enough to sit around all day getting' drunk and can't take the time to plant a garden and wonder why they have nothing to eat, that's not our problem."

For a moment, Law cringed, but calmly replied, "They're not dumb. They're victims of a cruel system."

"They're victims all right." Sludge said and looked directly into Law's eyes.

Law avoided Sludge's eyes.

Sludge continued. "They're victims of their own laziness. They're dumber than a bag of stones. And they're scared. That's why they like to cover their fat bodies with uniforms and march in stupid formations." As if exhausted, he sat down.

Fighting the urge to get angry, Law stared straight ahead. "Marching in formations is good training."

Bitterness filled Tommy's voice. "When they're part of a gang, who you choose to call soldiers, they feel safe. They are happy in a dictatorship where they know what is going to happen next."

"A dictatorship is the only way to run anything." Derrick's eyes turned mean. "It cuts the red tape and the whining. It's efficient."

The bitterness eased from Tommy's voice and was replaced with a sardonic chuckle. "Dictators fit into a predictable mold. They're usually people who are frustrated in life for some reason."

This hit Law. When the pig police had refused to help and threw him in jail, he had been frustrated, and he still was. Maybe he fit the mold. He tried to hide his sudden feelings of frustration.

But Tommy would have none of it. He shook his finger in front of Law's face. "You're not only disappointed, you're a frightened man."

As if he were contemplating moving in, Law defiantly looked around the kitchen. "Your little town here is not an island we cannot get to. We'll tear down your walls and destroy your town. Then we'll gather you all up. We'll take you back to Blue Town where you belong. You'll be the slaves you were born to be."

Tommy stiffened with hostility. "That is quite possible. But I would like to remind you that for over three hundred years, we have been prepared for that eventuality."

"That's right," Sludge said. "We ain't gonna be salves no more. We fought to be free and we're gonna stay free."

"You want to be free?" Derrick cut in. "Freedom is slavery."

"What are you trying to do?" Tommy asked. "Start a war?"

"If you don't come back to Blue Town, like you know you should." Derrick giggled with weird childish joy. "Then we will have no choice but to declare war."

Sludge leaned back and cast Derrick an arrogant stare. "I suppose the next thing you're gonna tell us is that war is peace."

Derrick's eyes indicated that a huge satisfied smile had formed on his cloth-covered lips. "You're no so dumb after all. When you think about it, war *is* peace. And ignorance is strength."

"If ignorance is strength" — Sludge bobbed his head with sadistic laughter — "you'd be the strongest man in the world."

The "terp, nerp, tnep" sickening sound came from deep in Derrick's throat. Yellow strings of snot, with the odor of glue, crawled, from under the cloth and stretched down onto the table.

Surprised and sickened, Tommy and Sludge leaned back.

Derrick's hair-less brows contracted into an angry arch. "What do you know about anything, you little mutated creeps?"

With his nose constricting and his eyes glaring with disapproval, Sludge managed to say, "I know that you stink like rotten glue." He covered his nose and mouth with the sleeve of his shirt.

"I may have a slight odor of glue," Derrick shot back. "But I don't have a lip that looks like a night crawler coming out of my mouth."

Leaning back away from the odor, Tommy held up his hand. "Gentleman, let's not reduce this meeting to name calling." He turned his head to the side and looked toward the window. "There are others outside who will be upset."

Ignoring his snot on the table, Derrick made a fist, stuck out his thumb, and pointed to his own chest. "We are not interested in the good of others. We are not interested in wealth or luxury or long life or happiness. We are different from all the

232

oligarchies of the past. We know what we are doing."

Sludge's face clouded. "You might impress your half-witted followers with fancy words, but we ain't fallin' for your crock of crap."

"It makes no difference what you do," Derrick said, and a rasping snort came from deep in his chest. "We *are* going to take control. After everything is the way it should be, we're stepping down."

"Sure you are," Tommy said sarcastically. "People before you were cowards and hypocrites. They claimed there was a paradise, just around the corner where pig-people and Dinkies would be free and equal."

"That is just the way it is going to be."

"You and I know that no one ever seizes power with the intention of relinquishing it."

"I'm glad you admitted that," Derrick said. "Would you care to elaborate?"

"Power is not a means. It is an end. You may have established a dictatorship for the pig-people, but you will not establish one here."

Derrick cocked his head in an insolent tilt. "What are you afraid of?"

Tommy's eyes bulged with puzzlement. "Under dictatorship, the object of persecution is persecution. The object of torture is torture. The object of power is power." His face filled with resentment. "We choose not to live that way."

As if devoid of all emotion, Derrick looked around the kitchen. "There is no need to get excited. Come with us. You won't have to live in these antiquated surroundings." He took his claw hand from behind his back and let it fall onto the table. "I'm sure after you have thought about it, you will surrender to us." He held up his claw hand. "And it will be of your own free will."

Looking at the claw hand, Sludge goggled with amazement. "Yeah right," he said. "And I believe you are a sane person with a claw hand, and there ain't no snot on the table."

Derrick clenched his claw and whirled around. With a scowl of truculence, he glared at Law. "What the matter with these Dinkies?"

Afraid Derrick may become combative, Law cringed. When he saw Derrick wasn't going to hit him, he pretended he hadn't been afraid and slumped with disgust. "If we can't tell them what is best for them, we'll just have to show them."

"Go ahead. Do whatever you want." Sludge shook his finger at Derrick. "You people are too ignorant to understand that we don't want or need you."

"And," Tommy added, "we don't need retards like you telling what to do. All we want to do is live in peace."

The cloth fell from Derrick's ugly face. Beneath the two holes where his nose used to be, his snot-coated mouth wreathed into a smile. "If you do as we say" —as if he were in pain his voice came out harsh and strained — "you will have peace."

"Why don't you just get it over with," Tommy said and lowered his eyes from the sight of

Derrick's face. "If you're going to declare war, then just do it."

With the scare tissue pressing on his throat, Derrick's voice was growing hoarse. He looked to Law.

Law sat extra erect and spoke as if he were reading from an ancient textbook. "The Friends of the Earth Corporation declares war on all Dinkies and takes title to all the land they possess or may possess in the future."

"You don't seem to be a very bright boy," Sludge said to Law. "Let me splain it to you. "Fish ain't never gonna live long enough to swim in your polluted water. A pig-person ain't never gonna breathe underwater. And you ain't never gonna live through a war against the Dinkies."

Derrick looked to Tommy. "How would he know that?"

"It doesn't matter how he knows it," Tommy snapped back. "Your ugly mouth has bitten off more than it can chew."

Derrick scooped the gold nuggets off of the table, stood up, and snapped to attention. With a stern expression on his face, he looked to Law. "Attention!"

Law leaped out of the chair so fast that the chair fell over. He ignored it and stiffened to attention.

Derrick continued. "Gentleman, prepare for war." He lifted his claw hand to his forehead and held a salute.

Tommy did not acknowledge the salute. "We already know you're an asshole. We're not going to confirm it with a salute."

Sludge stood up. "I'll give him a salute. He lifted his hand and gave Derrick a one-fingered salute.

Still holding his salute, Derrick placed the cloth back over his face. The odor of glue increased. He pulled the cloth away. Slobber stuck to the cloth and stretched into long sickening strings.

Sludge lowered his head and muttered, "You freak."

Holding the cloth to his face, Derrick puffed up. "What did you say?"

Sludge kept his head lowered. "I wasn't talkin' to you."

As Sludge and Tommy looked in disbelief, a shadow crossed Derrick's face. "It doesn't matter what you do," he said and snapped his claw hand from his forehead. "We are at war."

"Declare anything you want," Sludge said. "You're still a freak."

Derrick leaned toward Sludge. "If you didn't have your friends standing outside just waiting to come in, I'd rip that night crawler lip right off your face."

Sludge reached under the table and pulled out a pick ax and shook it at Derrick. If you think you can do it with this sticking up your ass, come on and try it."

Knowing that if Derrick injured or killed Sludge the Dinkies outside would overwhelm them,

Law reached out and touched Derrick's arm. "We don't have to listen to this."

"That's right," Derrick said and backed up. "If we have to, we'll use our secret weapon."

They stood ramrod straight, did an about-face, and stomped out of the room.

While Sludge waved his hand in front of his face, the odor of glue trailed behind.

CHAPTER 21

Hoping the ruse to lure the pig-people into Fake Dinky Land and trap them would succeed, Tommy was safely hidden in a tunnel. But nervous apprehension filled his entire body. He didn't know if the trap was going to work.

Standing next to Tommy and looking from under an opening in the steel trap door, Sludge scanned the wall that ran around Fake Dinky Land. Every few meters, towers, above the solid brick walls, rose sheer and vertical, and seemed to be only for looks. But they held an important part of the trap.

Tommy studied the walls and turned to Sludge. "Are the nets in place?"

Sludge placed a hand on Tommy's shoulder. "You ain't gonna see 'em. But don't worry. We got 'em ready to throw."

The Dinkies planned to lure the pig-people into Fake Dinky Land and use electric-charged nets to place them in temporary discomfort and imprison them within the walls of Fake Dinky Land until they agreed to stay away. That way, no lives would be lost, Fake Dinky Land would be spared to be used for another trap, and the pig-people would be defeated.

Tommy held up his hand. "Listen."

Sludge cupped his hand to his ear. "They're on the way."

"Get to the switch."

If the high-voltage switch was pulled, the nets would electrocute the pig-people. Sludge wanted to do just that. "Are you sure you only want to shock them?"

"We don't want to kill anyone," Tommy said. "And don't turn it on until they have all come through the gates and all the nets are out of the Dinkies' hands and down."

"I still think we should zap them with the high voltage, but I hope you're right." Sludge crawled a few meters into the tunnel and vanished in the darkness.

Tommy continued to observe through the opening in the trap door.

Derrick and Law came to the chain-link gate, stopped, and turned toward an advancing army of pig-people.

To Tommy's surprise, purple pygmies were massed behind hordes of pig-people warriors marching toward the gate. But they didn't look like they were ready to fight.

Law held up his hand.

The color guard held up orange flags that had the Black Sun symbol.

The warriors stopped marching.

Except for the flags flapping in a sudden breeze, all was quiet.

Law broke the quiet. "You have done well," he shouted, and Tommy figured Law was giving the pig-people another dose of ego building to help his cause.

An ear-piercing squeal of anguish keened higher and higher until it abruptly stopped. Already beginning to cower, the warriors mumbled amongst themselves.

Law's voice bellowed over the warriors. "Remember that sound. The Dinkies have already captured one of your comrades. Right now, they are torturing him."

Uneasiness filled the warrior ranks followed by a collective murmur.

Tommy wanted to run out and tell the mob of so-called warriors that Derrick was lying. The noise was coming from outside of the walls. It was a hidden pig-person pretending to be in pain. But patience and silence were needed to make the trap succeed. Tommy kept quiet and waited.

Law continued. "Although we are faced with the greatest crisis in our history, we need not be afraid."

The warrior's uneasiness seemed to subside.

Law nodded in approval and began his spiel of disinformation. "The Dinkies have lost their ability to intellectually process the obvious. The shortage of food indicates that more trouble is ahead. Race-wars and riots have surfaced, and masses of Dinkies are beginning to get primal and retreat back into their ethnic and racial identities. They are so busy fighting themselves that our victory will be simple and swift."

"Sure it will," Tommy muttered to himself and recalled what Law and Derrick had done when they had destroyed Shangri-la: They had used persuasive tricks to create a mob mentality, which had turned fear and vindictiveness into hideous ecstasy. It had given pig-people a strong desire to kill, a need to torture, and a never-ending desire to smash faces in with rocks tied to the end of sticks. It had turned docile pig-people into a screaming mass of lunatics. Law and Derrick had turned them into fighting men. They were trying to do it again.

"Warriors!" Law roared.

The pig-people warriors snapped their heads in his direction.

"It has been said that we could never defeat the pygmies at Shangri-la."

A series of boo's erupted from the warriors.

"That's right," Law continued. "We have achieved the impossible."

A cheer went up.

"Are we going to do it again?"

He didn't wait for an answer. "Yes!" He thrust his clinched fist into the air. "Yes! We are going to do it again. We are battle-hardened. We are ready for anything those dumb Dinkies can throw at us."

The warriors in the front ranks began thumping the ends of their spears on the ground and broke into a chant. "Kill the Dinkies. Kill the Dinkies."

Bass drums beat loudly. Warriors with rocks tied to sticks joined in. The chant grew louder, traveled to the entire mass of warriors, and to the purple pygmies, too. With the unstoppable mentality of a mob, the huge mix of brainwashed individuals merged into one mass.

With strings of slobber running from the red cloth covering his mouth, Derrick turned toward the chain-link gate. The "terp, nerp, tnep" sickening sound came from deep in his throat. He held the cloth to his mouth and swallowed. Then his loud voice thundered in the direction of the Dinky guard. "Dinkies tear down these gates!"

With a look of terror etched upon his face, the Dinky got up off his bench and unlocked the iron-grilled gate. "No need to destroy property," he calmly said. "These gates open easily." He opened the iron-grilled gate a meter, stepped through, closed it, and locked it. Then he went to the chain-link gate. Before he could open it, the pig-people had pulled it down.

The Dinky guard began ringing the brass bell in his hand and ran toward the iron-grilled gate. But he only made it as far as the lock.

With both hands, Derrick grabbed the Dinky's bell ringing forearm and lifted the Dinky into the air. Then he forced the Dinky's arm downward. It smacked on the side of the iron-grilled gate. A sickening dull snap filled the air and was followed by the bell clanging onto the ground. The broken ends of the radius and the ulna bones erupted through the Dinky's skin. As blood, from a severed artery, spurted into the air, a purple pygmy rushed up and took a huge bite out of the Dinky's arm.

Derrick removed the cloth from his face and looked down at the Dinky. Through a fiendish, slobbering mouth, he grinned. "How do you like me now?"

Even though he was in extreme pain, the Dinky guard reached into his pocket, took out the key to the iron-grilled gate, and tossed it through the bars. It landed in the dry dirt. A tiny puff of yellow dust enveloped it.

Wanting to help, Tommy tried to remind himself that a good leader always disconnects his feelings for his fellow man. Helping the broken-armed Dinky would mean death for himself and many others. But he couldn't watch and do nothing. He grabbed a sharp machete, hid it behind his back, and popped up out of the trap door. He ran to the iron-grilled gate, stood there, and confronted Derrick. "Let me cut you down to our size." His words came out with so much anger that if they had been venom, Derrick would have dropped dead right on the spot.

Before Derrick could react, Tommy ran the sharp machete through the bars of the iron-grilled gate. It flayed open the flesh on Derrick's bicep

Tommy knew he was no match for Derrick's strong body. He rushed back into the hole in the ground and slipped in. He closed the trap door until there was only a small slit and looked through it. Law was crawling over thick tarps that had been flung over the coils of razor wire at the top of the iron-grilled gate. If Law could get over the wire, he would get the key and unlock the gate.

Tommy let the trap door completely close. Before he could slide the bolt and lock it, Derrick reached down and yanked the trap door open. Too late, Tommy realized Derrick had climbed up over the iron-grilled gate before Law had.

Tommy crawled back into the darkness of the narrow tunnel and watched.

Derrick, who was twice as tall as Tommy, could not stand erect in the tunnel. "Damn," he cussed and held his hand over the rag he had tied around the cut on his bicep. "That tunnel's too small for me to go into. I'm not crawling like a dirty Dinky."

Law ran up to him and smiled. "We have a cure for that."

"That's right." Derrick turned toward the iron-grilled gate. Motioning with his hand, he yelled, "Get that key, unlock that gate, and bring in the propane." He slammed the trap door shut. "No dumb Dinky is going to outsmart me."

Tommy eased back to the trap door and slid the bolt home. "Let's see you lift it now."

A few minutes later: Clunk! Clunk! Sounded on the trap door. Tommy looked up. Whatever Derrick was using, with each hit, it was causing the metal to dimple. Tommy hoped the door would last long enough for the pig-people and the purple pygmies to get inside the walls so the Dinkies could drop the nets and Sludge could turn the electricity on.

Clunk! Clunk! The edge or the trap door bowed upward and created a little slot. Tommy peered out. The iron-grilled gate was wide open.

Leaning drunkenly against the wall, the Dinky guard with the broken arm defiantly thrust a crooked finger at an advancing pig-person. "You'll never get out of here alive."

The pig-person slammed the sharp end of a pick ax into the side of the Dinky's head. The end passed through the brain and out the other side. A spray of bone and blood erupted. For a moment, a cloud of blood hung in the air. With his eyes fixed in death, the Dinky's knees folded and dropped to

244

the ground. As the cloud of blood dissipated, he fell forward and lay still.

Tommy felt something on his shoulder. Derrick had slid a black hose under the trap door. Tommy looked to where the hose was coming from. A huge tank of propane gas sat on a heavy wagon. It would only be seconds before Derrick would turn the propane gas on. In a few moments it would fill the tunnel. If anyone in the tunnel survived the gas, it wouldn't matter. When Derrick ignited the gas they would be blown to pieces.

Just as Tommy reached up and pushed the hose out of the tunnel, a wave of pig-people warriors rushed through the gate. Behind them, purple pygmies followed. After the last pygmy had gone through the gate, Tommy crawled through the tunnel, picked up a chain and a lock, and exited outside the walls. Making sure no one was waiting in ambush, he did an end run and stopped at the iron-grilled gate. Then he closed it, ran the chain through the bars, and locked it. He had trapped the pig-people warriors and purple pygmies inside.

All along the outside of the second wall, Dinkies climbed to the top, unfolded wire nets, and threw them over the pig-people warriors and purple pygmies. Surprised, they struggle to free themselves from the nets. But the nets held them secure.

Inside the walls, the last three purple pygmies who had rushed through the gate had not been captured by the nets. They turned and rushed back toward the closed gate where Tommy was waiting.

Tommy just stood there.

The three purple pygmies began to turn red. One shouted, "We'll climb over."

They reached out and grabbed the gate. Their little arms vibrated with shocking electricity. They jerked their hands back. Infuriated, they turned bright red.

Tommy smiled. Like a parent scolding a little kid, he joking said, "You kids are going to stay in there until you learn to behave."

With their rat tails waving like slithering snakes, the pygmies glowed to a brighter almost neon red. As if it were a signal, one of the red pygmies let out a long ear-piercing shriek and pointed behind Tommy.

Tommy turned around. Down the road, a wake of dust boiled up. Something was moving. Whatever it was, it was coming fast.

Although the purple pygmies and pig-people were trapped in Fake Dinky Land, new waves of purple pygmies were swarming toward the gate. They were bigger and stronger, and there were more of them than Tommy could count. As he watched them, they let out high-pitched staccatos of "Yay! — Yay! Yay! — Yay! — Yay! — Yay!" It was so loud and ear piercing that it hammered into his brain, causing unstoppable pain. He had never wanted to kill anyone, but he would have to tell Sludge to turn on the high voltage. Holding his hands over his ears, he took off running.

When he got to the control station in the tunnel, Sludge turned to Tommy. "The voltage in the nets wasn't strong enough. The pig-people just threw them off. So I turned it up."

246

"Bigger pygmies are coming down the road. Do you think the voltage will be high enough?"

"I hope so, but when those pygmies turn red they git mighty powerful. There ain't no tellin' what they can do."

Tommy shrugged. "I guess we're going to find out."

They looked through the slit in the trap door. While the pig-people and purple pygmies who were trapped inside Fake Dinky Land searched for a way out, outside, a new wave of bright red pygmies hurled themselves at the electrified iron-grilled gate. Each time they hit the gate, they were electrified to the point of unconsciousness. Those who remained on the gate died with putrid smoke curling from their bodies. The odor of burning flesh and the propane gas freely flowing from the rubber hose and the leaking tank valve filled the air. But the red pygmies still charged the gate, their angry red bodies piling up, forming a ramp.

Three very red pygmies walked up to a dead pygmy, looked right and then left. Then they bent over, took huge bites out of the dead pygmy's rear end, swallowed with satisfaction, and ran up the growing pile of dead pygmies forming against the gate.

Irrational thoughts and actions were just a few of the many effects of cannibalism and the resulting karma of Kura disease.

Amazed, Tommy turned to Sludge. "They're goin' loco."

Sludge savagely cursed. "The Kura disease took over their minds."

"Alert the others. It's time to get out of here."

Sludge picked up a dented brass bugle, placed it to his lips, opened the trap door, and belted out a long sour blast.

The other Dinkies popped up from their hiding places. When they looked at the red pygmies, for a moment, they stared in astonishment. Then they scattered into the forest.

Before Tommy and Sludge could turn and crawl down the tunnel, a mesmerizing sight stopped their movements. A new wave of red pygmies streamed down the road and continued to march to the iron-grilled gate. Those in front lay down on the dead. The pygmy pile became higher and higher. When it was at the top of the razor wire on the gate, pygmies grabbed the razor wire. It cut deep into their red flesh. They turned bright-red angry and seemed impervious to pain. They just kept on turning bright-red and kept on advancing. After they had torn out the razor wire, they avalanched down the other side of the gate and invaded Fake Dinky Land. All along the walls, more and more red pygmies ran into the electrified nets of wire. The smoke from their frying bodies continued filling the air with the awful odor of burnt flesh.

Tommy looked at the switch box. Smoke curled from the edges of the closed door, and the muffled sounds of arcing sparks came from inside.

"They're too many pygmies on the nets," Tommy excitedly said. "They're grounding it out."

Sludge pointed to the huge propane tank that had the hose connected to it. Derrick had just snaked it back under the trap door. He turned the

248

valve on the tank wide open. Even though the valve was wildly hissing and leaking gas, he smiled.

Sludge's eyes grew wide. "It's a wonder the gas ain't already blown us to smithereens. When it hits the sparks coming from the control box, it's gonna to blow."

Tommy flashed a smile. "Yeah, I know."

Sludge understood.

With the odor of gas creeping into their lungs, Tommy and Sludge sprinted through the tunnel. Once outside, they breathed a few breaths of gas-less air and took off running.

At the edge of the forest, a mass of purple pygmies blocked their way. Tommy tilted his head to the side. It was the signal for Sludge to do something to divert the pygmies' attention. When he did, Sludge and he would run to the left and try to outrun them.

In great haste, Sludge and Tommy moved their heads from side to side, searching for something to throw. They saw nothing.

Tommy bent down. "Get ready to run."

Sludge tensed.

Tommy scooped up a handful of dirt and flung it at the purple pygmies. They jerked back. Squealing in pain, they jammed their hands into their dirt-filled eyes and turned red.

Tommy and Sludge ran over the top of a small hill that was at the edge of the forest and stopped at the bottom. Tommy looked up. A tree stood at the top of another hill. He looked to Sludge. "Let's go."

They ran up the hill. Tommy stopped at the top, but Sludge ran down the other side. Tommy grabbed a low-hanging tree branch and held it. He figured it was low enough.

At the bottom of the hill, Sludge waved his arm. "Come on. They're right behind us."

Tommy shook the low hanging tree branch.

A mischievous smile spread across Sludge's face. "You're gonna need help." He ran up the hill, stepped next to Tommy, and grabbed the branch. Together, they pulled the branch until it was about to break and held it.

They waited.

Nothing happened.

Sludge relaxed his stance. "Maybe they gave up."

"Either that or they're surrounding us." Tommy sniffed. The odor of propane hung heavy in the air.

Sludge waved his hand in front of his face. "It's gettin' hard to breathe. That propane tank is really leaking. Maybe the gas killed them."

Tommy looked to the top of the target hill. Purple pygmies stared back at him. As if they were getting ready to rip Tommy and Sludge to shreds, they excitedly wagged their rat tails and snapped their pointed teeth. Tommy and Sludge let the branch fly. It swished through the air. All but one pygmy ducked. Whap! The branch smacked that pygmy. Turning bright red, it went flying into the air. Thump! It landed on the hard ground on the side of the hill.

Tommy and Sludge ran down the other side of the hill. With their pointed-toothed mouths snapping, the red pygmies charged after them.

At the bottom of the hill, Tommy was running at full speed. To see how close the red pygmies were, he looked back over his shoulder. Whap! He ran into a low hanging tree branch. It knocked him to the ground. Before he could get to his feet, the red pygmies were snapping at his shoes. He looked to Sludge. "Save yourself. I'm not gonna make it."

Sludge hesitated. He could have easily run and gotten away, but as if petrified, he stood and helplessly watched.

The first pygmy's teeth were gnawing the leather on Tommy shoe. He kicked the red pygmy in the face. Its teeth broke. It screamed and rolled away. Three more pygmies charged. Six came from the right. More came from the left. Tommy sprang to his feet and prepared to jump over them. More snapping mouthed red pygmies came. All avenues of escape were blocked. Slowly advancing, they let out that high pitched staccato of "Yay! — Yay! Yay! — Yay! — Yay! — Yay!"

Just as Tommy and Sludge placed their hands over their ears to stop the loud and ear piercing sound hammering into their brains, BOOM! The explosion from the propane gas, Derrick had fed into the tunnels, had gone off.

The great force jerked the ground beneath Tommy's and Sludge's feet. Their knees flew up and hit them in their chests. All the pygmies fell to the ground. Woosh! The detonation in the tunnel had ignited the heavier than-air propane. It had traveled from the leaking tank and created a ground-hugging blanket of gas. Seeing the orange-blue fire rushing their way, Tommy and Sludge grabbed onto the tree branch and lifted their feet off the ground. The orange-blue flames crawled over the red pygmies. Heat caused the bottoms of Tommy's and Sludge's feet to heat up. But it seared the bodies of the red pygmies. They cried out in pain. But more were on the way. They would be chasing Tommy and Sludge.

Before the pygmies caught up with them, Tommy and Sludge dropped to the ground, leaped over the red pygmies fallen forms, and shoved past others too stunned to stop them. With their ears ringing from the loud explosion, and the wooden cabin burning behind them, Tommy and Sludge escaped into the forest.

CHAPTER 22

While the red pygmies continued to destroy Fake Dinky Land and feast on the dead, loud thumps of the warriors' drums signaled a call to formation. The pig-people warriors dropped what they were doing and scurried to the formation. For a moment, the red pygmies lifted their blood-covered mouths from the carnage. But they ignored the call to formation and went right back to gnawing on the dead.

Turning his back to the red pygmies, Law called the formation to attention. "Forward, march!" he commanded, and the pig-people warriors triumphantly marched back to Shangri-la.

Standing at the iron-grilled gate at Shangri-la, and surrounded by his followers, Law held a gold chalice filled with wine. With a smile lighting his face, he basked in the victorious mood around him.

A few meters away, Derrick stood extra erect. He thrust his hands behind his back and puffed up his thick chest. Although a red cloth covered his nose and face, his eyes seemed to be sending hate in Law's direction and toward the pig-people gathered around him.

Law held up his hand. Gesturing to the ruins of Shangri-la, he waved his hand in an arc. "This is all yours. You fine warriors have earned the right to take whatever you want."

Derrick relaxed his stance. With the tails of their open jackets streaming around them, the pig-people warriors rushed into Shangri-la.

While they scavenged the area for spoils of war, Law and Derrick walked through the ashes and debris and into Kaput's throne room.

Law thought he would enjoy its grandeur, its white marble steps, its sculptures, and its vaulted ceilings, but everything except the area around the throne had been broken or ruined. The place gave off an impending sense of evil. He shrugged it off, walked up the six white marble steps, and admired the gold crest and the jewels reflecting light off the throne. Fascinated, he eased himself into the comfort of the thickly-padded, red velvet of the high-backed golden throne and sat back.

Derrick's eyes grew wide with disbelief. Without warning, he ran up the steps and slapped Law across the face. In a thick guttural accent, his voice came out low and menacing. "Who do you think you are?"

Bewildered at Derrick's sudden hostility, Law jerked to the side. "What's the matter?"

As if he were a completely different person, Derrick began screaming at Law. "I was the one who made things on the list happen. Now you want to sit on *my* throne."

"What do you mean *you* made things on the list happen?"

Derrick violently jerked his thumb to his own chest. "Years before I arranged your early release from jail, I eliminated health care and let those who were too lazy to work die. I was the one who increased the pig-people's poverty level and provided everything for them to live and caused them to become too weak to fight back."

He threw his claw hand into the air. "I increased the debt to an unsustainable level and enabled the Friends of the Earth to increase taxes and produce even more poverty."

Derrick's ranting brought a profusion of pig-people into the throne room.

As if they weren't there, he continued shouting at Law. "And what did you when guns were about to be legalized?"

"I was in the culverts, barely surviving," Law shot back. "I couldn't do anything."

With a wave of his claw hand, Derrick dismissed Law's reply. "Likely story," he said, and snot flew from the two leather holes where his nose used to be. "While you were doing nothing, I created fake murders and robberies. The people couldn't wait to have their guns taken away." Snot flowed freely from his nose holes, but it didn't slow his rant. "Now, nobody can defend themselves from me and the police state I am about to create."

Law turned his eyes from the sickening, snot-spewing sight of Derrick's face. "That wasn't our agreement."

"I made no promises to you or any other useful idiots. I was the one who controlled what pig-people read and listened to. And I was the one who made it possible to deny pig-people an education and control what their children learned in school. As a bonus, I removed the belief in Orange Man from the land.

"But there is an Orange Man."

"Sure," Derrick sardonically replied, "and there are fairies, sprites, and space aliens."

Law fired back with his own sardonic response. "I suppose you created the earth, too."

The veins on Derrick's neck stuck out. "I am about to create the greatest kingdom pig-people have ever known. I have divided the people into the wealthy and poor and caused more discontent which made it easier to tax the wealthy, and the poor support the tax. I am about to take control of every aspect of their lives. Under my rule, it will be a new world."

As the pig-people warriors watched and took huge bites from the severed arms and legs of pygmies they had slaughtered, Derrick breathed heavily, wiped the snot from his face, and seemed to calm down.

Hoping Derrick would listen to reason, Law shook his finger at him. "It's all your fault!"

As Derrick's heavy breathing ceased, he tilted his head with puzzlement, and the scar tissue around his neck turned red. "What's all my fault?"

"You should have never gone in with those purple pygmies. We weren't supposed to kill the Dinkies, but the pygmies turned red and killed them all. We could have had Dinky Land and the Dinkies all for ourselves. It would be like it was before."

Derrick thundered, "You are wrong! Until the Dinky-loving Patagonia people are defeated, it can never be like it was before."

"There are not that many Patagonia people, and even though they will fight for the Dinkies, they are not a threat."

"You seemed to have forgotten that the Patagonia people never fight in groups. They go

256

out alone and ambush their enemies. We could never find them, let alone defeat them. As we speak, their individualism is letting the masses of red pygmies overwhelm them. Soon, the Patagonia people will be eliminated."

"That was no reason to destroy Dinky Land."

"Great towns are always destroyed," Derrick stated. "But we didn't destroy a great town."

Law squirmed uncomfortably on the throne. "I can't believe that."

"Listen up, bright boy. I've got a news flash for you. I wasn't fooled by the fake Dinky Land."

"What?"

The Dinky Land the purple pygmies destroyed was only a decoy, a trap. I know where the real Dinky Land is."

"But you gave me the map."

"Sure I gave you the map. But it was the wrong map. Fake Dinky Land was only a warm up for the real thing."

"How would you know where the real Dinky Land is?"

"I had the original map."

"Had? You don't have the map? You'll never be able to find the real Dinky Land."

Derrick tapped his skull. "I have everything depicted on the map in here."

"I hope and pray to Orange Man that you are not planning to kill those Dinkies, too?"

"That's the difference between us," Derrick said. "You only think about the accumulation of wealth. But wealth is not the important thing. It's the power that goes along with it. If you weren't so ignorant, you would realize that power is the only reason money ever existed."

"But I thought you wanted Blue Town to return to the golden age when Dinkies were slaves." He paused. "But most important of all, I thought we were friends."

Law placed his hands on his hips and leaned toward Law. "For your further information, pig-people only look for friends when they hate and become obsessed with a cause. Before a new order can be built, the old ways must be eliminated." He brushed his hands together and leaned back. "And that includes your stupid Dinkies."

Law let out a disgusted breath. "Why did I ever agree to join up with you?"

Derrick smiled big and let out a huge horse laugh. "Because, I forced you to."

Law sat ridged. "What?"

"I promised the purple pygmies they could have Dinky Land if they ate all your crops and burnt down your house."

"What kind of a person would deliberately burn down a man's house?"

Derrick jerked his thumb to his own chest. "My kind of person."

"But why?"

"I needed you to lead the pig-people."

"Why didn't you do it yourself?"

Derrick leaned in close. "Look at my face."

Law couldn't help but stare. Long strings of yellow slobber hung from Derrick's fat tong.

Law turned from the ugliness.

Derrick grabbed Law's shoulder and forced him to look into his face. "Take a good look."

From the two holes where Derrick's nose used to be, yellow strings of snot flowed onto Law's chest and the odor of glue blasted into his face.

He blinked in repulsion.

With the strings of snot swinging back and forth, Derrick continued. "Would you want a man who looks like me to lead you?"

"I believed you needed a friend."

Derrick's cheeks grew tight with fury. "So what?"

"With the belief that someday a friend would need you, I became your friend."

Derrick's hairless brows furled in puzzlement. "War changes everything."

Law wasn't buying it. "Do you actually believe war gives you a free pass to do things a sane person would never do?'

Derrick stuck his finger in the hole where he ear used to be, wiggled it, and shrugged. "You know how it is. War just does something to a person."

Even though Derrick's war excuse fooled others, Law knew war had exposed Derrick's true character. "Don't expect pity from me. Tell it like it is. You have committed war crimes."

Derrick jerked his finger from his ear. With a look of murderous antagonism, he defiantly stared at Law. "So what?"

"Your war crimes are not excusable. You are not a good person."

A rasping snort came from Derrick's two leather-like nose holes. "I'm not here to make friends." He raised his fist into the air. "I'm here to lead."

"After what you have done, it doesn't matter what you look like."

Derrick grabbed Law's shoulder. "Are you telling me that I can't lead?"

Looking at Derrick's hand gripping his shoulder, Law made a sour face. "You can't be trusted to lead anyone."

Derrick released his grip from Law's shoulder. "I don't need anybody to trust me. The purple pygmies and I have complete control."

"You can't tell me those purple pygmies are going to listen to your snot-dripping, ugly face."

"For your information," Derrick arrogantly said. "My looks paid off. The purple pygmies believe I'm some kind of a God or their alien creator sent me.

"Orange Man?"

"Call it what you want."

"It doesn't matter what they call you, the purple pygmies are cannibals. The Kura disease is already causing them to go mad. They're eating their own dead."

"So what? Their insanity will be my gain."

For a moment, Derrick seemed to calm. But as more pig-people warriors entered the room, he turned toward them and began again. Gesturing to the lavish room, he lifted his arm and swept it in an ark. "This is what we should have had all along,"

He pointed to Law. "It's this man's greed that has kept this from the real pig-people of Blue Town."

"What do you mean, it's my greed?"

"While you lived in your immaculate house and grew more food than you could possibly eat, my friends went without. Your greed caused the lack of food." He gestured to a clutch of purple pygmies eating pygmy meat. "But that isn't going to happen again."

Law looked toward the purple pygmies. Blood and burnt pieces of brown pygmy meat was spattered on their filthy faces, and their stomachs had expanded to huge proportions. Being on the verge of becoming red cannibalistic pygmies, they broke into fits of uncontrollable laughter and kept right on stuffing their mouths with raw pygmy meat.

"Thanks to me," Derrick said and pointed to the pygmies. "They are no longer hungry. Now, they will have clean water, and your solar panels will be shared. My friends will no longer suffer the horrors of no electricity." He leaned back and folded his arms across his chest. "What do you have to say now?"

"That's how much you know. Your pygmy friends smashed the solar panels."

"So what?" Derrick dismissively shot back. "We'll do just fine without them."

The thought of the ignorant act of his solar panels being smashed caused anger to well up in Law's chest. Trying to keep a sane mind, he suppressed the anger. But desperation seized him. With unblinking judgment, he stared at Derrick. "Don't you care about Blue Town?"

As if possessed, Derrick roared with blameless belligerence. "You don't realize what wealth really means. There is no end to it. Pounds and pounds of gold bring power, power far beyond your comprehension." He reached into his uniform jacket, pulled out the map to Dinky Land that he had said he didn't have, and waved it in front of Law's face. "I didn't need Peep. I don't need Blue Town, and I don't need you."

"What are you going to do?"

"About as much as someone like you could expect to live, you've already led a full, rich life. I'm going to do the same thing to you that I did to Peep."

Derrick's words caused Law to tense with trepidation. "What did you do to Peep?"

Derrick smiled his ugly smile. "You have to admit, the beer barrel was a nice touch. I had the purple pygmies kill him." He leaned forward and deliberately let the strings of slobber flow onto Law's arm. Derrick smiled, arrogantly leaned back, and stated, "What are you going to do about it?"

Law turned sideways. Pretending to be wiping the slobber strings on his arm onto the back of the red velvet throne, he reached down and pulled out his survival knife. "You scum," he roared. "You used me and everyone you could to peddle your lies. If you think you have complete control, you're wrong."

Before Law could lift the knife past his waist, in one swift motion, Derrick kicked the knife from his hand.

"Just as I thought." Derrick growled. "You can't even defend yourself from a freak like me. And for your information, the purple pygmies have eaten the Chief Earth Officer and all his cronies. I *do* have complete control."

Law charged into Derrick, his fists pounding his chest. Derrick grabbed him by the scruff of the neck, stepped to one side, stuck out his leg, and flipped Law. Thump! Law landed on the hard floor, flat on his back. Derrick sat on his chest and held him there. As a gob of yellow snot dropped into Law's eye, Derrick shouted into his face. "I have used up your usefulness. You no longer have value." He gripped the front of Law's neck and squeezed. Law couldn't breathe, and the glob of snot blocked the vision in one eye. He kicked, wiggled, and pounded his fists into Derrick's sides.

Law wanted to cuss into Derrick's face, but in shock at being betrayed and having Derrick's hand constricting his throat, he found it impossible to speak.

Trying to physically force him to respond, Derrick increased his grip on Law's throat. Law's throat constricted more. He still couldn't speak, and his air supply was being cut off by Derrick's grip. Law reared back and sunk his fist into Derrick's stomach. As if he were impervious to pain, Derrick held tight, but then he took his hand from Law's throat and stood up.

"Nice try," he crowed with malicious glee. I'm the master puppeteer here." Holding his head high and sticking out his massive chest, he swaggered a few steps away from the throne.

Law figured Derrick was calming down. He rolled over and crawled back onto the throne. As he tried to catch his breath, the lack of oxygen caused him to sag into a helpless slump.

Derrick turned and vehemently began shouting into Law's face. "I am the one pulling your strings."

Law's eyes opened wide with alarm. With a horrified start, he came out of his helpless slump.

Derrick yelled hysterically, "You are nothing without me. I am the elite showing the way for the unenlightened." He spun around and grabbed Law by the throat, again. "I should be sitting on that throne."

Law's muscles ached and the lack of air was causing him to loose strength, but Derrick's remark gave him the power of hate to fight back. He reached up, ripped Derrick's grasping hand from his throat, and breathed in much needed air.

Derrick grabbed him by the shoulders, effortlessly lifted him off the throne, and threw him to the side.

Law managed to stay upright but stayed slumped over.

Derricks face twisted strange delightful grin. "Now how do you feel?"

Law didn't answer. Faking fatigue, he kept his hands on his knees and looked into Derrick's crazed eyes. A ghost of a smile appeared. But Derrick wasn't joking. Law figure he could catch him off guard. He sprang forward and rammed his shoulder into Derrick's chest. Derrick slammed against the throne. The throne tipped back and toppled to the floor, but Derrick stood solid. His face contorted spastically. A horrible barking sound emerged from his twisted mouth. Although he hadn't seen Derrick raise the knife clinched in his fist, Law felt a burst of warm blood explode from his chest. He slowly dropped to his knees.

Standing over him, Derrick's voice came out horse and ragged. "Behind every great ruler there is crime."

In one swift, all-seeing glance, Law's eyes swept the scene. As if bored, pig-people nonchalantly stood around picking their teeth with splinters from broken bones. There would be no help from them. Law was angry with himself. Again, he had gotten so engrossed with the main goal that he had missed the obvious: Derrick could no more be trusted than the pig police. Feeling his life blood oozing out of the wound, he paused for a long moment. His quest had been the seat of his self-importance. It had given him a meaningful life's work. He had been a man who had tried to build something, not only for himself and those who followed, but also for his Blue Town and all the future Blue Towns of the world. He had been sure his efforts would enable others to put down roots and live satisfying normal lives.

As he watched Derrick upright the throne and sit in it, he realized his dream was over. He was going to die, and for what? For some sideshow freak to take over and make the land worse than it already was?

For one last lingering moment, Law stayed on his knees, but turned and fell on his face. Then he knew Derrick had cut his stomach open from pelvis to rib cage. As Derrick sat on the throne braying orders, with predatory eyes, the purple pygmies stared at the blood flowing from Law's body. In confirmation of how uncaring and rotten they were, the pig-people warriors cheered.

Law's world became soft and peaceful black. He felt no good feelings and no bad feelings and no pain. Beyond the black, he went to the world where there was no time. His physical life had come to an end.

CHAPTER 23

Where the high wall of the canyon surrounding Dinky Land threw a shadow over the acid pool, Tommy and Sludge stopped to catch their breaths.

Breathing heavily at the bottom of the steps that led to the top of the acid pit, Sludge bent at the waist, placed his hands on his knees, and lifted his eyes toward Tommy. "Did the others make it?"

Tommy ran up the steps and looked across the acid pit. Freddy was inside the cable car, resting his hands on the bridge bean controls. Tommy mouthed the words, Did they make it? Freddy gave Tommy a thumbs-up, flashed two fingers, and pushed the controller. The bridge beam began to extend over the acid pit.

With joyful but guarded relief, Tommy turned toward Sludge. "They all made it, except two."

Sludge walked up the steps. While they waited for the bridge beam to extend, Tommy warily studied the skulls and bones that had been scattered around the sharp, pointed stakes that had been pounded into the steep ground around the pit.

"Too bad our trap didn't work," he said. "I hope those red pygmies didn't follow us."

Sludge warily scanned the boulders that surrounded the area around the pit. "I never knew there were that many."

"Neither did I. There are just too many of them. Our trap didn't have a chance of working."

As if a cold chill had just run up his spine, Sludge shuddered. "Their teeth looked razor

267

sharp," he said shaking his head. "When they turned red and started eating their own dead, it was a big surprise."

"Hunger is a power force," Tommy said. "And Kura disease makes it even worse."

The bridge beam stopped. It was just a little too high for Tommy to step onto. He motioned to Freddy to lower the bridge bean.

Flashing a what-do-you–want–from–me look, Freddy shrugged.

Tommy shook his head. "He must not have gotten it fixed." He turned to Sludge. "I'll help you up."

Sludge grabbed the bridge beam, and Tommy boosted him up.

Before Tommy could get onto the bridge beam, as if someone were behind him, a warning shiver ran up his back. He looked back over his shoulder. Like a frothing maniac, a purple pygmy ran down the side of the boulders and stopped at the bottom of the steps. Then it picked up a skull and bit down on it. Part of the skull crushed. Opening and closing its ragged-toothed mouth, the pygmy crunched on the pieces of the skull and looked up. As if it had just seen Tommy, it dropped the skull and stared at him. The orange glow of its eyes showed no expression, but behind those eyes Tommy felt its urge to use those razor sharp teeth to buzz-saw him down to nothing.

Kneeling on the bridge beam, Sludge reached down. "Grab my hand."

Keeping a wary eye on the pygmy, Tommy reached up but lost his balance. He tried to compensate, but fell back, tumbled down the steps, and landed right next to the purple pygmy.

Surprised, the purple pygmy momentarily stared at Tommy. Tommy jumped up. Two strides and he was away from the purple pygmy. Hurrying away, he caught his foot on a solid stone. He fell and began rolling down the incline next to the acid pit. To stop his roll, he placed his hand and legs spread eagle. He came to an abrupt stop, flopped over once, and just missed being impaled by a sharp, pointed stake.

He looked back toward the acid pit. The purple pygmy had turned red. It was hanging onto the bridge beam. Sludge was tramping on its fingers. Freddy was rotating the bridge beam around in a circle. Sludge lifted his foot and tromped down, hard.

The pygmy went flying through the air.

Splash! It fell into the acid pit.

Sizzling and smoking, like something on a hot plate, for a moment, it managed to stay afloat. With its pointed, yellow teeth snapping, its red head slipped under the surging acid water. All that remained were a few bubbles on the surface.

Tommy crawled up the incline swearing. Sludge crawled off the bridge beam and pulled him up the steps. Tommy got to his feet and looked to Sludge.

Sludge's eyes were blazing. "Where did it come from?"

"I have no idea," Tommy said trying to catch his breath. "But I'm glad you go it off the beam."

Sludge brushed his hands together. "They ain't too much of a threat when there's only one of them."

Tommy looked toward the trap door that ran under the mountain of boulders. "Damn! Damn! Damn!"

Agitated, Sludge looked up. "Now what?"

Tommy pointed to the trap door.

Sludge looked at it.

The two straggling Dinkies had just come through it. Right behind them, one red pygmy stopped at the opening. Before the Dinkies could close the trap door, the red pygmy's body instantly became a whirling dervish, legs, feet, and arms thrusting, kicking, and spinning, its pointed teeth clacking like an unstoppable machine. Within seconds, it had immobilized the unprepared, unsuspecting Dinkies. Now, more red pygmies rushed through the opening and avalanched onto the Dinkies. While the fallen Dinkies screamed in pain and horror, the red pygmies bit off huge hunks of their flesh.

More purple pygmies were climbing over the top of the surrounding heavy boulders that rose fifty meters toward the sky. Their numbers were so great the boulders could not be seen.

As if the bridge beam were at waist height, with instant renewed energy from being scared, Tommy and Sludge jumped up onto it and frantically signaled to Freddy to retract it.

With eyes wide with fright, Freddy retracted the bridge beam.

The massive swarm of purple pygmies, turning red, stormed up the steps of the acid pit and dove in. Just as they had done at Fake Dinky Land, they were sacrificing themselves. Evidently, they were going to throw themselves into the pit until it was full and form a bridge.

Freddy released the brake on the cable car. It lurched downward. Before it dropped into the shaft, the last thing he saw were bright-red pygmies crawling over the sides of the acid pit, sizzling and boiling as the acid ate them alive

At the bottom of the cable car shaft, he breathed a sigh of relief. "We should be okay, now."

After they stepped out of the cable car, Sludge looked up. "I wouldn't bet on it."

Three purple pygmies were climbing down the cables of the cable car.

Sludge reached into the cable car and grabbed the control lever. "Watch this."

The electrical dynamo that powered the motors of the car whined to life. The slack in the cables played out and lifted the car. With its steel pulleys rolling along the cable, the cable car climbed upward. When the pulleys reached the pygmies fingers, it easily sliced them off. The purple pygmies turned bright-red and fell onto the roof of the cable car. Echoes of their pointed-toothed mouths, snapping, ricocheted all along the cable car shaft. They were still alive.

Freddy frowned. "So much for that plan."

A slight smile formed on Sludge's lips. "Don't get excited, young man."

As the cable car rose toward the acid pit, with the bleeding stumps of their hands, the bright-red pygmies clung to the roof of the cable car. When it stopped at the top, the pygmies climbed off the roof and into the cable car. When they opened the door, red pygmies poured into the car. More climbed onto the roof. After the cable car had been covered with a red slimy mass of pygmies, it started down.

Sludge held his hand on the brake release lever. "Get ready to run."

Tommy and Freddy stepped back.

Sludge pulled the brake release lever and ran from the cable car landing.

As the cable car free-fell, they all backed away.

When it hit bottom, in the explosive-like crash, red pygmies who hadn't been smashed to death tumbled out onto the landing, sprawling on the ground in a tangle of bright-red limbs. Painful screams filled the tunnel, but the surviving pygmies glowed red and kept snapping their pointed toothed mouths. Some stopped and snapped hunks of flesh from dead pygmies. Others picked up shreds of fresh pygmy flesh off the floor, jammed it into their mouths, and churned it between their jaws.

From the top of the cable car, more red pygmies rained down.

In horror, Freddy looked at them. "Where are they all coming from?"

"I don't believe it." Tommy said. "They have formed a pygmy chain. They're climbing down the shaft.

In disbelief, Sludge violently shook his head. "Let's get outta here."

They ran toward the tunnel and the silver craft.

When they swished past the dizzying whirl of wires, the electrical dynamo that powered the cable car whined to a halt, but they kept on running until they ran through the maze of tunnels and stopped at the silver-skinned craft.

The operator who had been sitting on a stool with his feet dangling jerked to his feet. "What's the rush?"

"Millions of pygmies have invaded the tunnels," Tommy excitedly said. "We need to get out of here, and fast."

The operator placed his hand on the control lever. "Get in."

Tommy pointed to the controls behind the stool. "Switch the controls to the inside of the craft."

"I'm not allow—"

Tommy cut him short. "No time to argue. Switch the controls and get in."

Bewildered, the operator held up his hand. "But," he said and looked to his left. Like wild, crazed animals, on all fours, a multitude of bright-red pygmies were crawling down the tunnel. Their high pitched staccato of "Yay! — Yay! Yay! — Yay! — Yay! — Yay!" caused unstoppable ear and head pain.

For a moment, the operator stood stunned with amazement."

Sludge yelled, "Don't just stand there like an idiot!"

As if being shocked back to life, with lightning speed, the operator switched the controls and jumped into the craft. "Let's go!"

Tommy and Sludge jumped in, too. The operator closed the dome. At the rear of the craft, the propeller thrashed the water. The craft lunged forward. With the spray flying in front of the dome, they took off. In a few seconds, the spraying water reduced to a low hiss. The craft stopped. They were on the other side of the tunnel.

Tommy lifted the dome. They all stepped out. "After we flood the tunnels," he said in great haste, "we should be okay."

"I hope so," Sludge said with relief. But that's a lot of pygmies. I hope there ain't enough of them to make a pygmy bridge across the canyon."

CHAPTER 24

Standing on the ridge of the canyon, Tommy and the other Dinkies looked down. The red pygmies were climbing down the other side of the canyon and forming pygmy chains. At the bottom of the canyon they tried to swim across, but they could not swim. Then they tried to build a bridge of bodies, but the edge of the water was covered with frothing rolls of air bubbles escaping from countless drowning pygmies. Too late, they discovered that the water was too deep.

The red-laced bit of hell had been stopped.

Tommy breathed a sigh of relief. "That should be the end of that."

The pygmies gave up but continued to search the shore for another way across. When they found none, the Dinkies cheered.

But their jubilation was short-lived.

Tommy pointed to a pig-person with a blaze of white hair. He was harnessed on the end of a rope being lowered into the canyon. The backpack strapped to his back looked to be full.

"What's he doin'," Sludge asked.

"Maybe he has a raft in that backpack and is going to float the pygmies across."

At an indentation in the side of the steep canyon wall, the pig-person stopped and dangled on the rope.

Tommy intently watched. "He isn't going all the way down, so he doesn't have a raft."

The pig-person pulled out a chisel and a hammer. He placed the sharp end of the chisel against the side of the stone canyon wall and hit the other end of the chisel once. A fragment of stone chipped out of the rock. Then he turned the chisel a half a turn and hit the end once again.

"He's making a hole," Tommy said. "He's getting ready to plant explosives."

Freddy, the bridge beam operator, stepped up. "No problem." He lifted a crossbow loaded with a plastic-tipped arrow. Sludge lit the plastic tip of the arrow. Freddy fired. The arrow zinged through the air. Swish! It stuck in the rope just above the pig-person's head. Whoosh! The rope ignited.

In disbelief, Sludge looked at Freddy. "I'll bet you ain't gonna do that again."

Before Freddy could answer, the pig-person, in the rope harness, stopped pounding on the chisel and looked up. The flaming plastic was burning through the rope. He frantically waved his arm and cried to pig-people above, "Pull me up! Pull me up!"

The pig-people pulled. The pig-person began his ascent. When he was just about to the top, the burning rope broke. The pig-person plummeted, hit the side of the canyon, and careened into the water below.

Another pig-person with another backpack began to descend.

Freddy shot another flaming arrow. This time he missed the rope.

Sludge chuckled. "Tole you, you couldn't do it again."

276

Freddy rolled his hand in encouragement. "Just keep lighting arrows. I'll hit it."

Three shots later, a flaming arrow stuck in the rope. This time, the rope burned quicker, and the dangling pig-person quickly fell to his death.

Derrick stepped to the edge of the canyon. Other pig-people helped him strap on a backpack.

"They'll never learn," Freddy said and readied another fire arrow.

But Derrick didn't harness himself onto the end of a rope. He harnessed himself to a steel cable, and the pig-people strapped a metal plate onto his back. Freddy's fire arrows would be useless. He lowered the crossbow. "Should we get the spotlights or the napalm barrels?"

Tommy looked toward the building that hid the napalm barrels. "It may be a good idea to get both."

Freddy and a few Dinkies ran to get the spotlights and barrels.

Derrick hung onto the steel cable with his claw hand and the pig-people lowered him down until he was below the rock shelf.

As if sensing danger, a dark cloud crawled across the sky and caused Dinky Land to be in semi-darkness. But Tommy could see Derrick. He was placing something into a crack that ran under a shelf of rocks.

As if in great pain, Tommy placed his hand on his forehead. "Oh no!"

"Oh no, what?" Sludge wanted to know.

Tommy pointed to Derrick. Derrick lit a fuse, jumped to the side, and signaled to the pig-people on top of the canyon. They began pulling him up.

277

The fuse flowered with a sudden red flame.

Sludge gasp. "He's gonna blow up the side of the canyon."

"Depending on what he's using," Tommy said in a rush, "those rocks could fly sky high and land on top of us."

Sludge turned. "Let's get outta here."

As they ran into the protection of the great pyramid, Boom! The earth shook. Rocks flew high into the sky and seemed to stay suspended. When they came down, they knocked the blades off the windmills, and pounded the ground. As if that weren't enough misery, more black clouds crept into an already leaden sky, and a tsunami of dust from the explosion churned toward Dinky Land.

As Tommy stood at the entrance to the great pyramid and the dust began to clear, he felt a deep hurt in his chest. It wasn't from the bass drum like thud from the explosion, but because the rubble from the explosion had created a road. With his ears ringing from the blast, he ran to the edge of the canyon and peered over. The rubble extended over the water and to the other side of the canyon, but that side of the canyon was too steep to climb.

While the purple pygmies stood in a state of confusion, caused by what had just happened, Derrick and his pig-people warriors begin to cross the road of rubble. Derrick signaled to pig-people warriors carrying explosives. They were going to blow the other side of the canyon.

After they did, the Dinkies, pygmies, pig-people, and humans would clash in anger. Tommy wondered if they were about to live the last moments of a final foolish battle.

This time, the explosives exploded with a muffled but more violent thud. A shock wave rocked the canyon, and a geyser of water hurled pygmies, warriors, rocks, and debris high into the air.

After another terrifying explosion and the dust had settled, the purple pygmies stayed back. Babbling amongst themselves, they seemed to be forming a huge crowd to attack in mass, but Derrick and a few of his pig-people warriors climbed up the steep road of rubble until they were close to the top of the canyon. Now that the top of part of the canyon had been blown away, the real Dinky Land could be seen. With mouths agape, Derrick and the pig-people warriors stopped and stared.

Derrick and his pig-people warriors were out of place. Compared to the decaying surroundings, they had grown accustomed to, the beauty of the real Dinky Land was another world.

For six hundred meters, the lush tops of green grass rolled under a slight wind. A clear stream, fifty meters from a stone guard house, babbled softly. The dust from the explosion had made it seem like twilight had come early, but the top of the canyon was beautiful in any light.

Tommy wasn't surprised at the pig-people's reaction. Years ago, when he had first glimpsed the top of the canyon, it had been the epitome of all he had dreamed of. And it still was. The crystal clear stream meandered around buildings, continued over the land and created miniature cascades and rapids

279

that rushed into wide ponds, surrounded by lush, green meadows. In the ponds, golden ducklings with black stripes swam behind their mothers. Beyond a flock of black-billed trumpeter swans that floated lazily on the water, the pond stretched for kilometers and flowed into timbered land, then narrowed suddenly into a bottleneck and created a roaring falls that fell into a steep cliff and denied passage to a desert stretching as far as the eye could see.

Tommy wouldn't have minded losing the desert, but he hated to lose such a treasure as the one preceding the falls. He signaled for the spotlights.

With electric lines trailing behind them, a line of Dinkies walked to the edge of the canyon and aimed the blinding beams of their powerful hand-held spotlights at the advancing pig-people. Squealing in the sudden pain, the pig-people reached for their eyes and shielded them from the light.

"Keep it on them," Sludge yelled. "Let them see the light."

Trying to avoid the blinding glare, the pig-people turned and slowly began to make their way back down the road of rubble. After they had walked ten meters, the spotlights went out. Without the windmills, the back-up batteries could not keep up with the huge voltage demanded of the spotlights. By the time four wires were spliced together, to power on spotlight from another source of power, the pig-people would be over the ridge and into Dinky Land.

Tommy signaled for the napalm.

Napalm-loaded catapults were pulled from the building.

They were ready.

Freddy peered down the road of rubble. Amazed at Derrick's ugliness, he pointed to him. What's a horrible sight like that doing in Dinky Land?"

"He's trying to destroy what little happiness we have," Tommy said and yelled down at Derrick. "Why do you have to destroy the land that gives you life?"

Derrick stopped and shouted up the road of rubble, "Everybody destroys. It is the way life is. Whoever has not destroyed, cast the first stone."

Tommy shrugged and nodded to a line of Dinkies standing on the top of the canyon. "Ask, and you shall receive."

The line of Dinkies bent over, picked up stones, and threw them at the advancing pig-people. The sharp point of one of the heavy stones took a true, swift course and imbedded itself into the top of a pig-person's skull. For a moment, as nothing had happened, the pig-person kept on coming. Then as if he suddenly realized he had been killed, his knees bent forward. He landed on his rear end and formed a helpless heap.

Thirty humans who had been secretly living with the Dinkies stood ready to defend the land they loved.

Tommy and the Dinkies stepped aside.

Matt McQueen, a big, hard-faced human, led the humans a ways down the road of rubble and waited for Derrick and his fellow pig-people.

When Derrick was right in front of him, Matt let out a savage roar. The humans and pig-people clashed in battle.

Matt used his superbly built body to swing a sword at Derrick. Derrick dropped down. The sword swished over his head, but Matt had swung the sword with so much hate and force he could not keep a grip on the handle. Hissing, it flipped around in circles. Its razor-sharp blade kept speeding and sliced a pig-person almost in half. His upper torso sagged to the right and bent over until it met the legs of his lower torso. Gushing blood, the pig-person folded over and splatted onto the ground. Like fat snakes, blue, red, and flesh-colored organs oozed out of the wound.

As Matt watched the nightmarish sight, keeping low, Derrick stepped forward, came up behind him, grabbed him by the waist, and lifted him into the air. As Matt scissored his feet, in an effort to break Derrick's grip, lines of cruelty formed on Derrick's face. A paroxysm of intense cruelty sank deep into his brain and shone in the flat light of his eyes. He threw Matt.

Flying through the air, Matt did one flip and landed on his feet, ready to do battle. He feinted with his right, then let loose with a left hook. Derrick slipped the hook and smashed a vicious right fist into Matt's body. Matt didn't flinch. He swung a powerful right of his own. It smashed Derrick's jaw to one side. Derrick went sprawling.

When he stood up, the "terp, nerp, tnep" sickening sound came from deep in his throat. Green strings of blood-filled slobber with the odor of rotten meat crawled from the two leather brown holes where his nose used to be and curled onto the front of his uniform jacket.

Matt rushed in, viciously punching Derrick's blood-flowing face. Derrick was knocked back. But he met Matt's charge with a jarring left jab of his claw hand that smashed Matt's upper lip into his teeth and knocked him back on his heels.

Derrick lowered his head and charged. Matt sidestepped and brought up a jolting uppercut. Derrick's body straightened. Matt wound up, whapped Derrick in the stomach. Derrick grunted one time, grabbed his stomach, and bent over. Just when it looked as if he were going to fall, he grabbed a sharp rock and hurled it toward Matt. Matt ducked. As he ducked, Derrick charged in, grabbed Matt around the knees, lifted him up and dropped him onto the sharp rubble. A shard of sharp stone pierced back of Matt's neck and came out the front.

Breathing in great drafts of air, Derrick challenged the next human.

It was a battle-weary Turk. He stood there, his body sagging, his breath coming in labored gasps, and as if he had just returned from the land of the dead, his rabid eyes stared. Somehow he had survived the slaughter at Shangri-la. But his purple pygmies were not with him. Tommy realized that before Turk had entered Dinky Land, Kura disease had caused his faithful purple pygmies to go mad.

Now they had joined forces with the other red pygmies. There would be no help from friendly purple pygmies today.

Raw anger and a sense of critical mass, about to explode, filled the air. The muscles on Turk's body thickened. Tommy could almost hear the blood surging through Turk's swollen arteries. Turk was more than ready to fight.

With a killing eagerness in his face, Turk's lips thinned, and his eyes blazed. He let loose a left hook that ripped the skin under Derrick's eye and spun him completely around. As Derrick backed away, trying to cover, Turk waded in and shot a wicked right hook to his chin. Teeth snapped. Derrick went down. Turk waited for him to get up. When he did, he was spitting teeth and dazed. Before he could assemble his faculties, Turk snapped his fist into Derrick's solar plexus. The jolt doubled Derrick over. He began to fall forward. To keep his face from hitting the rocks, he thrust his hands out to break his fall. Amazingly, his claw hand landed on the handle of the sword that had chopped the pig-person in half. With blood spraying from his toothless mouth, and wailing in outrage, Derrick used his claw hand to pick up the sword. He jerked to his feet and raised the sword to swing at Turk's windpipe. Turk smacked Derrick's claw hand. The claw opened. Before the sword could fall to the ground, Turk snapped it up. With both hands gripping the sword, he began the swing. Derrick lifted his claw to stop the blade.

Too late.

Turk got ready to reverse his aim and swing again. But he didn't have to. Derrick's head breathed its last breath and fell off Derrick's shoulders. With blood spurting from the arteries in Derrick's severed neck, his torso remained standing for three grotesque seconds. Then its legs folded, and it crumpled to the ground.

Tommy figured with Derrick dead, the pig-people would not have a leader. They would turn in bewilderment and go back to where they had come from.

He was almost right. The pig-people took a few steps backwards, but they didn't turn and run. They couldn't.

A loud threatening voice thundered up the rubble. "Where do you think you're going?"

The extreme volume of the voice sent chills along Tommy's back.

Right behind the fleeing pig-people, huge hog-people, with heavy necks and a multitude of chins rising from massive shoulders, came into view.

With their bald basketball heads, pinched faces, and small loathsome eyes, seething with hate, they deeply huffed and grunted. Although they were almost as wide as they were tall, they effortlessly walked up the steep road of rubble as if they were on a paved highway.

Tommy had never seen pig-people this large. For a moment he thought they may be coming to stop the slaughter.

But the sight of Derrick's dead body seemed to drive them loco. Tommy realized that these hog-people were the secret weapon Derrick had said he would use. And to make matters worse, the purple pygmies were coming up behind.

Concentrated evil like this had never tried to enter Dinky Land. In a maddening rage, the hog-people began attacking the humans. Weaving to avoid the hog-people's pawing blows, the humans threw blow after blow to the hog-people's monstrous forms. But they were unstoppable.

Disgusted, Tommy looked to the catapults. A Dinky, with an unshaven face and bushy black brows shading his cold eyes, nodded. He was the master of the catapults. The napalm-loaded catapults were ready to fire.

Three blasts from a bugle echoed down the rubble. The few living humans looked up. They had heard the signal to retreat. But they were going nowhere. The hog-people held them fast and continued to beat them into unconsciousness.

It didn't matter what Tommy did, in a few seconds, the hog-people would kill all the humans. Tommy gave the signal to launch the napalm barrels.

The Dinky pulled the rope that led to the trigger of the catapult. The barrels flew high into the sky and came down between the hog-people and the humans. The napalm ignited and flared into an incendiary display that lit the sky and spewed liquid fire in all directions. Ear-piercing squeals of hog-people being burned alive filled the canyon.

Death hung heavy in the air, and it looked like no one had survived. Tommy figured all humans and hog-people had been destroyed. He wanted to take a much needed break, but he couldn't.

Somehow, three purple pygmies had survived. They were cautiously sniffing their way up the hot smoldering road of rubble.

Dark clouds formed overhead and stayed there. When the three purple pygmies were at the top of the canyon they turned and wagged their rat tails. Like an army of ants, more purple pygmies, turning red, swarmed up the road of rubble.

Tommy signaled to the catapults. Again, napalm rained down. This time, it fried the crimson pygmies. When the smoke cleared, a few had survived. They were bright red and mad. Tommy wasn't worried. They could take care of a few leftover pygmies. Dinky Land would soon be safe.

When the few surviving pygmies made it to the top of the canyon, Dinkies with baseball bats batted the pygmies' snapping pointed-toothed mouths. As bits of their broken teeth flew from their faces, the Dinkies kicked the pygmies into the canyon.

When the last pygmy had been kicked into the canyon, Tommy breathed a sigh of relief and turned to go into the great pyramid.

Sludge grabbed him by the shoulder. "We ain't done."

"What?" Tommy turned back.

It didn't seem possible, but another wave of even more powerful red pygmies were swarming up the road of rubble.

As if a warning, black clouds obscured the sky. Tommy turned toward the sidewalk-fronted buildings. In the distance, street lamps swayed in the blowing wind, causing their light to form shadows on the stone sidewalks. The boughs of the trees, around the ponds, bent in the wind, shedding their healthy green leaves. A heavy rain slanted down from the dark sky and drummed on the roofs of the buildings and gurgled down the gutters. Thunder rolled. Strong winds rocked the empty catapults, and heavy rain changed to skinny, stinging sprays of black rain. It rushed out of a black cloud and lashed the red pygmies. But they continued to creep up road of rubble. The Dinkies were killing them, but for every red pygmy that was killed, thousands would be taking their place.

Just as suddenly as the rain has started, it stopped.

Contemplating what he could do next, a fleeing, black, fluffy tail caught Tommy's eye. It was Eippy. He was running toward the brine pool. Somehow, red pygmies had gotten into Dinky Land. They were chasing Eippy.

Fingers of fog still hazed the surface of the pool, and it still bubbled with greasy brine. But Spinach was waiting on the other side.

Eippy ran along the path that led to the little canoe and past the iron plaque poking above the thick magenta-and-white-flowered bushes.

At the pool, he stopped, got behind the canoe, and pushed it into the brine water. As the red pygmies stood on the shore, Eippy frantically paddled the canoe. It cleaved the surface so swiftly that it plowed a white furrow in the green brine. Spinach viciously barked on the other side of the pool, but more red pygmies ran to the pool where Eippy had entered. Jumping up and down, they encouraged each other to enter the pool. But the

288

pygmies who went into the pool sunk into its watery ooze and never came up.

Tommy wanted to see if Eippy had gotten away, but Sludge tugged on his shirt sleeve. "Let's go."

Tommy turned back. An unstoppable mass of red pygmies were coming to the top of the canyon. He cupped his hands to his mouth and let out a loud piercing Tarzan yell. All Dinkies turned toward the sound. They knew it was time to go into the great pyramid.

CHAPTER 25

When Eippy thought he had seen purple pygmies standing around a fire eating pig-people outside the wall of Shangri-la, he had dismissed it. Now he knew he had been wrong. The purple pygmies had been eating pig-people. They had gone mad. They were planning to have him for an evening meal.

With the canoe creasing the feted water and hissing with speed, Eippy wildly paddled the across the brine pool. When the canoe skidded to shore, twenty meters away, a band of red pygmies rushed toward him. And Spinach was gone.

Eippy jumped out of the canoe and began running to his left. The pygmies began running in that direction. They were going to head him off. He stopped. The pygmies reversed direction. Eippy didn't. His deceiving move created an escape opening. He ran through it. As much as his exhausted muscles could tolerate, he tried to run as fast as he could. But, under-brush snarled his feet, and unseen tentacles of overgrowth whipped at his face. The pygmies were snapping at his back. Cold terror gripped him. One misstep would be his last. He stumbled. He didn't fall but he slowed enough to feel the hot breath of a red pygmy on his neck.

He ran faster.

The red pygmies' high-pitched staccato of "Yay! — Yay! Yay! — Yay! — Yay! — Yay!" became a continuing stream of ear-piercing pain. Just as Eippy was about to place his hands over his ears, a single scream from a red pygmy, right behind him, stopped its streaming staccato. Eippy hurled himself into the air. He landed in dense foliage that bordered a stream. He stumbled, recovered, sprang out of the foliage, and landed on the grass behind it. Now he was out of the pygmies' lines of sight. But if he stood up, they would see him. He rolled to his left, then again. He rolled for all he was worth.

When he figured he was completely out of their line of sight, he stood up. His legs felt like heavy stones. He needed to rest his legs, but there was no time. He took one step, slipped, and crumpled to the ground. Shaking his head, he struggled to his feet. Before he could take a breath, ten meters away, the glowing, orange eyes of red pygmies bored into his very soul. Without warning, a purple pygmy crashed through the dense foliage. Although its frenzy was not in full force, Eippy could tell from the look in its maniacal eyes, it was looking for someone to eat. One more slip and Eippy would be in the pygmy's stomach.

Not in the mood to be shredded and eaten, Eippy began running.

Ahead, the stream began to narrow. If he could get to the other side, it could slow the pygmies advance. With the pygmies snapping at his heels, he leaped. He sailed across the stream but didn't make it to the other side. He landed knee-deep in water. And he was glad he did. On the other side, more red pygmies had been waiting behind a rock. They reached out to grab him. He backed into deeper water. Three pygmies on all fours jumped into the water. When they advanced toward Eippy, the current swept them downstream. The other pygmies stayed on the shore, reaching for Eippy. Making sure the three pygmies were gone, Eippy bent his knees, and let the current take him down the rapidly rushing stream. Sucking in much needed air, he was grateful he was out of danger. But it was premature. Roaring met his ears. The current was taking him to the falls that fell into the chasm. Figuring he could walk to shore and find a place to hide, he scanned the terrain. A few bushes were a possible place.

He put his feet down, but the water was too deep and the current too strong. He stroked for shore. His strokes powered him to it, but when he got there, there was nothing but round slippery stones to grab onto. With the roar of the falls in his ears and his chest heaving, he frantically grabbed at the round stones but it was useless. His hands only slipped off.

A few more meters and the current would carry him to the edge of the falls. There, he would plummet over and descend into the dark abyss. A meter before the falls, the current slammed him into a boulder. He grabbed the sides of the boulder, but his hands only pulled moss from it. The current pulled at his body. He resisted. But the force was too strong. Just as he had resigned that he would die, Spinach lowered his head to the water, grabbed Eippy's tail, and dragged him over the boulder and up onto shore.

Wanting and needing to take a rest, Eippy breathed in three great drafts of air. Spinach growled deep in his throat. Protectively he pushed tight to Eippy. The three drafts of air would have to do. The red pygmies were coming fast. He jumped on Spinach's back. They zipped away from the falls, but they were trapped between a mass of red pygmies crawling toward them and the cliff. Eippy frantically searched for a way out.

There was no escape.

As the red pygmies snapped their sharp teeth and advanced, Eippy figured it was only a matter of time before he and Spinach breathed their last breaths.

When the red pygmies were ten meters away, Eippy prayed to Orange Man for a miracle. But the red pygmies kept on coming. Now they were five meters away.

Eippy jumped off of Spinach's back, wrapped his arms around his neck, and whispered in his ear. "We'll die together."

Boom! Eippy felt like a bass drum had been placed on his chest and had been hit with a huge club. Without warning, the earth jerked. His knees bent and flew up to his chest. His ears rang and everything around him seemed to be spinning. He clutched Spinach and fell to the ground. All the red pygmies fell to the ground, too. Parts of pig-people, bits of red pygmies, and debris hurtled into the air. As a cloud of brown dust covered the land, Eippy realized what had happened. Hog-people had blown up another side of the canyon. They had created another road of rubble. Hoping he could use it to escape, he speculatively looked ahead.

Hog-people and advancing red pygmies were picking their way over the rubble. Here and there, a foot, a shoulder, or a mangled body part showed above the dirt and stones. Using the dim light, created by the dust, Eippy used Spinach's keen sense of direction and made it safely over the rubble and to the other side of the canyon.

A ways from the canyon they came to a path. It twisted right and left and was bordered by soft, foot-sucking mud. They navigated around that, and the land became dry, wild, and barren. Brush thinned out. And there were only stray blades of struggling grass. While the hot sun began scouring Eippy's face, dust rose from Spinach's steady trot. At the edge of the desert they stopped at a nest of boulders on a low hill.

Out of the nest of boulders, a huge hog-person sprang up. With full cheeks jiggling with sadistic laughter, he loomed in front of Eippy. His bluish, death-like face was heavily covered with loose fat. Like deadly daggers, his washed-out green eyes stared from the sides of his runny, lard-like nose. Except for his huge stomach, his body did not match his flabby face. Extremely wide shoulders and layers of hard muscle, stacked on short tree-stump-like legs, gave the impression that any attacking red pygmies would be no more dangerous than a few bothersome flies. As the hog-person waded toward Eippy, tendon and bone moved synchronicity and caused the huge hog-person to seem like an indestructible machine. The washed-out green eyes of his cadaverous face filled with contempt. He stopped laughing, bared his yellow teeth, and snarled.

Eippy prodded Spinach to turn and escape. But five red pygmies with green intestines hanging from their pointed-toothed mouths popped up out of the sand. Even though their unblinking eyes were pocked with sand, they glimmered with delight. As a bank of black clouds scudded across the sky, the pygmies aggressively hunched over. With their rat tails curving like crawling snakes, they rushed past Eippy and attacked the hog-person. Their pointed teeth clamped onto the ankles of his tree stump-like legs. Bones crunched and blood oozed. Eippy wondered why the hog-person didn't kick the pygmies or bend over and bat them away. But when the hog-person leaned over and tried to bend his ample waist and extended his hand toward the pygmies, he could only reach as far as the top of his knee. His fat stomach stopped him from bending over.

Instead of kicking the red pygmies, the hog-person viciously swiped his hand over their heads and attempted to scare them away. In response, they ripped strips of muscle from the bottoms of his legs and stuffed them into their mouths. Overwhelmed and immobilized, the hog-person tried to walk. But the pygmies had already eaten most of one of his legs. Dangling below the kneecap, the bleeding leg was about to fall off. One pygmy jumped up, clamped the leg in its mouth, jerked it free, and ran away. The hog-person tried to stand on his remaining leg, but the pygmies began to gnaw the bottom of that leg off. His body sagged. His chin slumped to his chest. His knee buckled. He staggered and managed to drop to both knees without falling over. The red pygmies bit the muscles from his thighs and swallowed it. With his face contorted in pain, the hog-person lifted his chin, leaned forward, and stared at Eippy. The bloody stumps of his chewed off knees skidded out from under him. Blood, from his severed arteries, squirted three meters into the air.. He pitched forward and flopped face-first into the sand.

More red pygmies popped up out of the sand. They had been laying in ambush. Now they were aggressively clamping their teeth into the hog-person and ripping huge hunks of fat-filled meat off his body.

Eippy didn't know how many more red pygmies there were, but he wasn't going to stick around and find out.

This time, Spinach didn't need to be prodded. He took off running.

Hours later, heat waves danced in the still air. With his eyes squinting against the surrounding glare, Eippy stared into a sky that was a white-hot bowl. A patient buzzard circled overhead. With Spinach at his side, Eippy lay on his stomach, hidden under a slanted piece of corrugated metal, he had stuck into the sand to create a little shade. While he waited for the sun to go down, red pygmies had surrounded him. Reluctant to end the festivities, they noisily slurped blood and munched on hunks of burnt pig-people they had carried with them.

Eippy wanted to jump on Spinach's back and flee, but an understandable reluctance to become another meal for the pygmies held him back. He stayed under the corrugated metal.

His and Spinach's thirsts were growing, but their only escape route would be over a dusty plain and across the desert. Even a few kilometers across a burning desert could be an immeasurable distance. If they tried to cross the kilometers of sand in the searing heat, without water, the odds against theirs survival would not be in their favor.

As a lone fly buzzed lazily in the hot sun, Eippy rubbed his hand over his face, narrowed his dark eyes against the chrome glare of the sun, and looked behind him. If the glare and threatening red pygmies weren't enough, a whirling dust cloud was headed his way.

When the dust-whipping cloud was at his feet, he covered his mouth and Spinach's head with the front of his shirt, closed his eyes, and waited.

Just as the dust storm began, he heard voices. He dropped his shirt from his mouth and looked to his left. Partially covered with a tarpaulin, two Dinky's and three children rose up out of the sand. They had been hiding there all the while. The heat must have gotten to them. Startled, they stared at Eippy. The male Dinky's face was haggard, and the bandage on his head was bloody. As if looking for a way out or for help, the Dinky nervously glanced around. The youngsters were sand-covered, hollow-eyed, and frightened, but the female Dinky had a flicker of hope in her eyes. For a moment, she reminded Eippy of Trinket. A dull pain entered his heart.

Hoping the dust would block their vision, Eippy looked toward the red pygmies. The dust cloud dissipated. The red pygmies lifted their pointed-toothed, bloody muzzles from the carnage, but they didn't attack. Staring at the Dinkies, the pygmies pressed on their bloated stomach and began disgorging what they had just eaten. They were not hungry. They were creating space in their stomachs for fresh Dinky meat.

Eippy wanted to save the Dinkies, but there was nothing he could do. The red pygmies began to enclose the Dinkies. The Dinkies tensed to run, but they would never outrun the red pygmies. If Eippy tried to stop them, he would also be eaten. He cringed.

Trying to conceal himself, he slumped flat to the sand. But the red pygmies kept on coming. Needing to feel simple uncomplicated loyalty at his side, Eippy kept one hand on Spinach. With his heart pounding in fear and his throat caked from dryness, Eippy felt he could not go on. Spinach licked his face. In terror, Eippy stared at red pygmies and waited for the end.

But the pygmies didn't fully enclose him or the Dinkies. As if savoring the chase of their next meal, they just stood there. When the Dinkies began slowly walking away, little puffs of dust rose from their feet, and the red pygmies stood still.

Eippy didn't know how long the pygmies would wait until they devoured the Dinkies. But if he could stay hidden until the sun slid down behind the mountains, the sky would darkened and give birth to new stars. After the cold hand of darkness gripped the desert, it would be twenty degrees cooler, and he wouldn't need as much water. Just before the morning sun chased the darkness away the temperature would be just above freezing. Maybe the cold would slow the red pygmies advance, and he could easily slip away. But the cold wouldn't last. By midday, it would be boiling hot, again.

After the Dinkies had walked almost out of sight, Spinach sniffed at an unfamiliar odor. Instantly, movement behind the corrugated metal caught Eippy's attention. With his back to the bright sun and putting its full glare into Eippy's eyes, a hungry-eyed, red pygmy, with dirty-blue intestines hanging from its mouth, popped up, its wide, staring eyes filled with incredulous horror.

Eippy felt his jaw drop

Then more snapping, pointed-toothed red pygmies popped up.

They had only been resting for the big chase.

Three red pygmies grabbed the corrugated metal. They were going to pull Eippy's shield away. But instead of yanking the metal away and exposing Eippy to the full force of their open, snapping mouths, an electric shock surged into their hands. They jerked back. Their feet slid forward. They landed in the sand. Unknown to the pygmies, the dry air and the dust storm had created a static electricity build up on the metal. It had shocked them. Now they were even madder and turning bright red.

Before they completely recovered from the surprise of being shocked, Eippy jumped on Spinach's back and hung on. Spinach took off at a full run.

In front of them, as if heat waves where the curtains of a stage, dust devils did unexpected dervish-like dances above the hot white sand and seemed to jeer, "Hant! There is no water."

If Eippy could make it across the desert, a green meadow hid somewhere at the end of a rarely used animal path. There, water would flow clear and cool. The big problem was that he had never been there. It was only a story an old Dinky had told him while he had been in Dinky Land.

In the vast desert wilderness of white, the sun stabbed him like lances of fire and blasted heat all the way into his bones. As he rode on, he nodded off or stared at the unchanging desert. His back ached and the sun was getting hotter. His face throbbed with every prod of Spinach's paws. As Spinach gasped for breath, his jaw gaped open, and his tong hung limply out the side of his mouth. Eippy realized being on Spinach's back was causing him to become overheated.

Eippy urged Spinach to a stop. He searched the area for red pygmies. When he saw none, he slipped off Spinach's back and narrowed his eyes against the glare. No breeze sent a shaft of coolness through the dancing heat waves, and he was at least twelve kilometers away from the mountains.

After a little rest and with Spinach walking by his side, they continued the long trek.

Three kilometers later, it didn't get better. Now, the area looked like a place where a nuclear reactor had hemorrhaged. No desert flowers or cacti grew here. Every now and then, a few strands of sickly yellow grass looked ready to keel over. Even the land looked worn and powdery. There was nothing around them but desert and sky. Under intense heat from a brilliantly glowing-white sun, a scorching wind tore across the sand, sending huge hurling huffs of sand in their direction.

Eippy pulled Spinach to the ground and lay down, head to head. Eippy placed his shirt over their heads. As they waited for the blowing sand to stop, Eippy wondered if taking unhurried walks over green hills in the magic place his father had talked about was an archaic dream of two old men that had never come true.

After the storm, they stood up. The sand fell from their bodies. Eippy tried to spit sand particles from between his teeth, but his mouth was too dry. Coughing out sand particles, he continued walking at Spinach's side.

When they walked into a bowl of alkali dust, they had four kilometers to go. Eippy drooped his weary head, prodded a few steps, and gasped through his dry mouth. Spinach's tired ears tipped forward. Right in front of Eippy's feet, the unmistakable bare foot prints of a red pygmy glared back at him.

He couldn't understand how a red pygmy could have gotten ahead of them. It was the speed of Spinach and his endurance that had gotten them away from Dinky Land before the red pygmies had a chance to snap their bodies to shreds. And Spinach had given him enough lead to take a little rest, but that little rest hadn't been enough time for the red pygmies to catch up. For hours, Eippy had a taken his course from a distant mountain peak. As he and Spinach had gradually worked their way across the desert, Eippy had not seen a single living thing.

Then it dawned on him. The red pygmies were everywhere. With an unending food supply of pig-people and any living thing they wanted to eat, the red pygmies had been reproducing at a rapid pace. To them, the heat and lack of water of the desert was not a barrier.

Weather-beaten and wind-blasted, Eippy looked far ahead. Dark clouds over the mountains had let loose. The clouds were losing their water. It was falling upon the steep slopes of the mountains. He wished it were falling on him and Spinach.

Trudging forward, Eippy hoped the old Dinky was right. It would be a slim chance, but to get where he needed to go, he and Spinach would have to cross two shallow gullies that cut into the slope and ran down into a bottom of flat land. If they made it across the gullies before it happened, they could get to high ground. Then they would be safe.

Although he couldn't see them, Eippy could feel the red pygmies creeping closer. Rain began to fall on him and Spinach, and flashes of jagged lightning brightened the darkening sky. Eippy was thankful for the rain, but couldn't stop to enjoy it. He looked back over his shoulder. The red pygmies were a kilometer away. Some carried the severed arms and legs of pig-people over their shoulders. Some held hunks of purple pygmy's body parts in their hands and occasionally bit into them. Others just kept on snapping their pointed-toothed mouths, and in their high-pitched staccato they continuously cried out, "Yay! — Yay! Yay! — Yay! — Yay! — Yay!"

Eippy needed to move faster. He jumped on Spinach's back. Spinach tried to run but only managed a swift jog.

Up ahead, a wide dry river cut through the face of the desert. Without hesitation, they rode into the first gully. A skinny stream of new rain water snaked along its bottom. Eippy wanted to bend over and take a drink and wash the sand particles out of his dry mouth, but there was no time. The snaking water was a preview of what was coming. Up in the rock-sided mountains, nothing was stopping the rushing water.

Spinach and Eippy raced across the stream. On the other side, Spinach slowed. Panting, he stopped. From far away, a loud roar of thunder echoed. Eippy leaned over. With labored breaths, he talked in Spinach's ear. "We can't stop here. We have to get to the next gully."

Spinach lunged forward. They were moving, but it was almost a kilometer to the next gully. And the pygmies were still coming. Spinach stopped. Eippy jumped off his back. Glancing back at the advancing pygmies and fearing their snapping mouths, Eippy ran along side of Spinach.

The next shallow gully loomed before them. Any other time, the sixty meters across the gully and going up the trail on the other side would be a leisurely walk, but not only did the snapping and clacking of the pygmies filled their ears, the continuous high-pitched staccato of "Yay! — Yay! Yay! — Yay! — Yay! — Yay!" caused their ears to ring and their heads to feel like they were going to burst with pain.

Spinach cringed.

Eippy rubbed the back of Spinach's neck. "We can make it, boy."

Down the bank they ran. Eippy hoped they weren't running to their deaths. At the bottom they saw the water. It was a flash flood, at least twelve meters high. The rolling, black wall of angry water was rushing right at them. Racing beside Spinach, Eippy sprinted for the trail.

They made it

But at the same instant, the thundering wall of water swept behind them.

Eippy looked skyward and thanked Orange Man.

Standing on the high ground of the mountain and under a frowning peak, a little spring bubbled out of a break in the stone.

Here, Eippy and Spinach washed the sand particles from their dry mouths and took long drinks. Wiping his mouth, Eippy looked up and pointed. "Look, Spinach."

The rushing water had trapped the red pygmies between the two gullies. They stood bewildered and idle. When a few tried to cross the mighty flowing water, it swept them away. Then the great wall of water doubled in size and washed them all away.

With rain lashing his face, Eippy allowed himself a grim laugh. As if celebrating the red pygmies' demise, Spinach planted his four paws firmly on the ground and wagged his tail so violently that his whole body shook.

After he quit shaking, with pleading eyes, Spinach looked up at Eippy.

"We can take it easy now," Eippy said. "But we still have to find a safe place to live."

CHAPTER 26

Inside the great pyramid, Tommy and other Dinkies who had managed to escape the snapping mouths of the red pygmies stood around the base of white limestone steps. The steps led to a gold platform where a small, snow-white pyramid stood. Six meters high and six meters wide, its surface reflected concentrated beams of diamond-like light.

After Tommy and Sludge walked up the marble steps and stood in front of the pyramid, an electrical hum filled the air. Tommy placed his forehead on the side of the pyramid and peered through a secret opening. Translucent tanks, containing green crystals, approximately four meters high and two meters in diameter, lined the inside of the pyramid. Submerged in a translucent golden liquid, emerald crystals sat in proximity to a gold bubbler that aerated the liquid and created some sort of chemical reaction. It was the source of the electrical hum. A large number of orange wires snaked from the center of a floor of red-rubies, up the sides of the tanks, and into the lip of each tank.

Tommy and the other Dinkies didn't know how the emerald crystals in the liquid created electricity, but it had provided way more than enough electricity to power Dinky Land. Outside, for all to see, solar panels and windmills were used to power the blue light on the outside of the pyramid but were not really needed. They only operated to hide the real source of electricity in the pyramid. Over the years, Dinky Land had grown. With that growth, the demand for electricity had increased. Knowledge of how to increase voltage had been handed down to many generations of Dinkies. Like many before them, Tommy, Sludge, and a few other Dinkies were entrusted with the knowledge, and for security measures, the process required two Dinkies.

In the past, when the pyramid couldn't keep up with an increased power demand, two Dinkies had carefully increased the voltage. They had been taught that if they increased the voltage too much and too quickly, it would result in a chain reaction that would destroy all of Dinky Land. But before that happened, lightening-like bolts would jump off the outside triangular walls of the great pyramid. For miles, around the outside of the pyramid, every living thing would be electrocuted. Only those inside the great pyramid would escape the deadly volts of electricity.

It would be risky, but Tommy and Sludge figured that if they increased the voltage to the point of causing lighting to flash off the pyramid, it would kill the red pygmies.

Apprehensive about the life and death decision of increasing the voltage, Tommy lifted his forehead from the side of the pyramid and turned to Sludge. "Do you think we should do it?"

With his forehead wrinkled in thought, Sludge shrugged. "I'm not sure."

Clunk! Clunk! The sound of the blocks being hit with a heavy object echoed through the walls of the great pyramid.

A Dinky with a broken arm yelled in fright, "They're trying to break in!"

"Damn," Tommy said. "If we do nothing, they'll break the cycle of the grid on the outside of the pyramid. Not only will the electricity stop, they'll break in. Without electricity the slab that seals the tunnels might not lock into place. In the time it takes to seal it manually, they'll swarm the tunnels. We'll be eaten alive."

Sludge slowly lifted his hand and pointed to the secret opening in the little pyramid. "We gotta do it."

Pain and fear rushed into Tommy's chest. He did not want the responsibility of doing something that could destroy Dinky Land. He turned to Sludge. "Maybe if we wait, they'll give up and go away."

Clunk! Clunk!" Was followed by the angry voices of red pygmies.

"We can't fool ourselves," Sludge said. "They're not gonna go away. They're breakin' the stone blocks."

"You're right." Tommy turned and placed his forehead on the side of the pyramid. Looking through the secret opening, he told Sludge, "Go ahead, pull it."

Five meters away, Sludge pulled on a small block in the small pyramid until it hit a stop. The hum increased with an angry roar.

Tommy reached in front of his stomach and pulled on a small block until it reached its stop. As if a prelude of things to come, one harmless spark arced from the top of the small pyramid.

Tommy lifted his forehead from the side of the pyramid and turned toward Sludge. "We both have to pay attention. One slip and we're done for."

Sludge took a deep breath and slowly exhaled. "I'm ready when you are."

With apprehension, Tommy placed his forehead back onto the side of the pyramid. Reaching just above the secret opening, he pushed the right side of a block. It rotated out. In its curved center, a knurled knob waited to be turned. He placed his fingers on the knob and looked to Sludge for confirmation. "Okay, Sludge, push the block in."

Sludge pushed his block in and held it. "Dial it in."

Watching the emerald crystals in the tanks, Timmy delicately began rotating the knob.

The bubbler rapidly aerated the translucent golden liquid. The chemical reaction was increasing. As the electrical hum increased, Tommy's apprehension increased. He lifted his fingers from the knob and looked to Sludge. "Let's try that."

Clunk! Clunk!

"It ain't working," Sludge said, alarmed. They're still trying to break in."

Tommy cursed, placed his fingers back on the knob, and turned it.

The bubbler hissed and sent a continuous stream of bubbles into the translucent golden liquid. The emerald crystals glowed softly.

Clunk! Clunk!

In fear, Tommy turned the knob, more.

Bubbles no longer flowed into the liquid. Now the end of the bubbler profusely sprayed a ruby red Jell-O-like stream.

Clunk! Echoed through the walls but wasn't followed by another.

"It must be workin'," Sludge, said.

Tommy lifted his head from the secret opening. "How long should we keep it this way?"

Sludge shrugged. "How should I know? We ain't never did this before."

The hum increased to a tooth-hurting pitch. Tommy placed his forehead back onto the secret opening. The emerald crystals had turned bright white. He turned the knob back.

But it was too late.

They had been in a hurry. They had gone too far. As if complaining in protest, a constant low bass vibration of the mighty pyramid shook the earth.

The insulation around the orange wires inside the small pyramid melted. The bare wires curled down and slapped onto the red ruby floor. Welding to the floor the wires arched and threw a bright white flash into Tommy's unprotected eyes. The low bass hum increased. Blinded by the flash, Tommy spun the knob. The hum vibrated in his ears. The knob was useless.

He turned to the gathered Dinkies. With his voice vibrating from the hum, he shouted, "Get into the tunnels!"

As if they were being poured into the tunnel opening, the Dinkies flowed through the opening and into the darkness. To make sure no one else

310

was in the pyramid, Sludge and Tommy made one quick look around. Then they jumped into the tunnel, and pulled a lever. Moaning in protest, the huge stone trap door grated in its stone guides and slid shut.

As if a detonator had been activated, from deep in the earth, a loud, dull clunk thudded through the ground. A moment later, one great flash spread over the land. In the brightness, the last thing the red pygmies saw were X-ray images of their red pygmy partner's bodies. All their bones and sharp pointed teeth clearly defined in the nuclear overload.

CHAPTER 27

Spinach and Eippy trudged through the wildest, densest forest they had ever seen. After they had climbed into the jagged wilderness of a mountain side, a howling wind beat the warmth from their bodies. It was then that Eippy realized the trudge through the forest had been only a warm up for things to come. They ascended higher and higher. When they reached the fringes of the eternal ice fields, their breathing became a great effort, and winds wailed just meters overhead. A blinding curtain of snow was ahead, but they kept on climbing. Winds picked up, parted the snow, and revealed what was just ahead of them: A huge hog-person. Eippy wanted to turn and run, but if they went back down the mountain, the red pygmies would be there.

Hoping they sneak past the hog-person, Eippy and Spinach inched forward. But the hog-person didn't move. Misted with blowing snow, he was half-buried in a wall of ice. He had frozen to death. Cold and exhausted, Eippy wanted to stop, lay on the snow with Spinach curled beside him. With his tail tucked around his body, they could take a rest. But if they stayed in one place, he and Spinach would end up like the hog-person. They would freeze to death.

Although the bitter cold bit their bodies, they had no choice. Hoping they could get away from the red pygmies, they passed the frozen hog-person and kept trudging upward until they went over the top, and began the decent.

After they had finally made it down the other side of the mountain, it was a great relief. The air was warm and breathing became easy, but only a few healthy green trees and dark green shrubs dotted the terrain. In the distance, an abundance of lush green vegetation and tall trees surrounded what seemed to be a secret valley. Eippy wanted to go there.

After an hour of Eippy riding on his back, Spinach twitched an ear. Eippy glanced to where Spinach was looking. With both ears pricked and his nostrils expanding, he was looking into a clearing next to a line of pine trees. Eippy hoped it wasn't an ambush spot for red pygmies waiting to attack. He spoke softly to Spinach, "Get ready."

A cautious advance brought them to a campfire of ashes and a few partly burned sticks. Searching for embers, Eippy stirred the ashes. He found no embers. But the ashes were still warmth. Whoever had been there hadn't been red pygmies. The red pygmies had gone mad. They were now eating their kills raw. They didn't need to take time out to build a fire.

A ways beyond the ashes, a web fence of chrome wires stretched along an area of pine trees. The web fence didn't stand straight up like an ordinary fence. Instead, it slanted upward at a thirty-degree angle for a distance of twelve meters.

As Eippy watched a little whirlwind blow a swirl of leaves around his feet, he heard familiar sound: Children running and screaming in their play. He looked toward the sound. Beyond the web of wires, a snow-white rooster with a red comb was pulling a laughing, little pie pygmy in a wooden wagon. Behind them, half-naked children, as high as Eippy's waist, playfully chased the wagon. With their black-silky tails flowing behind, they laughed and shouted with glee, "Go, Frank, go!"

Frank, the rooster, playfully zigzagged around the pine trees and vanished into a stand of tall grass. When the little pie pygmies chasing the wagon saw Eippy they stopped. With their black-silky tails curling into an S, they stared for a moment, then they ran back into the pines.

Eippy had always felt that the main thing wrong with people was that they didn't laugh enough and love enough. The sight of the rooster and the laughing children brought a warm happy feeling into his heart. Maybe it was because anyone who had a rooster for a pet couldn't be bad. He hoped whoever was inside the fence were civilized and weren't raising pie pygmies to eat.

He looked up at the web fence. Its thirty-degree angle made it appear as if he could simply walk up to the top, drop off, and land inside the fence. He looked to Spinach. "Wait here. I'll be right back." He placed one foot on the bottom of the fence and hesitated. The climb seemed too easy. It could be a trap. After all, no one would put up a fence that couldn't keep people out.

He took his foot off the fence. Spinach barked a warning. Eippy turned. A red pygmy came barreling out of the bush. Eippy jumped to the side. The pygmy ran right up the web fence. When it was a meter from the top, the wire glowed orange hot. Wisps of electrical smoke snaked around his body. As if it were soft butter, the pygmy's body oozed through the hot squares of the wire. In a haze of sizzling smoke, the red pygmy gurgled to its death. The resulting rectangular, smoking strips of his body plopped to the ground. More red pygmies rushed toward Eippy. He jumped on Spinach and they took off.

Racing along the web fence line, Eippy searched for a way to get inside without having his body melted into rectangular strips. Hoping someone inside the fence would hear him, he called for help.

No one answered.

Spinach stopped, looked ahead, and barked.

A pie pygmy with a silky-black tail walked out of the brush with his hands up. "Are you friend or foe?"

"I would like to be everyone's friend."

The pie pygmy dropped his hands and gave Eippy a long hard stare. In a submissive posture, Spinach walked up to the pie pygmy. The pie pygmy patted Spinach on the head and smiled. "You dog's a good judge of character. "My name's Ned." He extended his hand in friendship.

Eippy grasped his hand and shook.

Ned released his grip. "Are you afraid of height?"

Eippy had no idea why Ned had asked that, but he figured anyone who had laughing, playing children and a rooster named Frank wouldn't harm him. "I'm not afraid of height. My name's Eippy."

Ned's eyes grew wide with delight. "Did you say, Eippy?"

Wondering why Ned had become excited, Eippy nodded.

A huge ear-to-ear smile spread across Ned's face. "Welcome home, Eippy!"

"Home?" Eippy questioned. Could this be the magic village his father had talked about just before he died? Eippy wanted to ask Ned, but there was no time.

"The red pygmies have gone mad." he said in great haste. "They are eating every living thing."

Ned lifted his hand to his forehead, hooded his eyes, and searched the area behind Eippy. "We should be able to make it." He turned and took a step. "Follow me."

Ned led Eippy and Spinach through a maze of stone walls, around a circular tunnel, and stopped at the entrance to what seemed to be the tracks of a roller coaster inside a cage.

Ned reached under the steps and pulled a switch. The steel gate to the cage opened. They walked in.

Bewildered, Eippy stared at what was before him. A roller coaster sat on steel tracks. Bolts of white lightening had been painted on the sides of five orange cars.

Eippy turned toward Ned. "What is this?"

"It's an antique roller coaster called the Orange Streak. We found it to be an amusing way to get over the fence."

The clacking of red pygmies teeth echoed over the walls of the maze. Ned stiffened and motioned with his head toward the clacking. "They're getting close. We better get on."

Eippy stepped into the coaster car. The sides were smooth and polished to a slippery surface. Spinach jumped in and sat next to him.

Looking at Spinach, Ned frowned. "That may be a problem."

Alarmed, Eippy defensively held onto Spinach. "What may be a problem?"

The restraining bar may not hold your dog." As if in thought, Ned lifted his hand to his chin. "I may have a solution." He reached down and unbuckled his belt. "Take your belt off, too."

Puzzled, Eippy took his belt off. "Now what?"

Ned reached under the car and pulled a lever. A restraining bar popped out in front of Eippy and Spinach. "The bar may not hold your dog in place." He offered Eippy his belt. Put our belts around him and secure them to the restraining bar." He paused. "When it happens, the belts should hold him, but just in case, keep a good hold on him."

"Why am I doing this?"

The snapping of the pygmies grew louder.

"No time to talk." Ned jumped into the front car. "You'll find out." He released the brake. The string of cars coasted down a slant and hooked up to a moving chain. As the chain clacked, the cars were pulled to the top of a tall hill.

Eippy looked back over his shoulder. Far below, because they were twice as tall as the pie pygmies, the red pygmies were squeezing into another string of coaster cars. Before Eippy could say anything, Ned shouted, "Hang on!"

The car rolled down the hill. Gaining speed, it swished through the air. The sudden force pushed back the skin on Eippy's face. His hair flew straight back. As if glued to the back of the seat, he hung onto Spinach. Through the fur, Eippy felt Spinach's muscles tense.

At the bottom of the big hill, a small hill loomed up. The coaster hit the top of the small hill. As if it were on the end of a snapping whip, the car jerked. In a gut-wrenching swoop, Eippy and Spinach were bucked up off their seats. The belts around Spinach went taut and held him secure, and the restraining bar held Eippy and Ned in the car.

When the car came to a stop, Ned jumped out, ran to the railing, and frantically waved his hand. "Come on, Eippy, you'll miss it."

Eippy unbuckled the belts. Spinach jumped free. With his pants drooping, he held the belts, jumped out of the car, and ran to Ned.

He handed Ned his belt. As Eippy fastened his own belt, Ned pointed to the little hill at the bottom of the big hill. The coaster was jam packed with red pygmies who had managed to squeeze themselves into the smooth-sided cars. When the coaster snapped over the little hill, the red pygmies flew out of the cars and sailed high into the air. With their pointed mouths snapping and clacking, they uselessly flailed their arms and legs. When they came down, they made a glancing blow on a metal slide, slid down, splashed into an acid pit, and sizzled to death.

Ned laughed.

Eippy wondered if Ned laughed because it was like waiting for approaching red pygmies: Everyone knew they would be awful, but nobody knew when they would arrive. But until they did, there was nothing to do but carry on and try to have a good time.

Befuddled, Eippy stared at Ned.

Ned shrugged. "The best way to fight evil is to mock it."

"It may be," Eippy said, but won't the other red pygmies crawl up the hill and get to us?"

"We've thought of that. Right after a coaster full of red pygmies departs the caged entrance, three fences of web wire come down and block it. Those red devils can climb on that all they want." He paused. "And we have one more obstacle."

Ned led Eippy behind a line of green bushes with red berries, past the pine trees where he had seen Frank pulling the children, and stopped at the base of a tall stone wall. Flat stones butted next to the bottom of the wall and formed a walkway. Eippy wondered why a walkway had been laid right next to the wall, and he wondered why it had been swept clean of all debris and dust.

Ned picked up a stick from the ground, placed it into a hole in one of the blocks, and pushed. The block slid inward. A small tunnel, scarcely big enough for a pie pygmy to slip through, appeared.

Now Eippy knew why the walkway was there. Its smooth flat surface being swept clean everyday would make it difficult for anyone to leave footprints on the flat stones.

Ned stepped aside, gestured to the tunnel, and bowed. "Be my guest."

Eippy stepped to the tunnel entrance and stopped. "What about my dog?"

"No problem," Ned said and walked a few steps into the tunnel. He reached up and pushed a rock. It curved outward and clunked. He motioned to Eippy. "I need your help. Come on in."

Eippy went into the tunnel. Ned placed one hand the side of the square tunnel. "We have to push this block to make the tunnel bigger. We only use it to bring in large items. And you will notice that only people as big as us can enter the tunnel and unlock the bock." He placed both hands on the wall.

Eippy did the same.

"Okay push."

They pushed. The block at the side of the tunnel slid outward and rolled on steel rails until it stopped a meter on the other side of the tunnel.

Ned brushed his hands together. "Okay, call your dog."

Eippy walked half-way into the tunnel. Spinach was there waiting. Eippy led him out of the tunnel.

After Ned and Eippy pushed the block back in place, Spinach pointed his nose in the direction of something on the ground. Afraid that the red pygmies had somehow gotten through the tunnel or he had been led into a trap, Eippy's heart thudded with apprehension. He whipped his head around and looked to where Spinach was pointing. In the shade of a flowering red rose bush, blue birds with orange chests scampered on the ground.

Eippy exhaled a sigh of relief.

Twaaa-wheeet! Twaaa-wheeet! Came from somewhere in the distance. Spinach looked toward the pleasing sound. Right away, Eippy knew it was the song of a red-winged blackbird.

Now that they were safe, Eippy needed to know something. He turned toward Ned. "Why did you say, 'Welcome home?'"

"You may not remember, but when you were only a few years old you got into the wagon with the rooster pulling you."

"I saw a rooster pulling a wagon. It did spark fond memories, but I didn't know why."

"Maybe the wagon tipped over and you hit your head or something. You loved to ride in that wagon."

"Was it pulled by a rooster, called Frank?"

"A rooster pulled it, but that rooster was called Clyde."

Faint memories of a rooster came to Eippy's mind but faded. "If I liked it so much, how come I didn't stay here? And how did I get through the web fence?"

"We didn't need the web fence then. All we know is that you went riding one day, and Clyde came back with an empty wagon." Ned shook his head. "After that, Clyde moped around for days."

They walked across a field of clover. Honey bees buzzed from pink blossom to pink blossom. Off to the left, a row of cherry trees stood in a straight line, their leaves green and healthy. The trees caused Eippy to hunger for a cherry pie.

Ned noticed Eippy staring at the trees. "Do you miss the cherry pies?"

Eippy could almost taste and smell a cherry pie. "I don't know why, but all of a sudden I *am* hungry for a cherry pie."

"You should be. You are in the land of the pie pygmies."

Memories of pies enter Eippy's mind. "Pie pygmies?" he questioned.

A huge smile spread across Ned's face. "We are pie pygmies. The pig-people call us pie pygmies because they like to make pies out of us. But we are really called pie pygmies because we make and bake all kinds of pies. Apple pies, carrot, tomato, sweet potato pies, and peach, cherry, and berry pies. If we can grow a vegetable or pick a fruit, we make it into a pie."

When they walked over a hill of green grass, Eippy thought how nice it would have been to share a cherry pie with Trinket. Remembering how they could have been together seemed to bring a melancholy tenderness to the air around him.

At the end of the field, a group of pie pygmies, just like Eippy small and furry with silky-black fluffy tails, stood, close-pressed and silent.

Ned cupped his hands to his mouth and announced, "Eippy's home."

The pie pygmies' fluffy tails flared out, and their eyes shone with excitement. But what was behind them amazed Eippy even more. A small village with houses, none taller than a brown pygmy's waist, stood in an attractive array. Eippy's home where he had lived with his mother and father had been half the height of a pig-person's waist, but here, the houses were half that size. Each house had its own characteristics. Rich green lawns with flower gardens led to luxurious front doors. He was definitely in a pie pygmy village. He had come home.

As Ned led Eippy and Spinach along a white gravel path that curved around the houses, soft, golden light glowed in every window. Eippy wondered where the power was coming from.

Ned noticed the bewilderment in his face. "Look over there," he said. "That is just one of the many things that can be done when pig-people are not in charge."

Eippy looked. Off in the distance, rows of what looked like golden dish reflectors ran across a high stone wall. "What are those things?"

"They're gold sun catchers. They catch protons of energy from the sun and provide clean and free power to everyone." Ned frowned. "We should have more, but we have a difficult time getting enough gold."

Eippy patted the gold-attracting magnet in his pocket. He was glad he still had it. If this place turned out to be a safe place to stay, he could easily find more gold to produce more sun catchers. Then even on the coldest days, he could warm an outside area with a sun-catcher-powered heater. He would lean back in a lounge chair and the heater would warm him into dozing contentment.

A voice suddenly screamed. It was a piercing but happy shriek that had traveled far over the sun catchers. Cheering pie pygmies muted its echo.

Eippy looked to where the scream had come from. Girlish giggles came from a cluster of female pie pygmies. They moved to one side. A silky-black tail excitedly swiping back and forth caught Eippy's immediate attention. With his tongue lolling to one side and his eyes bright, Spinach loped toward the cluster of female pie pygmies and stopped in front of Trinket.

As she reached up and patted his head, Eippy couldn't believe it. Although Trinket's lovely eyes were red from crying, she brought sunshine back into his life. She was absolutely radiant. Overcome with emotion, he fell to one knee. Although he was totally spent, his arms ached to enfold her. He stood up. With Spinach barking with joy, Trinket ran into Eippy's arms. When they embraced, the crazy world he had existed in, stopped its insane pace. Spinach stopped barking, and whined with glee. When he stopped, stillness surrounded Eippy and Trinket. In her arms, Eippy felt peace and comfort. Trinket was someone he was going to enjoy being with the rest of his life.

"I missed you so much." Eippy released his embrace. "Let me look at you." Trinket slowly dropped her arms to her sides. Eippy stepped back. She was even more stunning than before. Her face was smooth and stress-free, with dark, doe-like eyes, long lashes, and full sensual lips. He looked at his hands. The filth from his struggles was still embedded under some of his fingernails. He suddenly realized that his black and white striped polo shirt had been torn and was spotted with dirt. His dirty fingernails and his dirty polo shirt seemed to underscore that his life had been useless without her. He had believed Trinket was dead and had not kept himself as clean as he usually had done. Now he was ashamed, but for only for an instant.

Trinket lowered her pretty head. "I'm sorry," she said. "I should have had a welcoming gift for you.

"The only gift I want is you."

"That can be arranged."

As she stood there, the thrill was more intense than it had been before. They tightly embraced. Swaying, they held each other. As she nervously clawed at his back and their silky-black tails slowly swished, as if making sure she was real, Eippy lovingly ran his hand over her back, and their lips sought each other out a hundred times. When they were satisfied that they were together their passion slowly mellowed to contented sighs.

Eippy placed his hand on her waist. As Spinach followed, they walked lazily under the shade of willow trees and stopped at her house.

This house was a far cry from Trinket's hut in Shangri-la, and it was like no other house he had ever seen. Green vines filled with pink roses climbed over the white picket fence that surrounded the manicured front lawn. When he opened the gate, a stone pathway led to the spindle-enclosed front porch. Off to the right, a wooden porch swing, with hearts carved on the back, sat back waiting for relaxing evenings. A short distance from the swing, a bowl waited in front of a straw bed. Spinach walked to the bowl and stopped. As if he had finally come home, he lay down on the straw bed.

Clean shiny brass hinges and a door latch plate decorated the majestic mahogany door.

Eippy pressed the brass latch and opened the door for Trinket. "We should be married."

He received a smile of pleasant surprise: She nodded. "Yes."

Eippy's heart soared. He was overwhelmed with love. The magic was still there. She still felt the same thing as Eippy. It was simple and natural. They could be married, sit outside on the swing, and finally have a safe place to live.

When he stepped into the dining room, two place settings, folded linen napkins, crystal goblets, and gleaming silverware had been meticulously placed on a table that could easily seat twenty people. He stared at the two plates and then looked at Trinket. "Did you know I was coming?"

Trinket blushed. "Hoping you'd come home, I have always set two places."

Eippy nodded and looked back at the table. Artfully arranged fish and baked potatoes sat next to a bed of green salad, and a cherry pie, on the side reminded Eippy how hungry he was. He looked at his semi-dirty hands. "Where can I wash up?"

"Right through there." Trinket pointed to a long hallway with six doors. "Your bathroom is the second door on the right. While you wash up, I'll feed Spinach."

Eippy rushed to the bathroom. Although the sink and indoor plumbing were extravert and he

326

wished he could stay and admire the beauty and connivance of it all, he was in a rush to get back to Trinket. He quickly washed and was about to rush back to the table, but a welcome sight caught the corner of his eye. Hanging on a hanger on the back of the bathroom door was a brand new black and white striped polo shirt. He tore his dirty polo shirt off, slipped into the new one, and walked to the table.

He sat at the head, and Trinket sat to his immediate left which allowed him to look out through a row of French doors. Outside, a wide veranda with small trees and shrubs created a relaxing view. But Eippy's mind wasn't on a relaxing view. Although he hadn't eaten a single bite, his huger pains were being erased by the sight of Trinket. And she didn't seem to be hungry either.

She leaned toward Eippy. "After we have eaten, I'll show you our bedroom."

Now, Eippy wanted to eat, and as quickly as he could. He took a few quick bites and looked to Trinket.

A puzzled look filled her lovely face. "We should give thanks to Orange Man."

"I'm sorry." Eippy set his fork on the table, took her hand in his, and bowed his head. "Oh mighty Orange Man, bless this food we are about receive and thank you for bringing us back together. Amen."

He grabbed his fork and looked up.

Trinket held up her lovely hand. "You haven't eaten for a while. Slow down."

Eippy didn't want to, but he slowed to a more non gluttonous pace.

After moments that seemed to be hours, Trinket lifted her napkin and gently dabbed her lips. "Are you ready?"

Eippy jumped up so fast that the back of his legs slammed into the edge of the chair and sent it back. Slightly embarrassed at his eagerness, he blushed and lowered his head. "Yes."

Trinket let out a girlish giggle and sprinted down the hall.

Almost stumbling over his own feet, Eippy followed.

Trinket stopped at the last door on the left. Before she could open it, Eippy was at her side. He opened the door for her.

Inside, enormous sprays of fresh flowers had been mounted on the walls, and a white curtained bed with swags of purple velvet ropes was only a few meters away. The heavy bed was higher than any bed Eippy had slept in. Letting her shoes silently slip from her feet, Trinket walked to the bed and climbed up onto it. It was so elegant that Eippy wondered if she wanted to muss the covers or riffle the curtains.

He stepped closer. The spread had to have been created from the finest, softest cotton ever spun. The feathery soft pillows were an interwoven with rich, raised designs, and had been perfectly placed. They seemed to be waiting to cradle their sleepy heads. A bed like this had never been so beckoning. Eippy pictured him and Trinket lying there in comfort. It was going to be a beautiful life.

Seductively smiling, Trinket lifted her hand and wiggled her finger in a come-here gesture.

Eippy stepped out of his shoes and jumped up onto the bed.

Just as their lips touched, Crack! A lightning bolt arced outside. Its extremely bright sharp flash cut through the curtains of the window.

Eippy and Trinket jumped to their feet.

"What was that?"

Trinket's face filled with fear. "I don't know."

They ran outside.

With alarm written all over his face, Ned ran toward them. As he neared, his face looked like the unhealthy, red face of a man who had been out in the sun too long. Out of breath, he stopped in front of Eippy.

Eippy's eyes probed for danger before it appeared. "What's the matter?"

"A flash of light lit up the sky," he said and gasped for breath. "It must have made the red pygmies angry. A slew of the crimson devils have stormed the first fence. I never knew there were that many." His eyes flashed with fear. "They have blown the transformer."

"Will the other two fences hold?"

Ned whipped his head around and looked up at the golden sun catchers. They were gleaming, but the power seemed to be fading. "I don't know."

"Will the web fence keep them out?"

Ned tilted his head toward the sun catchers. "It's a delicate system. If they overload them, it's all over."

Somewhere, off in the distance, thunder rolled and grumbled. In a lifeless air, the leaves on the willows hung still.

A great change was coming.

CHAPTER 28

With his flowing white robe gracing his smooth orange skin, Orange Man sat in a plush, red leather chair in front of a brass pipe organ, playing church music. As he gracefully pressed the immaculate, white keys, the translucent fingernails on his long fingers flashed silver, and although his almond-shaped eyes gave off a clear glow, his black irises broadcasted a deep dark feeling.

He looked over to his purple pygmy assistant who had been trying to create a prolonged association between multiple different organisms of different species that would benefit each member.

Frowning, his assistant shook his head.

Orange Man quit playing the organ and smiled. As he did, the sides of his long drawn face looked like they were being pressed between a wine press.

He placed a gentle hand on his assistant's shoulder. "Are you having trouble with your little symbiosis experiment?"

His assistant stood on his toes and leaned over the edge of the rolling universe. "We may have to pull the switch."

As if he were deeply troubled, Orange Man slowly shook his head. "The end of their existence is a high price to pay to save the planet. Let's take a look."

As sprays of dawn broke through a filth-filled sky, Orange Man and his purple pygmy assistant looked down on the masses of sprawling red pygmies. They were gnawing away, eating, or destroying every bit of flesh and every living thing on the planet.

Disgusted, Orange Man looked to his assistant. "We have had sociopaths with Neanderthal minds with little ability to separate truth from lies and right from wrong. Now, we have red pygmies, and they're going to invade the pie pygmy village."

Hope leaped into the assistant's eyes. "Do they have a chance?"

"The Dinkies couldn't stop them," Orange Man said with sadness in his voice. He lifted his translucent finger-nailed finger and pointed to a never-ending mass of red pygmies surrounding the pie pygmy village. "The pie pygmies will fare no better."

"Is it over?"

"We have given those creations billions and billions and billions of years, but they were never satisfied. We gave them one thing, and they always want something more. And that greed has constantly caused global destruction." His lips trembled at the thought. "Then when they back off and the earth just about recovers, they poison it again. Instead of using the free power we have given them for peaceful purposes, they are again destroying their world." With tears welling up in his large almond shaped eyes, His voice edged upward. "It isn't ever going to work."

The assistant leaned back in his chair. "Their world is devoid of empathy." With an injured look, he looked to Orange Man. "Before we pull the switch, do you want to freeze them again?"

Limply sagging, Orange Man said, "We have frozen and heated the earth until almost every last living thing was destroyed. And they came back. We flooded them. And they survived."

"It is a shame that their mental abilities do not equal their physical abilities."

With extreme discomfort, Orange Man stared at the planet. "In an effort to guide them toward a better order and hopefully better morals, we have sent saviors. We have given them many different Gods." His almond eyes blinked away tears. "But their disordered minds only created another bewildering world beset by conflict of species. Their minds continue to be disordered. It would be too disturbing to introduce another lesson they will not learn."

The assistant slumped with resentment. "I can see all future efforts will be useless."

Orange Man placed both hands on the assistant's shoulders and looked into his eyes. "You made man in your own image. And we saw that it was good." He stepped back and frowned. "But not this time. Our creations have become uncivilized. Civilization must end."

The pygmy assistant nodded weakly. "We can send Hog to another planet to agitate, but I'll have to agree. The rest are useless." He reluctantly sank back into his green leather chair. "We'll salvage what plant life we can and go on to the next experiment."

Orange Man turned to go but turned back. "Wait a second. The experiment isn't a total failure.

The pie pygmies have not abused the power of the gold magnet. They could have become Gods."

"But they did not."

Nodding, Orange Man continued. "The pie pygmies are the only ones who have learned enough to come back home. Activate a final roll of thunder, send the craft, and pick them up."

"Should we pick up Frank, too?"

A big grin spread across Orange Man's face. "Sure. Life wouldn't be the same without Frank." He motioned toward the big orange switch. "After they're aboard, block out the stars and turn the sun off."

"What about the Dinkies?"

"They were almost ready to come home. For a while, they'll live underground where the red pygmies can't get to them. After the red pygmies are gone, perhaps a new species will come. Make a note to revisit the place."

After the craft picked up the pie pygmies, a single sharp flash of light cut the night. As the last rays of the sun bathed the earth for the last time, a sudden halo appeared. Except for the orange glowing eyes of mad red pygmies devouring themselves into extinction and crying stars falling, for just a moment, the image of a Black Sun design based on a sun wheel with twelve L-shaped spokes leading to a smaller center circle appeared, and everything went back to black.

THE END

DOUBLE DRAGON NOVELS BY RONALD K. MYERS

Action/Adventure/Mystery
DILLINGER'S DECEPTION
IMPOSSIBLE GOLD

Military Espionage/Action Adventure/Thriller.
ALMOST FREE

Humorous/Historical Fiction/Action Adventure
I'M GONNA CUT YOUR EARS OFF
FREE RIDE

Futuristic
STAY ON THE BLUE GRASS
THE ORANGE TURN
PYGMY WARS